MW00585801

KEEPING BAD COMPANY

The Liberty Lane Series from Caro Peacock

DEATH AT DAWN
(USA: A FOREIGN AFFAIR)

DEATH OF A DANCER
(USA: A DANGEROUS AFFAIR)

A CORPSE IN SHINING ARMOUR
(USA: A FAMILY AFFAIR)

WHEN THE DEVIL DRIVES *

KEEPING BAD COMPANY *

* *available from Severn House*

KEEPING BAD COMPANY

A Liberty Lane Mystery

Gillian Linscott

Writing as

Caro Peacock

U.S. Publication Date:
June 2012

This first world edition published 2012
in Great Britain and the USA by
Crème de la Crime, an imprint of
SEVERN HOUSE PUBLISHERS LTD of
9–15 High Street, Sutton, Surrey, England, SM1 1DF.

British Library Cataloguing in Publication Data

Peacock, Caro.
Keeping bad company.
1. Lane, Liberty (Fictitious character) – Fiction. 2. Women private investigators – Fiction. 3. London (England) – Social conditions – 19th century – Fiction. 4. Detective and mystery stories.
I. Title
823.9′2-dc23

ISBN-13: 978-1-78029-020-1 (cased)

All Severn House titles are printed on acid-free paper.

Severn House Publishers support The Forest Stewardship Council [FSC], the leading international forest certification organisation. All our titles that are printed on Greenpeace-approved FSC-certified paper carry the FSC logo.

Typeset by Palimpsest Book Production Ltd.,
Falkirk, Stirlingshire, Scotland.
Printed and bound in Great Britain by
MPG Books Ltd., Bodmin, Cornwall.

ONE

A footman refilled our champagne glasses so smoothly that the gentleman talking to me didn't pause in the story he was telling about a certain minister on a recent visit to Paris. The gentleman was keeping his voice low because the minister in question was at the other end of the room, in a group around a minor royal. Half the cabinet were present, in court dress of tailcoats, breeches, silk stockings and buckled shoes. It was very much a 'decorations will be worn' occasion, so the men's chests blazed with orders from all over the globe, gilded, jewelled and enamelled. It struck me as a pity that by the time a man had earned the right to wear silk stockings and jewels, he was usually well past the age when he might look dashing in them. There were exceptions, of course, like that rising politician, Mr Benjamin Disraeli. He was in the group with the minor royal, doing most of the talking as usual. His calves were svelte in silk, his black curls flowing, waistcoat ornamented with some multicoloured honour he must have managed to acquire on his honeymoon European travels. On the edge of the group his wife, Mary Anne, in ill-advised frills of purple silk, watched him adoringly.

Mr Disraeli had greeted me soon after I arrived, in company with a young gentleman from the Foreign Office.

'What a pleasant surprise to see you, Miss Lane. May I say that you're looking particularly well this evening?'

The second part of his remarks might have been true. I'd taken trouble for the occasion and was wearing my new amethyst-coloured silk with the low neckline and puffed sleeves, my favourite dragonfly ornament in my hair. The first part was untrue. It wasn't a surprise to see me because he'd been partly responsible for my attendance at this diplomatic gathering. I sometimes carried out work of a confidential nature for the Foreign Office. Although Mr Disraeli was too ambitious and mercurial to be much trusted by the authorities, he was known to be an acquaintance of mine so was occasionally used to see whether I'd undertake particular assignments.

On this occasion, the task was straightforward and I'd accepted. The gentleman to whom I was listening was, to put things bluntly, a spy in the pay of a foreign embassy. He'd been involved in a nasty piece of work that had caused the suicide of a British diplomat. All I had to do was to slip a particular fact into our conversation that would make clear I was aware of it and see how he reacted. In return for my report, I could expect ten guineas, the knowledge that I'd helped expose a traitor and the possible gratitude of the Foreign Office. My target was near the climax of his grubby story. He leaned towards me confidentially, giving himself the chance to look straight down my bodice. I resisted the temptation to swing my elbow into his ribs. The question I was going to ask him as soon as his story finished would be a much more effective weapon. Only, I never managed to ask it.

I glanced over his shoulder across the room and saw a young gentleman break away from a group of people and come striding towards us, frowning. The sense of urgency about him made me wonder if my employers had, for some reason, changed their minds at the last minute. Nothing distinguished him from all the other young diplomats, except possibly that his face was redder than most. He was in his mid twenties, slightly plump and wore a decoration with crossed swords that looked as if it might be Indian. Something about him seemed familiar. I searched my memory, wondering where I'd met him before and what in the world I might have done to annoy him so much. As he came nearer it was worse than a frown, positively a glare, and directed straight at me. My target must have sensed he was losing my attention because he raised his voice.

'. . . then, would you believe, the chambermaid said to him . . .'

Then he gasped and pitched forward, nearly knocking me over. That was because the glaring man had cannoned straight into him, catching him with all his weight on the shoulder. My target was gulping indignant noises. Apologies were in order, but the glaring man didn't make them. He disregarded his victim entirely, looking me full in the face, his eyebrows a black bar.

'Liberty, what do you think you're doing here?'

His voice carried. People were staring. I returned his glare with one of my own.

'I believe you have the advantage of me, sir.'

Meaning that he was a boor twice over, first for barging then for addressing me by my first name. By now the other gentleman had recovered enough to ask him what the devil he thought he was doing. Again he was ignored.

'I'm taking you home this instant, young lady.'

I thought the red-faced young man had taken leave of his senses. So did some other gentlemen, including my escort for the evening, who were rushing over to protect me. They closed round the young man and tried to hustle him away. He resisted and stood his ground.

'Kindly don't interfere. This is a private matter.'

'Insulting a lady isn't a private matter,' one of the gentlemen said.

'I'm not insulting her. I'm simply removing her from bad company.'

'Why should you suppose you can dictate my company?' I said, furious.

And yet, even as I said it, an impossible thought was taking shape in my mind. It came from his voice and the defiant way he was standing. So perhaps, deep down, I wasn't as surprised by his next words as the gentlemen to whom he spoke them.

'So if you'll all excuse me, I am taking my sister home.'

TWO

My brother, Thomas Fraternity Lane, should have been four and a half thousand miles away and on that first evening I heartily wished that he still were. Which was sad, because for the past seven years the dearest wish of my heart had been to see him again. Seven years ago I'd stood with my father, now dead, on the shore at Gravesend and watched the waving white glint of Tom's handkerchief from the rail of the ship that was carrying him away to India. Tom was fifteen then, I eighteen. Letters from India every six months or so recorded Tom's career as a rising young administrator with the East India Company. Letters from me, slightly more frequently, recorded all the things about my life that I dared tell him without driving him into a frenzy of worry or disapproval. He wasn't due for home leave for several years. By that time, I might even have found a way to tell my only brother that his only sister was earning a living as a private inquiry agent. Or perhaps my life would have changed in such a way that I could tell it glancingly, as something that belonged in the past. His sudden and unexplained presence in London had ended that hope. Within seconds of being reunited, we were fighting as if we were back in the nursery.

Given our surroundings, the fight had to be more decorous than when the weapons were shuttlecocks and toy soldiers. Tom, myself and my escort for the evening, Mr Calloway, took ourselves into the lobby where a few footmen were leaning against the wall, waiting for their masters to come out to their coaches.

'What are you doing here? Why didn't you tell me you were coming home?' I said to Tom.

'I didn't have a chance. In any case, I didn't expect to find my sister practically in the arms of a man with one of the worst reputations in London.'

'I was *not* practically in his arms. Anyway, how do you know?'

'Because one of the men I was with was looking at you both and sniggering about old so and so making another conquest. Conquest! My sister!'

'I can assure you I'm nobody's conquest. If you want to know, it was quite the reverse.'

'I don't want to know. Don't move from here. I'm going to find a hansom.'

'And carry me into it with a sack over my head?'

'If necessary, yes.'

Mr Calloway gave a diplomatic cough. He'd collected my cloak and had it over his arm.

'Mr Lane, may I suggest that we both escort your sister home.'

He had such a reasonable air about him that my angry brother unbarred his eyebrows and lowered his voice.

'May I ask who you are, sir?'

'Malcolm Calloway, of the Foreign Office, at your service. I had the honour to be introduced to Miss Lane by our mutual friends, Sir George and Lady Talbot. She very kindly consented to accompany me to the reception this evening.'

It was the first I knew of George's knighthood. Trust Mr Calloway to be ahead of the Gazette. His explanation left out a lot of things, but it calmed Tom a little.

'But that appalling fellow . . .' Tom said.

'I entirely agree with you, Mr Lane. Unfortunately, my attention was diverted. If I'd known he was inflicting his presence on Miss Lane, I should certainly have taken the action which you so promptly did.'

I tried not to catch Mr Calloway's eye. He knew very well why I was there that evening. Part of my anger with my brother was that he'd made me fail in a professional obligation and, probably, cost me a much-needed ten guineas. My cloak wafted itself round my shoulders without visible assistance from Mr Calloway. His glance to the footman by the door produced a carriage as soon as we stepped out on to the pavement, not a hansom but a hireling two-horse landau with room for the three of us. Mr Calloway handed me in and stood back so that Tom could sit beside me.

'Where shall I tell the driver, Miss Lane?'

More diplomacy. From a past perilous occasion, Mr Calloway was well aware of my address, but it wouldn't have improved Tom's mood to know that.

'Abel Yard, off Adam's Mews, Mayfair.'

The landau creaked and rattled over the cobbles. It was mercifully too noisy for conversation but I was aware of Tom beside me, tense as a gun dog. At Abel Yard they both got down to help me out. In the light of the carriage lamps, I could see Tom wrinkling his nose at smells of cows and chickens wafting from the far end of the yard. At the bottom of my stairs I thanked them both, wished them goodnight and closed the door before Tom knew what was happening. I needed time. Now I was recovering from the surprise, my heart was singing out that my brother was back. But there'd be explanations and quarrelling to come, I knew that as surely as I knew the sun would rise. For my part, I wanted to know what he'd been doing at a reception in Whitehall when he should have been in Bombay. All next morning I waited in, sure that every carriage going along the mews, every footstep coming into the yard, was my brother's. By then, the desire for explanations had become a simple wish to see him again. When a knock came at the door in the yard, around noon, I practically threw myself down the stairs and flung back the door, ready to fall on his neck. This impetuosity must have surprised the footman who was standing there in a livery jacket of a strange bright brown colour, but he managed to keep his face a professional blank. I composed mine and accepted the card he was holding out to me. It had a gilded deckle edge and informed me in engraved copperplate that Mrs Benjamin Disraeli would be 'At Home', at Grosvenor Gate, that afternoon, from half past two until half past four.

I carried it upstairs, puzzling it out. If Mary Anne Disraeli knew of my existence at all, it would be for reasons that would not have made me particularly welcome at her 'At Homes'. So the invitation clearly came from her husband, who must want to speak to me. All too likely, it would be to pass on a message from my employers about my failure the previous evening. Not a pleasant prospect, but no help for it. The afternoon was mild and sunny so I put on my green-and-blue printed cotton dress and walked the short distance from Abel Yard to Grosvenor Gate. Mary Anne was receiving her guests in the huge upstairs drawing room. The place was a skirmish of colours, gold silk curtains, crimson carpet, chairs and sofas upholstered in yellow damask, the whole riot reflected in tall mirrors with ornate gilt frames. My hostess, in sage-green satin, welcomed me with a vagueness that confirmed my guess about the invitation. I kept apart from the groups of chatterers and waited, sipping tea and turning over the pages of a book of engravings of Italian ruins that had been left open on a piecrust table and, sure enough, Mr Disraeli appeared at my side within minutes. This afternoon he was relatively soberly dressed in blacks and greys, but his waistcoat was figured gold silk.

'I trust you enjoyed the reception last night, Miss Lane.'

His voice and a lift of his eyebrow showed he knew very well that I had not, so I kept quiet and waited.

'It must have been a great pleasure to see your brother again. I'm sure you had a lot to talk about.'

Was he being sarcastic? I glanced at him and realized that for once Mr Disraeli was not thoroughly well informed.

'There's always a lot to talk about,' I said.

'Quite so. I hope he's not feeling too nervous about giving evidence to the committee.'

I took a sip of tea, hoping to hide my surprise and probably not succeeding. It was becoming clear that whatever he wanted to talk about, it wasn't my failure of the evening before.

'I don't think Tom's a nervous man,' I said.

'Just as well. It can be an ordeal being questioned by a parliamentary committee, especially in the circumstances.'

I wanted to yelp out: *What committee? What circumstances?* It sounded terribly as if my brother had been recalled from India in disgrace, but surely, at his comparatively junior level, whatever he'd done shouldn't be serious enough to concern a committee of MPs. I hid my anxiety, knowing that you always got more out of Mr Disraeli if you knew a lot already.

'I hadn't realized Parliament was so directly concerned with East India Company internal affairs,' I said.

In fact, it was a strange relationship. The vast concern that some people called John Company had grown, in around two hundred years, from a group of merchant adventurers to an organization with its own army that ran the whole subcontinent of India and much else besides. After a series of scandals, parliament had taken away some of its powers. Not enough of them, according to a lot of people.

'The McDruggies have had some of their opium shipments confiscated by the Chinese,' Disraeli said. 'They're yelling for compensation and war. When trade's going well, the last thing they want is Government interference. As soon as they take losses, we're supposed to sail in and save them.'

McDruggies? I tried not to let him see that I didn't know what he was talking about.

'I don't suppose my brother's to blame for any of that.'

'No. He's had the bad luck to be caught up in this affair on the fringes of it. Strictly speaking, it shouldn't concern the parliamentary committee. Still, when it comes to one of the Company men probably committing murder, I suppose we have to take a decent interest.'

At this point I might have given in and asked him who'd been murdered and what it had to do with Tom, but Mary Anne had spotted us and come rustling across the room, ringlets bouncing, obviously concerned that her husband had been speaking for too long to one woman.

'Dearest, the Claverleys want to know about Vienna. Do come and talk to them.'

'Of course, dearest. You'll excuse me, Miss Lane. We shall talk further.'

He let himself be rustled away, leaving me with half a cup of cold tea and a head spinning with questions.

I knew Tom must come that evening. I'd made everything in our parlour as ready as I could. A fire of best coal burned in the grate with the kettle on the hob and the teapot standing beside it. A bottle from the dozen of good claret a grateful client had sent me was decanted, the finest cold pie that money could buy standing on the table in case he was hungry. The cat was dozing on our new hearth rug. Mrs Martley, the very picture of respectability, knitted in her chair by the fire. My ex-street urchin apprentice, Tabby, was on duty in the yard, ready to whistle up as soon as a gentleman appeared. The whistle came at around eight o'clock, just after we'd lit the lamps. I flew downstairs and this time it really was Tom. Before he could say anything I threw my arms round him and hugged him tightly, trying to make up for those seven years of missing him. For all I knew, he was intending to carry on our quarrel from where he'd left off, but for a while at least I wanted to enjoy the sheer wonder of his being back. He hugged me in return, but with some reserve, then followed me upstairs and stood in our parlour like a stranger, holding his hat and gloves in his hand. When I introduced Mrs Martley as my housekeeper he gave her a polite nod of the head and she bobbed a curtsey. I felt like crying for the time lost but took his hat and gloves from him, made him sit in the other chair by the fire, wildly offered tea, claret, pie.

'I'll take a glass of claret,' he said. 'Our tea tastes fresher because we're closer to China. When you're accustomed to tea in the East, you have no taste for what they do with it in England.'

I made a clumsy business of pouring, hiding my dismay. I'd parted from a brave boy who'd been my follower and companion in adventures. I thought of us racing our ponies over logs in the woods, diving from rocks into the sea, daring each other to climb out of our bedroom windows at night and go watching foxes and badgers under the light of the moon. This young man's face and figure were rounded, his dark hair sleeked down. He seemed at least five years older than I was, rather than two years younger. When we'd parted, his voice had only just broken and his laugh was still a boy's. Now he spoke as if tea were a matter of grave policy. I couldn't tell what to do with this stranger who'd returned in my brother's place. Then, as I handed him his glass, I looked into his eyes and saw Tom hadn't gone away after all. They were still the fine dark eyes he'd had at fifteen. And, as so many times on our adventures together, the look in them told me that Tom was very worried or scared and doing all he could to hide it.

I touched my glass to his.

'To your return.'

'I'm not sure that it's worth toasting,' he said.

Discouraging. I poured a glass for Mrs Martley and handed it to her with a nod and an upward glance that told her to keep her promise: go upstairs and leave me and my brother alone. She went. Tom emptied his glass at two gulps.

'Liberty, I was very surprised to find you—'

'Never mind that,' I said. 'What's all this about you and a parliamentary committee and a murder?'

That stopped him in his tracks. He almost dropped the glass.

'How do you know about that?'

'It seems to be pretty well common knowledge.'

That was hardly fair to Mr Disraeli, whose knowledge was anything but common but I wasn't ready to tell Tom about that particular friendship.

'It was supposed to be a deadly secret,' Tom said. 'That was why I couldn't write and tell you I was coming.'

'So secret that you attend a Foreign Office reception with half the world there, but can't tell your sister?'

'We were ordered to go to the reception. I suppose they wanted to see me and size me up before the formal proceedings.'

'They being the MPs on this committee?'

A nod.

'But why do they want to speak to you?'

'Because I'm a witness. Except I'm not really a witness. There were no witnesses. That's the confounded thing about it.'

Those dark eyes were full of misery. I refilled our glasses.

'You'd better tell me about it,' I said.

THREE

The story Tom told me took us into the early hours of the morning. It ranged the entire distance across India, from Calcutta in the east to Bombay in the west, and then a death just before dawn by some red rocks on a hill. Here it is as he told it.

'The man who died was named Burton. He was the assistant of a merchant, Alexander McPherson. McPherson runs a company that exports opium from India to China and imports tea from China to Britain. They say he's well in with the Governor and a lot of the senior men in Calcutta. He used to work for the Company, but then branched out on his own. He's away trading in Canton half the time. He's supposed to be as rich as Croesus, built himself a house that's practically a palace, stuffed with plate and jewels. But like the rest of the opium men, he took a bad knock recently when the Chinese confiscated whole shiploads of the stuff. I've never worked in Calcutta so all I knew about him was from gossip, until he arrived in Bombay about eight months ago. It still wouldn't have been any concern of mine, except for the effect it had on the deputy head of my department, a man named Edmund Griffiths.'

Tom's voice was warm as he said the name, unlike his tone when talking about McPherson.

'Although he's senior to me and a lot older, Griffiths and I hit it off as soon as he was transferred from Calcutta to Bombay. You'd like him, Liberty. He reminds me of father. He's spent most of his life with the Company, mostly as a local magistrate. He never cared much about money or promotion and as far as I can tell he lives on his pay. What he loves is India. He speaks dozens of the languages and dialects and even writes poetry in some of them. I've seen him joking on equal terms with a prince and hunkering down in the dust to talk to some old holy man. Of course, a lot of people in the Company don't care for that sort of thing. They call him "The Mad Griff". Even before he joined us in Bombay, some of the older men were laughing and gossiping about him. They were wondering why he was being transferred all the way there from Calcutta. Then the story got out: he was being sent pretty well in disgrace because he'd made public threats against McPherson. And I have to tell you, Liberty, if I'd been in Griffiths's place, I hope I'd have been making threats against the man as well.'

Tom's eyes blazed and he ran a hand through his carefully combed hair, disordering it. He was beginning to look and sound more like the brother I knew.

'Why?' I said.

'Because the man was little better than a bandit. A long way back, in his magistrate days, Griffiths kept coming across natives who'd been deprived of their little bits of land by McPherson. The method was that he'd advance the farmers small loans, get them into debt then take over their land to grow opium. All legal, so there was nothing Griffiths could do about it, but he says it drove him nearly mad. He's never been a man to keep his views to himself, so he started trying to kick up a fuss about it, appealing to the Governor and so on. Eventually he realized it was a waste of breath. After all, who's going to worry about the opinions of some obscure employee against a man with McPherson's money and influence? So for years he kept on with his work and his language studies and tried to forget the likes of McPherson existed.'

'So what happened?'

'The latest trouble in China. You know the Chinese authorities don't want our opium? They keep trying to ban it, but McPherson and his like bribe the officials and get it in anyway, then just put the price up to cover the bribes. Quite recently, the Chinese have been taking a stronger line. They confiscated thousands of chests of opium, including a lot of McPherson's, and burned them. McPherson comes rushing back to Calcutta, expecting the Governor to pay compensation and send in warships. Well, the Governor's pretty powerful, but he can't do that without the say-so from Westminster.'

'Hence this committee?'

'Yes. Luckily the government won't be rushed into anything,

though McPherson and his gang are doing their best. Anyway, to get back to Calcutta. With McPherson rampaging round making so much noise, it stirred up all the old feelings in poor Griffiths. He stood up in public, at some dinner or another, and told McPherson to his face that he was no better than a pirate and the government shouldn't pay him one single rupee of compensation.'

'Brave.'

'I agree. If I'd been in Calcutta, I hope I'd have said so. Griffiths added for good measure that McPherson was a disgrace to his country and men like him, if they weren't checked, would get the British thrown out of India.'

Tom thumped his fist into his palm, caught up in Griffiths's oratory.

'And the threats?' I said.

'He told McPherson that if he went on cheating Indian farmers out of their land, one of these fine days he'd be found on a lonely road with his throat cut, and serve him damned-well right.'

'You heard all this from gossip?'

'No, I heard it from Griffiths himself. He said the only thing he regretted was that they'd hustled him out of Calcutta before he could say worse.'

'I can see why the Company wanted to put the whole breadth of India between them,' I said. 'But has Mr McPherson been found on a lonely road with his throat cut?'

'No. He's here in London, bursting to give his views to the committee. He and his gang came over on the same ship as I did. But the point is, that's exactly what happened to his assistant, Burton. He was supposed to be meeting McPherson one morning. McPherson found him dead, and his luggage looted.'

'But how does that concern you as a witness, since you were in Bombay all the time? Or Mr Griffiths, come to that?'

'Because Burton wasn't killed in Calcutta. He was killed just outside Bombay. McPherson and his people were honouring us with a visit.'

'Why?'

'McPherson was making his way back to London, to pull

strings here. He was travelling by way of Bombay because he wanted to realize some of his assets there, he made no secret of that.'

'Assets?'

'Calling in loans, mainly. Even a fellow as rich as McPherson can't stand the loss of five thousand chests of opium without taking some harm. Then there were jewels. Everybody knew he was bringing some of his collection back to London with him to sell. While he was waiting, he used his spare time in Bombay trying to make things as difficult as he could for poor Griffiths.'

'Did he succeed?'

Tom looked into the fire and sighed.

'Yes. Griffiths is a stoic. He tried not to let it show. But the sight of McPherson parading around as if he owned Bombay made him furious. His health's not good either. He's had warnings from the doctor about his heart and should be leading a quiet life, but with this business going on, he can't rest. I'm sure McPherson knows that.'

'But would it matter to him what Mr Griffiths thought, if he was so lacking in influence?'

'You'd have thought not, but there's something between them that goes a long way back. I don't think Griffiths has told me the half of it.'

'What about this Burton who was killed?'

'I don't know much about him, except that he was about my age and supposed to be McPherson's right-hand man. McPherson must have trusted him to have him carry the jewels.'

'The ones from Calcutta?'

'No. They came by ship, as you'd expect. These were another collection, from somewhere inland. Nobody seems to know quite where. McPherson's interests stretch all over the place. Anyway, Burton was bringing them from wherever it was and McPherson rode out on his own in the early morning to meet him. There are some big red rocks by the road that make a good place for an ambush. He found Burton and a native servant dead by the side of the road, with their throats cut. Their luggage had been looted. The other servants had run off.'

'The jewels were gone?'

'Some of them. But the most valuable, Burton had carried in a belt under his clothes. They were still there.'

'Were you or Mr Griffiths present when any of this happened?'

'No, of course we weren't.'

'Then I don't understand how you're involved.'

'Because of a diamond hawk,' Tom said.

I stared at him.

'Hawk?'

'Swooping on its prey, head and body set with diamonds, ruby claws, eyes and beak. It's a brooch the size of your hand. I thought it a vulgar thing, but it was supposed to be worth a fortune.'

'How does that come into it?'

'It was part of McPherson's hoard. I found it on Griffiths's desk.'

The fire shifted in the grate and coals fell on the hearth. I scooped them up without taking my eyes off Tom's face.

'It happened two days after Burton was killed,' he said. 'Griffiths had asked me to fetch some report from his desk. I moved the papers, looking for the report, and there was the hawk.'

'What did you do?'

'Picked it up and took it to Griffiths. Of course, I had no idea that it belonged to McPherson. But Griffiths recognized it. He told me I was to go straight away with him to the Governor and explain exactly what had happened. So that's what we did.'

'Did Griffiths have any explanation?'

'None at all.'

'How had he recognized it as McPherson's?'

'He said it had belonged to a lady he knew.'

'So what was it doing on his desk?'

'He said he had no idea.'

'Did the Governor believe him?'

'I don't know. I think he'd have liked to believe him. I don't think he cared much for McPherson either.'

'So was there a trial?'

'No. Officially Burton was murdered and robbed by bandits. But of course the Governor had to send a report to London. Months later, word comes back that there's going to be a parliamentary committee looking into the affairs of the Company. It's mostly about the opium compensation business, but because of McPherson it's all connected. Griffiths and I were ordered to London.'

A lot of questions were in my head, but Tom looked mortally tired and the loud clock in the nearby workhouse was striking two. Tom told me that he was lodging in a house in the City which the Company owned, but I persuaded him that it would be madness to walk across London at this time of the morning. He consented to eat a slice of the pie and drink a cup of despised English tea, then I lit a candle and showed him through the little doorway into the room that I keep as my own study. It looked cosy by candlelight, with its bookshelves and daybed piled with shawls and cushions. Tom could sleep there. I could see his eyes going round the room, looking for things that would help him understand what sort of person his sister had become. If I'd found him changed in seven years, what might be going through his head about me?

In the morning, I was up before Tom and going quietly downstairs in my riding clothes. As usual, my great friend the groom Amos Legge, was waiting for me on horseback at the gate into Abel Yard, holding the reins of my mare Rancie. We had our morning canter in Hyde Park, before the fashionable world was up and about. I told him that my brother was back, but no more than that because I supposed Tom had been talking in confidence. As he helped me down from Rancie, an idea came to me.

'Tom needs exercise. Would you take him riding in the park one day? Not on Rancie, more of a weight-carrier.'

Upstairs, Tom was sitting at breakfast in the parlour, being waited on by an obviously enchanted Mrs Martley. The remains of bacon and eggs on a plate suggested she'd used up most of our week's supply on him and a smell of toast hung on the warm air. I sat down by the fire in my riding costume and made some for myself from what was left of the loaf.

'There are things we must discuss, Liberty,' Tom said.

My heart sank. That pompous tone was back. I buttered my toast, poured tea and ate and drank with deliberate slowness. Tom passed an impatient hand over his chin.

'I need a shave.'

'You've got too accustomed to having servants,' I said. 'A man won't suddenly appear and do it for you.'

We went upstairs to my study, leaving Mrs Martley clearing up. I sat on the daybed, leaving Tom the armchair.

'Who's paying for all this?' Tom said.

'My palace here, you mean? I am.'

'From giving music lessons?'

'Only a few, these days. Chiefly, I'm an investigator.'

'Of what?'

'Of anything. I try to solve problems for people. When they can afford it, they pay me.'

'It must stop,' Tom said.

I managed not to say anything, biting my tongue.

'I didn't sleep much,' Tom said. 'I've come to a decision on what to do about you.'

I released my tongue. It was probably bleeding.

'Oh yes?'

'When all this is over, you're coming back to India with me.'

'I am, am I?'

Tom wasn't even looking at me.

'I can borrow your fare against my future salary and rent a small bungalow for the two of us. I don't suppose it will be for long because I dare say you'll be married within a year.'

'Oh really. Have you anybody particular in mind for me?'

'Nobody in particular, but there are a lot of Company men in their thirties and forties who don't want to go all the way back to England to find a wife. Good, intelligent men, some of them. You'd like them.'

'Should I indeed? Just as well.'

He'd failed entirely to notice my sarcasm and grinned with relief at having got a difficult scene over. The grin faded when I stood up.

'Did it occur to you at any point to consult me about this great plan?'

'You love travelling. You'd like India.'

'I'm sure I should, under other circumstances, but I'm not going to be shipped out with a label round my neck: "Surplus to requirements. Please marry."'

'Libby, you know very well it's not like that. My responsibility to our parents . . .'

'Your responsibility to our parents is to remember what they taught us about the rights of men and women. That doesn't include trying to tyrannize a sister who is doing perfectly well leading her own life – and is two years older than you.'

I went on in this vein for some time, quite possibly sounding pompous myself. Tom kept trying to interrupt. The noise we made probably carried to Mrs Martley downstairs. Eventually we exhausted ourselves and just stood glaring at each other. The sight of us back in nursery mode again left me quivering between laughter and tears. I sat down on the daybed and held my right hand towards him, palm flat, our childhood sign of truce.

'Pax.'

'What you won't see, Liberty—'

'Pax.'

He saw he'd get nothing out of me until he did it, so reluctantly held out his own palm and said the word. I made myself speak in a calm voice.

'Tom, the trouble is that you know very little about the life I lead. It's mostly my fault. I should have told you more, but it's not easy in letters. In any case, it means you're assuming things about me that simply aren't true. I promise you that in the seven years you've been away, I've done nothing that I couldn't have told our mother and father about if they were alive.'

'It's not a matter of what you've done or not done. It's your reputation that's—'

I held my palm out again and went on talking.

'You don't have to take my word for that. There are two people I'd like you to speak to. One of them's our father's old friend, Daniel Suter.'

'I want to call on Suter in any case. I hoped you were going to marry him.'

'We thought we might, for a while. Only he married Jenny and they're two of the happiest people I know. Tell Daniel that he's to answer any questions you care to put to him about me.'

Daniel could tell Tom a lot, including the events that had led me to my unusual trade. A lot, but not everything.

'Then there's another friend. You haven't met him, but he helped our father in the last few days of his life, and he brought Rancie to me. His name's Amos Legge. He's head groom at a livery stables in the Bayswater Road . . .'

Tom seemed about to protest again.

'. . . and he's been the best of friends to me. I shall see him tomorrow and tell him that he's to answer all your questions, only you'd better be prepared for that to take a long time, because he won't be hurried. I've already told him that you'll go riding in the park with him.'

That seemed, at last, to silence Tom. I wrote down the addresses of Daniel Suter and Amos's stables, then we went downstairs where Mrs Martley was making an ostentatious noise washing up. So our voices had carried. She brought Tom his hat and coat and said she was sure we'd be seeing a lot of him. I went to see Tom to the gates of the yard and told him that he'd find a barber to shave him somewhere around the Burlington Arcade. As I watched him walk away down the mews, I thought that he hadn't replied to Mrs Martley's remark about seeing a lot of him. We shouldn't see him again until he'd spoken to Daniel and Amos. When he'd heard all there was to hear from them, should we see him at all? I only hoped I hadn't lost my brother all over again.

FOUR

The next few days brought no more visits from Tom. The only news of him came from Amos, who had twice taken him riding. I gathered that both rides had been long ones, but it would have been unfair to Amos to press for more details. I tried to distract myself with a case that Tabby and I had been working on for a while, involving a silver coffee pot and a remarkable amount of silliness from a family that should have known better. We concluded it to everybody's reasonable satisfaction and so were five guineas richer. Still no sign of Tom, and I began to wonder if he'd washed his hands of me altogether. Then one evening he appeared as Mrs Martley and I were clearing up the supper things. He looked tired and thinner in the face.

'Griffiths wants me to bring you to see him.'

Here was a surprise. Then I thought I could guess the reason.

'You've been discussing me with him?'

'Yes.'

'And all the things you found out from Daniel Suter and Amos Legge?'

'Yes.'

This time I managed to stop myself flying into a rage. Tom had no business to discuss my affairs with anybody else, but he had no friends or relatives around him to share his problems, so perhaps it was natural to confide in an older man whom he admired. I was sure that I knew the purpose of the proposed visit. Mr Griffiths would support Tom's plan for taking me to India on a husband hunt. Well, I could listen and say a polite no. Also, if I'm honest, I was curious to meet this combative Mr Griffiths.

'When?' I said.

'I'll call for you tomorrow morning at eight o'clock.'

'Isn't that a little early for visiting?'

'He's living out at Richmond. We'll take the stage from St Paul's.'

He drank tea with us, but wouldn't stay the night. He had things to discuss with men from the Company about his appearance before the parliamentary committee. He seemed sad and preoccupied and it went to my heart to know that I could do nothing to help him.

Next morning Tom brought a cab to collect me. The journey to St Paul's was too noisy and the stagecoach too crowded to have any chance for conversation, which was something of a relief. When Tom took off one of his gloves I noticed that the nails were bitten down to the quick, an old habit. When we came to Richmond he handed me down from the coach and gave me an assessing look. There was nothing for him to criticize. I was wearing my grey-and-blue wool dress and a bonnet so sober it was practically Quakerish.

'Well, am I respectable enough to meet your Mr Griffiths?'

He hesitated.

'Liberty, I don't want you to have the wrong impression of him. He may seem eccentric, but I promise you he's as good a hearted man as you could wish to meet.'

'Well then, I shall be respectful of him. More than that I won't promise.'

He looked as if he wanted to say more, but led the way across the green towards a neat brick-built cottage with a front garden that was a froth of wallflowers and forget-me-nots.

'Is it his?' I said.

'I believe he's rented it.'

In living so far out of town, Mr Griffiths must be taking great pains to distance himself from his Company colleagues.

We walked up the red brick path and Tom knocked on the door. It was opened at once by an Indian lad wearing a turban, tunic and white trousers. He was clearly expecting us and showed us into a sunlit room overlooking the garden. The man standing to meet us there reminded me of a heron. He was thin and angular, shoulders a little bowed. His face was clean-shaven and as brown as oak bark, with a bony wedge of nose and eyes that were probably grey, but had a bright and lively look that made them seem blue. His hair was bright silver, worn almost collar-length, but neat. He was simply dressed in a grey cutaway coat over a shirt and neckcloth of dazzling whiteness and a plain grey waistcoat.

'Tom, my boy, it's good to see you.'

He looked at me and smiled, but waited correctly for Tom to introduce us.

'Miss Lane, it's a pleasure to meet you. If you take that chair there, the sun won't be in your eyes. You'll join me in a cup of tea?'

His voice was pleasant and cultivated, rather old-fashioned. The tea was brought in by the lad as soon as he'd finished speaking. It was served in small cups without milk and had a startlingly fresh taste. As we sipped and made polite conversation – the company on our stagecoach journey, the pleasantness of an English April – I looked round his room and liked it. The architecture was as rustic as you'd expect in a cottage, with great ceiling beams that threatened the head of anyone more than five and a half feet tall, with mostly plain wooden furniture. Books and maps were everywhere and the open desk crowded with papers and pens. I noticed that the inside of our host's index finger was deeply ink stained and there was an ink spot on his otherwise immaculate shirt cuff.

We finished our tea. Mr Griffiths turned to my brother.

'Tom, since it is such a very fine day, I'm sure you won't object to taking yourself off for a walk for half an hour or so, while your sister and I enjoy a *gup*.'

'Gup?' I said.

He smiled.

'It's what Indians say for gossip. *Gup*, or even *gupgup*. Expressive, don't you think?'

I glanced at Tom and saw from his face that Mr Griffiths's more-or-less order to absent himself had come as a surprise to him. Still, since Mr Griffiths's silver hairs made our being alone together respectable, he could hardly object. Tom gave me a look that told me, as plain as speaking, to behave and allowed himself to be shown out.

'May I?'

Mr Griffiths was politely waiting for my permission to sit

down. When I nodded he sat at the chair by his desk. His long-fingered hand wandered towards one of the pens as if it didn't like being parted from it. I steeled myself for the likely lecture about what a fine young man my brother was and how it was my duty to go with him to India.

'You're fortunate in your brother, Miss Lane. He's as fine a young man as I've ever encountered.'

I sighed mentally, staring down at my gloves. Just as I'd expected.

'And I hope you won't resent the fact that he's told me something about the remarkable life you've been leading.'

No use saying that, yes, I did resent it. One of my gloves was developing a split in the seam.

'I'm afraid he's worrying a lot about his evidence to the committee. He feels he's being used as what one might call a witness against me,' Mr Griffiths said. 'I've told him that all he can do is speak the truth and trust me to deal with the consequences.'

'Tom will always speak the truth,' I said, looking him in the face now.

'Yes. To quote our Bard, he is "as true as truth's simplicity". But then, is truth always simple, do you think?'

He was looking at me as if he really wanted an answer. This interview was not going quite the way I'd expected.

'Yes, I think truth is simple,' I said. 'It's what we do to hide it that makes things complicated.'

He nodded, as if that had confirmed something.

'You see, Miss Lane, there are things I can't talk about to Tom.'

'What kind of things?'

'Who killed Burton and how that jewel came to be on my desk. Any talk we had about that would be only speculation, and unfair to Tom. His best way out of this is by telling the truth of what he heard and saw, pure and simple. He's all too ready to do battle on my behalf, and wreck his own future. I don't want that. But you're in no danger of having to give evidence to that committee, so I can talk to you.'

He saw the look of surprise on my face and added courteously, 'If you'll permit it.'

'But what can I do?'

I was mainly bowled over with relief that we weren't talking about Tom's plans for me.

'Share some thoughts with me. It's clear from what your brother says that you have an original way of looking at things.'

'I'd like to help you if I could, but . . .'

'I'm not asking you to help clear my name. I don't care one iota whether my name is cleared or not in the eyes of those rogues and fools who make up public opinion. It's not a murder trial and the committee can't hang me. But I do want to understand what happened.'

He waited, looking at me in a deliberately droll way, like a spaniel waiting to be thrown a biscuit. He might have been trying to hide the seriousness of his request so it would be easier for me to refuse.

'But this all happened with people I don't know, in a country I don't know and, I suppose, months ago.'

'Yes, it's more than six months since Burton died. Things move slowly between England and India. And yet your brain doesn't move slowly, does it, Miss Lane? I have a distinct impression that there are things you'd like to ask me.'

'You told Tom that the diamond hawk belonged to a lady. How did you know that?'

He'd invited questions but this one surprised him. His eyebrows went up.

'I'd seen a lady wearing it a long time ago.'

'How long ago?'

'Twenty years.'

'May I ask who the lady was?'

'Her identity is irrelevant to any of this. Twenty years is a long time ago to most people.'

The barrier was polite, but firm. No progress down that path.

'So how did it come into Mr McPherson's possession?'

'I don't know.'

'Was it one of the jewels his assistant was bringing him?'

'So we're led to believe. I believe your brother has told you the sequence of events. He discovered the hawk on my desk. We took it to the Governor. McPherson later identified it as one of the collection that Burton would have been carrying.'

His eyes were on me, waiting for the next question. For all his courtly politeness, I had an idea that he was testing me.

'Is there any reason to doubt that it was?' I said.

'I know of none.'

'Does it strike you as strange that Mr McPherson should have left his assistant to carry a valuable consignment of jewels by road?'

An emphatic nod.

'Very strange. Most people thought so.'

'Shouldn't they have expected an attack by bandits?'

'Possibly, yes. Though the roads of India are safer on the whole than you might imagine. That's one of the achievements of the Company. Still, in a country where wealth is so unequal, men will try to cure their poverty by violent means.'

'Did Mr Burton have an armed guard?'

'No. Only half a dozen servants. There was some sense in that. If you were moving something valuable by road, it might be safest not to draw attention to it. Safety in few, rather than safety in numbers.'

'Only they weren't safe. Somebody knew about the jewels,' I said.

From where I was sitting I could see Tom on the garden path. He stood, trying to see into the room to find out if we were still in conversation. Griffiths didn't notice him. After a while he walked away, presumably to make a few more circuits of the Green.

'Somebody would have known,' Griffiths said. 'I want to explain something about India, if I may, without trespassing on your patience. Every European there, even the most humble, is surrounded by an army of servants. Even his servants have servants. Your *mali*, your gardener, will have a boy to carry the watering cans and that boy will give another boy a few mouthfuls of chapatti to fill the cans for him. Your syce will have three or four boys at least to do the hard work around the horses that's beneath his dignity. The kitchen of even a single man will employ enough people to staff a fair-sized inn in England. Mostly, they're invisible to Europeans.'

'Not noticed because there are so many?'

'Exactly. Fine people in England make an affectation of not

noticing their servants but in India it's truly the case. If we even began to think about all those people we depend on for our daily lives we might lose our confidence altogether, and that wouldn't do, would it.'

'So you think McPherson's or Burton's servants would know about the jewels being transported?'

'That's what most people thought, yes. Apart from the poor man killed, the other servants with Burton ran away and were never found. A lot of people concluded they were in league with the robbers.'

'And yet you've come under suspicion for having something to do with it.'

He might well have taken offence, but his openness made me risk it. To my relief he beamed at me, like a tutor encouraging a pupil.

'Is it so surprising? Tom will have told you I threatened McPherson?'

'Yes. But surely nobody suggests you rode out at the head of a robber band.'

He laughed.

'Ah, but you see, Miss Lane, I didn't need to. My influence among the natives is so strong that I only have to crook my finger and they'll go out and kill whoever I please. It's all part of this annoyance with me for actually liking the company of the Indians and learning their customs. As far as some people in the Company are concerned, it's like being in league with the devil.'

'As bad as that?'

'Very nearly. There's fear at the bottom of it, of course. If the Indians realized their power, they could sweep our military bands and our magistrates and our bridge parties off the face of the country more easily than a dog shaking off fleas. In their hearts, the Europeans know that and if they think about it, it scares them.' Then he seemed to check himself for being too serious and smiled again. 'Miss Lane, forgive me for being heated. I must keep my rhetoric for this.' He gestured with his pen holder towards a considerable pile of paper on his desk.

'My pamphlet.'

It looked like a fair-sized book.

'On McPherson?'

'On the opium trade. It's already wrecked the Indian farmers, stupefied tens of thousands of poor addicts and if it goes on like this, it will have us at war with China. All it needs is the order from the government and hundreds of men will die to protect the fortunes of McPherson and his like. I'm hurrying to finish my pamphlet, so that I can publish while the committee's still sitting. If I do nothing else in my life, I want to wake the country up to what's being done in our name.'

'What about your position with the Company?'

'This is a higher duty than to the Company. As soon as this inquiry's over and my pamphlet out, I intend to resign my post and go back to India as a private person. I'll have done what I can and shall spend the rest of the days that are left to me studying.'

Tom was walking down the path now, with a determined air.

'So you had nothing whatsoever to do with the death of McPherson's assistant?' I said.

'Do you know, you're the first person in all this who's actually asked me that outright. The answer's no. I did not.'

The Indian lad showed Tom into the room.

'I hope you'll excuse us, sir,' he said to Griffiths. 'The next stage for town leaves in ten minutes and there's a long wait if we miss it.'

'Then you must go, with my thanks for allowing me to meet your sister. Miss Lane and I have had a most interesting conversation. You must bring her to see me again very soon.'

There were other passengers in the stage back, so Tom had no chance to ask the question that was obviously burning in his mind: had Mr Griffiths managed to convince me? I avoided his eye and mostly looked out of the window, wondering how much to tell him. Lying to Tom was clearly impossible, but Mr Griffiths had decided not to burden Tom with more speculation about Burton's death and that seemed a wise course. When we got down at St Paul's, we walked for a while, looking for a cab.

'So what did you make of him?' Tom said.

'An honest and interesting man.'

He beamed.

'I'm glad you thought so. What did you talk about?'

'Life in India.' And death rather more, but no need to say that.

'So has he convinced you?'

'I'm not sure he was trying to convince me.'

'That's Griffiths's way. He doesn't push you to a conclusion, just gives you some gentle guidance.'

'And we talked about his pamphlet.'

Tom's face clouded.

'You disagree with him?' I asked.

'No. I agree with him entirely. Only it's going to make a lot of trouble.'

'I think that's what he wants.'

A cab came. When we got down in Adam's Mews, Tom escorted me to the foot of my staircase but wouldn't come up.

'I'm supposed to be back at East India House. They get worried if I'm out of their sight for long. They haven't told me not to talk to Griffiths, but they'd like to.'

'As bad as that?'

'They're all worrying about what I'm going to say to this confounded committee. They know how I hate giving evidence against Griffiths.'

As he turned to go, I said: 'Do you think Mr Griffiths meant it, about wanting to see me again?'

'If he says it, he means it.'

'So we'll be going again?'

'If this committee business allows, yes.'

I was surprised how eager I was to see Mr Griffiths again. I'd liked him, but it was more than that. He'd piqued my professional curiosity with a puzzle I couldn't see how to solve and I knew I couldn't let it rest.

FIVE

For the next ten days or so, Tom and I existed in a state of more or less amicable truce. Once, he escaped from his duties at East India House to come riding in the park with Amos and me. We raced along Rotten Row and although Rancie and I easily beat him on his hireling hunter, we ended our race breathless and laughing, much as in the old days. But I couldn't help noticing his suspicious looks when gentlemen recognized me and raised their hats, though he said nothing. At least he had the sense to treat Amos as a friend. It might be 'Thank you, Legge' and 'Yes, Mr Lane' in the stable yard, but out in the park they rode side by side and talked, mostly about India. Amos was endlessly curious about it, and not only the horseflesh. He couldn't have enough of the sights and customs of the country.

Tom had seen the Gurkhas from the hills with their curved knives, a line of a hundred jewelled elephants in procession, the dervishes whirling. Once, when they thought I couldn't hear, he told Amos about the religious processions called *carkh puja* with men dancing with iron spikes stuck through their tongues or knives in their arms and legs, to win favour of the gods.

'Would you believe that one of them had made a hole in his arm with a dagger and threaded a live snake through it? But when his friends drew out the snake and bound up his arm, the wound hardly bled at all, no more than from a cut in your finger.'

And then again: '. . . the most beautiful women in the world. They wear a light silk garment called a sari, and have a way of drawing it across their faces, just so, with their eyes looking out at you over the top. And such eyes . . .'

But mostly he talked to Amos about the beauty of the country, the wonder of riding out in the cool of the morning into a world that seemed new-made, the variety and beauty of the people, the Bombay sunrises. I knew that was meant for me as well and, just as Tom hoped, it did make me want to see them for myself, only not on his terms. Sometimes, too, it made me think of another traveller in a distant country. When Robert set out on his travels, he'd written to me every week. We'd come close to each other through a dangerous time and he'd wanted me to marry him. I thought we should wait, not sure that he knew his own mind, and he'd gone abroad on a journey that would keep him away all year. He should be near Athens by now. I hadn't heard from him for two months.

Tom came to tea in the parlour with Mrs Martley and me several times. I'd taken the trouble to buy the finest China tea and served it without milk. He said it was almost as good as his *khitmutgar* made in camp over a fire of dried horse dung when they were travelling. I took that for a compliment. As we talked and drank, and exchanged some childhood memories, the strain that had been obvious on his face when he arrived would begin to drain away. Gradually he relaxed enough to talk about what was worrying him. I suppose he had to talk to somebody, and the men from the Company who'd been brought over to give evidence to the committee were Calcutta men. They were senior to him, older – and enemies.

'You have to have been out there to understand it, Libby, but there's a coarseness about the Calcutta men. It's the capital of the country, where the Governor-General lives, and all very grand; palaces on every corner and some of the streets you'd think you were in Bath. And it's the centre of our trade to the east, with Burma and China, so it's where the money men are. The Calcutta men pretty well look down on us in Bombay.'

I said I could see that Mr Griffiths wouldn't fit in there. It sparked an outburst from Tom.

'They hate him, Libby. Only now, I'm seeing how much they hate him. Back in India, it was more like contempt: "Mad Griffiths" or "Old Griffiths has gone completely native". The Calcutta men didn't want to be dragged back to give evidence to this committee, but now they're here, they're using it as a chance to discredit him.'

'Just as he's hoping to use it to make the case against compensating them for their opium.'

'That's partly why they want to destroy him. Though it's more personal than that. And I have to listen to them dripping their poison every day.'

'Couldn't you move out of Company lodgings? Come and stay here, if you like.'

'Too far away from the City. I'm still a servant of the Company. In theory, they've found me some temporary work in the accounts section in East India House, but it's so that the Calcutta faction have me under their eye. And their influence – they think.'

'Influence?'

'Going over and over my evidence to this confounded committee. Suggesting things about Griffiths's behaviour that might have slipped my memory and that I might care to include. Sheer bunkum.'

'But once you get in front of the committee, they can't influence what you say.'

'Of course not, and they shan't. I shall say exactly what I saw and heard, nothing else. But even that's bad enough.'

No denying it. What with the comments made about McPherson and the discovery of the hawk jewel, my poor brother was one of the main witnesses for the prosecution.

'But it's not like a court case,' I said, clutching at straws.

'No, it's worse. In a court case, there are rules. The judge won't allow hearsay evidence, for instance. A parliamentary committee can do what it damned well likes – sorry, Mrs Martley – just what it likes.'

'I've been thinking about your finding that hawk on his desk,' I said.

'I wish to goodness I'd thrown it straight in the waste-paper basket.'

'Did Mr Griffiths often ask you to fetch things from his desk.'

'Almost never – that's the ill luck of it.'

'Why not? I should think an assistant would be always fetching papers.'

Tom laughed, though not cheerfully.

'We discovered early on that it was a waste of time to ask me.'

'Why?'

'Because of what we called his poppadom filing system.'

He saw my puzzled look and explained.

'Poppadoms are a sort of flat bread the natives make, crisp and thin as parchment. They serve them in stacks, twenty or so at a time. That's how Griffiths kept his papers, in a lot of different stacks, all the papers on top of each other. He could plunge his hand in at any time and draw out just what he wanted, but nobody else could find anything.'

'And yet he sent you to find a report?'

'It surprised me at the time, but he said it was near the top of a pile, and it was.'

'Did everybody know about his way of keeping papers?'

'Yes. It was part of his eccentricity.'

Something didn't quite fit here. For the moment I put it away in my mental stack of poppadoms. There was something else I wanted to discuss.

'Mr Griffiths says you all have a lot of servants in India.'

'There's no avoiding it, and it would be inhumane even if you could. The few rupees we pay them are the difference between starving and not starving.'

'How many do you employ?'

He had to think about it.

'I share a bungalow with another man. There's the gardener, and two boys, or it might be three. A cook and his boy. Three or four cleaners, plus one who empties the chamber pots but isn't allowed to do anything else. The laundry woman we share with the bungalow next door, the punkah wallah and his assistant . . .'

'The what?'

'The man who pulls the rope that works the fan. You can't do without a punkah in that heat. Then there's the syce for our horses, another couple of boys, the bearer who runs messages . . .'

He stopped to think.

'That's already seven and a quarter servants for your share,' I said.

Tom laughed, entering into the game.

'Oh, that's only at home. When we ride out, there's the boy to hold the horse and a bearer to carry our guns or our work papers. In the office, half shares in another punkah wallah and quarter shares in the boy who brings round the tea. Of course, when we ride out on an inspection tour, that's another lot of bearers to set up camp, the mahout for the elephants and their boys and an escort of native soldiers.'

'It sounds as if you're never alone,' I said.

'You're not. That's one of the first things you have to get used to about India. But you will get used to it, I promise you.'

He'd noticed I was looking thoughtful, but mistaken the reason. Just as well.

'So there's always a lot of gossip among the servants. What was the word Mr Griffiths used?'

'*Gup*. Yes, and not just the servants. You wouldn't believe how the Europeans gossip, men as well as women. *Gupgup* all the time, even worse than London. It comes from not having enough to do.'

And, dear gods, he wanted to drag me into that world. I pressed on.

'So the whole of Bombay knew about this business of the hawk on Mr Griffiths's desk?'

'Pretty well, yes.'

'And they were saying that Mr Griffiths had got some of his Indian friends to kill Burton and steal the jewels?'

He shifted uneasily in his chair. The relaxed mood was draining away fast, but I needed to know.

'Some of them, yes. I mean, not actually saying so in terms, but . . .'

'And nobody asked Mr Griffiths outright?'

'I don't suppose so. You can't just sit down with a man and ask him if he's killed somebody.'

'I did.'

'What!' Tom nearly fell off his chair.

'To be precise, I asked him if he had anything whatsoever to do with the death of McPherson's assistant. He said he didn't.'

Tom had gone red in the face.

'You were talking about all this to Griffiths?'

'Yes.'

'Liberty, how could you? What must he have thought?'

'Probably that I was taking a decent interest in something that affects him and you very much.'

I didn't tell Tom that it was Mr Griffiths who'd brought up the subject. He wasn't listening in any case.

'I'd have thought I could have trusted you to behave with normal politeness. I must go to him at once and apologize. As for you—'

'He wasn't in the least offended. I can't believe that everybody was accusing him behind his back but nobody thought to ask him. Not even you.'

'Least of all me. Are you seriously suggesting that I should ask a man old enough to be my father, who also happens to be my friend, if he's a murderer?'

'Why not? You could have asked him at the same time why he sent you to find that hawk on his desk.'

At that point, my brother had a simple choice. He could explode through sheer indignation or he could start using his brain. It was a relief, on the whole, when he decided against explosion. Instead, he scowled at me and told me to stop talking nonsense.

'Unless India's addled your brain completely, it must have occurred to you,' I said. 'Mr Griffiths seldom sends you to find anything on a notoriously disorderly desk, but that day he does and you put your hand on the hawk almost at once. Just as he knew you would.'

'But anybody could have put it there.'

'That's true. But if somebody besides Griffiths himself put it there, he still knew it was there.'

'In that case, why leave me to find it?'

'Because he wanted a trustworthy witness.'

'Of what?'

'I don't know.'

Tom repeated, routinely, that I was talking nonsense but with less conviction in his voice.

'There's another thing,' I said. 'Both you and Mr Griffiths

have told me you can't go anywhere or do anything in India without servants. But that morning, McPherson rode out to meet Burton alone. Does that mean really alone, or with only half a dozen or so servants?'

This time his reply was prompt. 'Really alone. People were commenting on that.'

'And what did they say?'

'Even the man's enemies admit he's got good nerves. There were suggestions that the jewels Burton was bringing were more valuable than McPherson had let on and he didn't want a lot of gossip about them.'

'Did anybody see the jewels that hadn't been stolen, the ones in the wallet on Burton's body?'

'I suppose some people did. I don't know.'

'Since McPherson found the body, I suppose he must have taken the jewels off Burton's body himself.'

'I suppose so. What are you driving at?'

'Don't you think it's odd that the robbers didn't strip Burton's body and find the rest of the jewels?'

'They were disturbed, I suppose.'

'But I thought most of Burton's servants had run away. Those must have been very timid robbers.'

Tom ran a hand through his hair.

'I just don't see where this is heading.'

The truth was, I didn't either. It had all happened four and a half thousand miles away, mostly to people I'd never met. What was the use of being nagged by questions, and nagging my brother? Still, I risked one more.

'What happened to the hawk after you and Griffiths took it to the Governor?'

'I suppose he gave it back to McPherson. Now stop this, Liberty. I don't want to hear any more about it. And if I do take you to see Griffiths again, I expect you to promise that you won't talk about it to him.'

When I turned back from seeing Tom on his way, Tabby was waiting for me in the yard. I hadn't introduced her to him, thinking he had enough on his mind.

'I might be going away for a bit,' she said.

There was a truculent look about her.

'Is anything wrong?'

'Nah. Just fancy it.'

It was no use cross-questioning her, but my heart sank. The fact was, Tabby and I had a business disagreement. Life as an investigator was not all diplomatic parties. In quiet times, tracing the pet animals that so often went missing around the Park was one of our staples. Tabby, with her gang of urchins from her days of surviving on the streets, had always been an accomplished tracker of dogs, parrots and monkeys. As she picked up an increasingly polished way with clients, I'd turned more of that side of the business over to her and even had cards printed, 'Lost Animals Found', with our Abel Yard address, so that she could deliver them to the big houses. I'd not entirely given up hope of converting her to the advantages of being able to read and write.

Then it had come to my attention that Tabby and her gang did not always wait for the animals to go missing of their own accord. The urchins had taken to kidnapping them, then sharing the proceeds of returning them, as finders, to their grateful owners. When I'd told her it must stop, she'd been annoyed.

'We've never hurt none of them, not a hair nor a whisker.'

'I should hope not. But that's beside the point. It's dishonest.'

'People are happier when they get them back than if they'd never lost them in the first place.'

'That's also beside—'

'And it's only the rich ones we try it on. What they give us is only small change to them.'

I didn't say that was beside the point too, because it wasn't entirely. Working with me, Tabby had seen the way some rich people lived and been unimpressed. I couldn't blame her. How could I preach to a girl who'd had to fight for halfpennies in gutters that she should be content with her station in life?

I looked at her, in her neat grey dress with her hair clean and tied back. She was scuffing her shoe on the cobblestones as she did when her mind was uneasy. It was often the prelude to a dip back into her urchin mode. She'd sometimes vanish for a day or two, then appear suddenly and take up from where we'd left off. Something told me this was more serious and I was surprised that she'd taken the disagreement so much to heart. It had happened weeks before and should have blown over by now. Perhaps I should have taken more trouble to explain at the time, but I'd been much occupied then with one of the nastiest cases in my experience and had been determined to shield Tabby from it, so we hadn't been talking as much as we usually did.

'You'll come back?' I said.

All I got was a nod. I took a handful of coins out of my pocket and gave them to her.

'Don't need it.'

'Take it anyway. Let me know if you need me.'

I turned and went upstairs, to stop myself uselessly pleading with her. She was like a young fox that might consent to live with you for a while but will never surrender its freedom. That night there was no candle gleam from the cabin at the end of the yard where she lived.

At the start of the week, when Tom was due to give his evidence to the parliamentary committee, I received another invitation to a Mary Anne Disraeli 'At Home'. Considering that I'd exchanged hardly ten words with her on my previous visit, she seemed to have developed a surprising taste for my company. This time I waited on a sofa by the window, playing with somebody's lapdog, and sure enough the elegant figure of Mr Disraeli appeared beside me.

'May I?'

He flung back his coat-tails and sat down beside me, giving a passing stroke to the lapdog, just in case it was ever given a vote, I supposed.

'So what did you make of our friend Mr Griffiths?' he said.

The skill in dealing with Mr Disraeli was never to let him see he'd surprised you, so I just stopped myself from asking how he'd known.

'A very interesting gentleman,' I said.

'So I gather. He should certainly annoy most of the committee. You know it's loaded with friends of John Company, all wanting an excuse to go to war with China? Those McDruggies – I mean those excellent and reputable gentlemen in the opium trade – have packed the committee so thoroughly that they might as well conduct their deliberations reclining on divans and smoking pipes.'

He gave a lightning impression of an MP leaning back and inhaling, so droll that I almost laughed out loud.

'Why do you call the merchants the McDruggies?' I said.

'They do seem to include a remarkable number of Scotsmen. Fresh from Canton with a million of opium in each pocket, denouncing corruption and bellowing free trade, like Jardine and Matheson.'

'And Mr McPherson?'

'Indeed, like Alexander McPherson. I believe he's seeking a cool quarter of a million in compensation.'

'Is there nobody on the committee against them?'

'There's an earnest young man named Gladstone who's dead set against the war, but nobody listens to him.'

'So you're not on the committee yourself?'

He shook his head.

'So many demands, so little time.'

Which went a long way to explain Disraeli's interest. In spite of his failure so far to gain a ministerial post, he refused to believe that anything in the political world could happen without him. If, as was likely, he'd tried to be appointed to the India parliamentary committee and failed, he wouldn't rest until he knew more about its proceedings than any of the MPs involved.

'If you happen to meet Mr Griffiths again, you might warn him that McPherson and friends are doing their best to shred his reputation before he gives evidence to the committee,' he said, serious now.

'I think he knows that already.'

'Does he? He's an eccentric who spends his spare time talking to Indians instead of drinking whisky with his fellow countrymen, a troublemaker and quite probably a murderer. The committee will swallow it whole.'

'Then there's his pamphlet,' I said.

A sudden glint in his eye was the only indication that Disraeli hadn't known about that. I hoped I hadn't blundered, but then surely a man putting out a pamphlet doesn't wish for secrecy.

'Indeed. I'm sure we're all looking forward to that,' he said.

Two women were approaching, obviously intent on conversation with him.

'You'll excuse me, Miss Lane. Please give my good wishes to your brother. Do tell me if you think there's anything I should know about our friend.'

As often in my meetings with Mr Disraeli, I was left wondering if I'd found out more from him than he had from me. Honours equal this time, I hoped. But given his taste for sailing in stormy waters, his interest worried me.

SIX

I delivered Disraeli's message to Mr Griffiths the following afternoon, when he and I were taking a decorous walk in the sunshine beside the Thames at Richmond. Once again, he'd managed neatly to get us apart from my brother. The cottage was a chaos of straw and packing cases because Mr Griffiths had suddenly decided to move himself closer to the centre of things in London. He'd brought few possessions with him from India – a trunk of clothes, half a dozen carpets, some pictures and ornaments, several hundred books – but packing them for the carter seemed such a business that he greeted our arrival like a man besieged.

'Tom, my boy, I'm being driven mad. You know how I like things. Could you very kindly see to the last of the packing and spare your sister to take me for a walk in the fresh air?'

So we left Tom and the Indian lad, whose name was Anil, loading books into tea chests, with the carter's horse dozing in the shafts outside. As soon as we were through the garden gate, Mr Griffiths resumed his spry air, striding out and swinging his walking cane. He nodded when I passed on the warning about McPherson being determined to damage his reputation.

'Of course he is. Still, thank Mr Disraeli for his goodwill.'

'I told him about the pamphlet. Does it matter?'

'Of course not. I'm sending copies to all the MPs. I don't suppose more than a dozen will read it, but we must do what we can.'

He sounded quite cheerful about it. We stopped to watch some children with their nursemaid, throwing bread to the swans. I think he needed a rest from the brisk pace he'd set, but was trying to hide it.

'Tom's annoyed with me,' I said. 'He wanted me to promise that we wouldn't talk about what happened in India.'

'And did you promise?'

'No. He thinks I did, but that's only because he expects me to do as I'm told.'

He laughed. 'He should have more sense. So have you come to any conclusions?'

'How can I? I don't know anywhere near enough. All I've come up with are some more questions.'

'Such as?'

'Such as why Mr McPherson went out to meet the assistant on his own, and why the robbers only took some of the jewels and missed the really valuable ones.'

'Yes, those had occurred to me too.'

'Did they occur to anybody else in Bombay?'

'I believe there were questions, yes. But nobody discussed them with me.'

'This assistant, Burton, was he well known?'

'In Bombay, hardly at all. The first most people there knew about him was his funeral.'

We left the children and swans and walked on at a slower pace beside the river.

'There was another question,' I said. 'It's even occurred to Tom, though he wouldn't dream of asking you.'

'Oh?'

'Why did you send him to find that diamond hawk, when you knew it was there anyway?'

He said nothing for a few steps and I thought I'd gone too far, but when he answered his tone was calm, even amused.

'So Tom suspects that, does he?'

'If he thinks about it, only he won't let himself think.'

'He's very loyal to his friends.'

'Yes, so there's an obligation on his friends not to misuse his loyalty,' I said.

'I hope I'm not misusing it. He's told no lies. I sent him and he found it, just as he describes.'

'But you knew it was there?'

He swished his cane through a clump of cow parsley, setting it swaying.

'Miss Lane, if I answered that question, you'd feel obliged to tell your brother?'

'Yes.'

'Then you'll excuse me for not answering it at present.'

'So the answer is yes?'

'The answer is: wait.'

'Wait how long?'

'A week or two.'

'Until Tom's given his evidence to the committee?'

'And until my pamphlet is out. It will explain many things to you and others. Then we shall talk again.'

The tone was still perfectly good-humoured, but there was no budging him and we didn't talk again until we'd turned back towards the cottage. Then he broke the silence.

'There is one respect, at any rate, in which I'm not playing entirely fairly with your brother.'

'What?'

'He believes that I'm halfway to persuading you to join the fishing fleet.'

'Fishing?'

'Forgive me. That's the disrespectful term some men in India have for ladies sailing in search of husbands.'

'In some more words from our Bard, I'd sooner "lead apes in hell".'

'I'm sure of it. You'd hate life in India very much.'

'But you love the country.'

'The country, yes, but not our countrymen within it. And – with a few brave exceptions – our countrywomen even less.'

'Are they so ill-humoured?'

'In essence, no worse than most ladies here. But India makes caricatures of them. You know the way society ladies live in London – the calling cards, the dinners, the charity concerts by bad amateur musicians, the shredding of each other's reputations over the teacups?'

'All too well.'

My work sometimes took me into these horrors. Seeing them at close quarters was one of the reasons why I'd resisted my friends' efforts to marry me off to socially acceptable men.

'Well, imagine all these things with the thermometer at ninety degrees in the shade, with husbands absent on tours of duty, children at school thousands of miles away, sick with low level fever half the time, and so many people attending to your wants that you never even have to open a sunshade for yourself. All the tedium of being a fine lady in London multiplied a hundredfold.'

He smiled when I shuddered.

'Poor Tom,' he said.

We arrived back in town ahead of Mr Griffiths, who said he had business to finish off in Richmond, and Tom suggested that we should go to his new lodgings to superintend the unloading of his things. Mr Griffiths had rented rooms in the City, not far from where the coach set us down at St Paul's, so we strolled there slowly to give the carter time to arrive. On the way, we passed Tom's temporary workplace, the headquarters of the East India Company. It dominated Leadenhall Street with its great columned front, like an overgrown Greek temple but with top-hatted businessmen instead of priests pacing up and down the steps. A few minutes' walk away, Mr Griffiths had taken two floors of a tall grey stone house. The rooms were elegant and decorated in modern taste but had the lifelessness of a place let out by the month. A porter came up from the basement and helped us oversee the unloading of the packing cases, mildly curious about the new tenant. Would the gentleman be bringing his own servants? The porter's wife could oblige with meals sent up and laundry done. Would the gentleman be staying long? One servant only, Tom told him, and probably not long. He left the question of meals and bed linen for Mr Griffiths.

The cottage in Richmond had seemed much more cheerful and homely. I was surprised he'd decided to leave it when he could easily have travelled in and out for the hearing. Tom admitted he was surprised as well and said it had been a decision made in the last couple of days. We both wondered if this restlessness might be a sign that Mr Griffiths's nerves were not under such iron control as he liked to pretend. When I suggested that we might unpack to make the place more welcoming for his arrival, Tom instantly agreed. We spent a pleasant couple of hours unrolling carpets and silk wall hangings and placing books in the bookcases. Most of the books were leather bound and gilded, with titles in Latin, Greek,

Arabic and others that Tom identified as Sanskrit and Hindi. Tom unpacked Mr Griffiths's personal kit and laid out in the bathroom his sponge, razor and razor strop and bronze mirror. It was a fine room, with a gauze curtained window looking out over the street, black-and-white tiled floor and a fixed bath. You only had to turn a tap for a rush of cold water, presumably from a tank in the attic. Two gleaming cans stood beside the bath, ready for the servant or porter to carry up hot water from the basement. We walked round the rooms, satisfied with our efforts, and left the key with the porter for Mr Griffiths's arrival later.

That was the day before Tom's evidence to the parliamentary committee on East India Company affairs. I knew he didn't want to talk about it, so had just wished him good luck when we parted. When the day came, I couldn't help thinking about him and around midday I put on my cloak and bonnet and walked through Green Park and St James's Park to Westminster. I knew that the committee was holding its sessions in a room off Westminster Hall. The great hall, nearly eight hundred years old, had miraculously survived the fire that had destroyed the rest of the Palace of Westminster six years before. While our legislators argued about plans for rebuilding, they had to carry on their business as best they could in what was left to them. Of course, the public weren't allowed into the committee but there was nothing to stop anybody lingering in Westminster Hall. I thought I'd just wait there to watch Tom come out. If he looked reasonably composed and had people with him, I should keep in the background and not ever let him know that I'd been there.

Inside, the hall was like a cathedral – stone-flagged floor, great wooden roof beams, dim light from small windows high up. But the atmosphere was alive with men walking and talking, quietly in conspiratorial groups or calling to each other loudly, like boys in a playground. Frock-coated servants of the House hurried around, with messages for MPs. Ordinary people, nervous in best clothes, stood on the edge of things, probably hoping for a word with somebody willing to listen to their problems. Lawyers in wigs and silk gowns swept past, clerks loaded with papers trailing behind them. There must have been two or three hundred people there, dwarfed by the size of the hall, and only a few women. Other committees beside the one I was interested in were sitting in various rooms off the hall and each one had its own group of men waiting outside. In one group, some of the faces between the tall black hats and white stocks looked more sun-browned than the rest. A clerk confirmed that, yes, this was the East India committee. I found an inconspicuous place by the wall, where I could keep the door to the committee room in sight and waited.

It was the glint of the thing that caught my eye. In the dim light, with most of the men in black coats, it flashed like a sudden jet of water. A group of men, five or six of them, had come in to the hall and were walking in my direction. The tallest one was leading the way, the others following him like courtiers. He was perhaps in his early fifties with a square, forceful-looking face. His broad nose looked as if it had been broken and reset badly. Even in this setting, there seemed a piratical air about him, as if he'd be in his element superintending the firing of cannons. Dark eyebrows with traces of grey jutted over narrow eyes that were moving all the time, as if observing the people round him then discarding them as not important enough for lingering. None of these were the first things anybody would notice about his appearance. What was drawing most of the eyes in this part of the hall, as well as mine, was the ornament he wore on the lapel of his coat: a diamond hawk as big as a woman's hand, with ruby eyes and talons. On a man who was otherwise in conventional business clothes it should have looked absurd, but the fierce beauty of the thing and the confidence of the man wearing it made it look like a declaration of power.

A buzz went through the group waiting outside the committee room. Some of them walked up to the man. I didn't need the 'Hello McPherson', to tell me who he was. He asked a question I couldn't hear and nodded at the answer. Watching him, I didn't at first notice the man who was walking in our direction from the far end of the hall. As he came closer I saw it was Mr Griffiths, strolling along and looking up at the great roof beams as if simply out for a constitutional walk. I guessed that, like me, he'd come to meet Tom and probably had no idea that McPherson was there. Then one of McPherson's group noticed him and said something. McPherson had been chatting to his neighbour, but instantly his head came up. Almost at once his posture became challenging, bull-like, feet braced, eyes glaring. Almost at once, but not quite. I doubt if the men around McPherson saw it, but from where I was standing I had caught the first expression on McPherson's face and it had looked very like alarm. By then, the men around McPherson had gone quiet and were all staring at Mr Griffiths. It must have been a shock to him when he looked down from the roof beams and caught that collective stare, but he held his nerve and kept walking. When he came to a halt, a few yards away from them, there was a smile on his face. Everybody had gone quiet so that it seemed as if the great hall was concentrated on the meeting between the two enemies.

Mr Griffiths spoke first, in a conversational tone, but loudly enough for bystanders to hear.

'Good afternoon, McPherson. Sporting your jewellery collection, I see.'

McPherson gave him a hard look down his boxer's nose. 'I'm surprised you've got the face to come here. Or are you getting up a protest meeting?'

His voice was a deep and arrogant drawl. If he'd ever had a Scottish accent, it had vanished in his time out east. Some of the men round him tittered as if he'd made a good joke. It seemed an unfair encounter, McPherson surrounded by his cronies, Mr Griffiths very much alone.

'I don't need protest meetings,' Mr Griffiths said, sounding quite unworried. 'I think actions are better than words. Although words have their uses too.'

'Are you threatening me?'

McPherson's voice was a bull-like roar. It looked as if he was having to restrain himself from charging at Mr Griffiths and tossing him aside.

'With words?'

If McPherson was the bull, Mr Griffiths was taunting him like a picador, though it was hard to see why what he said should annoy his target so much.

'You're determined to slander me, aren't you?' McPherson said.

'How could any words of mine hurt the reputation of a man so prosperous and well regarded?'

Mr Griffiths's tone was satirical, but it seemed an odd thing to say for a man who had spent years bombarding McPherson's reputation with words.

'If you have anything to say against me, why not come out with it?'

Mr Griffiths smiled. 'I shall, in the fullness of time.'

'So I suppose I must wait and tremble,' McPherson said.

His attempt to meet sarcasm with sarcasm sounded forced, but it brought louder sycophantic titters from his supporters.

'Just so,' Mr Griffiths said. 'Meanwhile, make the best of what's left to you.'

He nodded towards the hawk, turned and walked away and out of the hall as steadily as he'd walked with me by the river the day before.

McPherson stood looking after him, the men round him chattering and laughing as if he'd scored a victory. I was worried about Mr Griffiths and might have gone after him but at that moment the door to the committee room opened, Tom came out and McPherson was called inside. It was his turn to give evidence. Tom was pale-faced and miserable. Some of the men who'd been waiting closed round him, obviously wanting to know what had happened. When they'd got their answers they strolled away, leaving Tom standing there on his own. By this time, there was no sign of Mr Griffiths. I went up to Tom. He might have been angry that I'd come there, but I could no more have left him than when he'd been lost and alone in the woods at home. He came towards me and gripped my hand.

'Oh Libby, I feel like Judas.'

I tried to reassure him that none of it was his fault. We walked together through the hall and out into the sunshine.

'Was it worse than you'd expected?'

'Not really worse, but bad enough. Some of them were really out to destroy Griffiths, every little rumour and sneer from cutting one of the governor's dinners to wearing native dress sometimes. Why shouldn't a man dress as he likes in his own bungalow?'

'I can't see what that's got to do with the proper government of India.'

'Disrespect for the authorities, bringing the English into disrepute. As if some of the wine-swilling bullies we send out there weren't doing that all the time. McPherson will twist that committee round his finger. I suppose he's in there now, demanding compensation for his opium.'

We walked alongside the river for a while, watching boats going up and down. The tide was out and even this early in the summer the smell was so bad that we walked back to St James's Park. In the sweeter air by the lake he relaxed a little and sighed.

'At least it's over now.'

I didn't like having to tell him about the scene between McPherson and Mr Griffiths, but it would be worse if he heard it from anyone else. I tried to play it down as much as I could, but it depressed his spirits all over again.

'It won't help him,' Tom said. 'Griffiths himself has to appear before the committee on Monday. After the poison McPherson and his cronies had been spreading, what I had to tell them and now this, they'll tear him apart.'

'I don't think he's so easy to tear,' I said.

But Tom wouldn't be comforted. We stood for a while, watching ducks upend themselves in the water.

'So what happens to you, now you've given your evidence,' I said.

He shrugged.

'Another few weeks here, I suppose, then back to Bombay.'

My heart lurched. Having found Tom again, I dreaded losing him.

'Only a few weeks?'

'A month perhaps. Now the other men have come all the way to England they're in no great hurry to go back, and I suppose they'll send me on the same ship.'

With men he thoroughly disliked, to a career he'd probably blighted by being on Griffiths's side.

'Must you go back? I'm sure we could find work for you here.'

I had a few influential friends, but not many. I'd struck the wrong note and Tom frowned.

'Using my sister's kind influence to get me a job on a clerk's stool? No thank you. Liberty, I want to talk to you seriously.'

I'd known this was coming, though I'd hoped it wouldn't be today.

'Well?'

'I've done what you wanted. I've talked to Daniel Suter and Legge. I know the life you've been leading while I've been away.'

'Quite an eventful one,' I said.

His grave manner was sparking off the spirit of contradiction in me again, even though I felt sorry for him.

'I can see that in some cases you had no choice . . .'

'And in others I made a choice.'

'. . . and your motives have been honourable on the whole . . .'

'On the whole! I've never done anything that's dishonourable.'

'I'll accept that. But setting up to earn your living as . . . as . . .'

He was almost choking on it.

'As a private inquiry agent,' I said. 'It's more interesting than giving music lessons, though not much more profitable on the whole. Still, we live.'

'It's got to stop, Liberty.'

We walked on in silence for a while, and his next words were in a lower voice.

'So is there somebody in this country, Libby?'

What could I tell him that was true? Yes, I'd thought there was somebody, only he wasn't in this country now, probably in Athens already or beyond that for all I knew. He'd offered to marry me, only I'd thought he wasn't sure of his own feelings and had sent him travelling. Still no letters. It was a big world, full of women, and Robert was a romantic at heart. In other circumstances I might have confided my loss, and possibly my foolishness, to Tom.

'No, not really.'

'I hoped Griffiths might have convinced you by now.'

Naturally, I wasn't going to tell him about his friend's treason in this respect. I asked him if he intended to call on Mr Griffiths.

'Yes, tomorrow afternoon or Sunday. He'll need to know what line the committee's taking.'

We didn't say much more as we walked through the park and across Piccadilly to Abel Yard. We parted at the bottom of the stairs. I watched him walk away, his shoulders slumped, and felt an unreasonable anger against India and everybody in it for doing this to us.

The weekend passed without a visit from Tom. I rode in the park with Amos on the Saturday, walked with Mrs Martley. Although she didn't realize it, our walk took us to some of the places in the park where Tabby's urchin friends congregated. I hoped I might see Tabby at least, even if she wouldn't talk to me, but there was no sign of her. All the time I was wondering about Tom's meeting with Mr Griffiths. I hoped that Mr Griffiths would do a better job of cheering him up than I'd managed. Soon after eleven o'clock on Monday morning, Tom's call from the bottom of the stairs told me that had not happened.

'Libby, are you up there?'

His voice was sharp and urgent. He came rushing upstairs, hat in hand, face white.

'Tom. What's wrong?'

It was in my mind that he and Mr Griffiths must have quarrelled, but his next words were much worse.

'He's dead, Libby. Griffiths is dead.'

SEVEN

I took him to my own room upstairs and sat him down on the couch.

'What happened?'

'He's killed himself.'

'No!' Then, uselessly, 'Are you sure?'

'I found him, Libby.'

'Tell me.'

If Tom had been less shocked, he might have tried to spare me the details. As it was, he poured the story out, trying to come to terms in his own mind with the reality of it, still hardly believing.

'I told you I was going to call on him over the weekend. I went on Saturday afternoon. His boy, Anil, came to the door and told me Griffiths sahib was sorry but he had a visitor and couldn't see me. He sent down a message inviting me to come to breakfast with him this morning at eight o'clock. That surprised me a little, that he hadn't suggested I should call on Sunday instead of Monday morning, but I thought he might have overstrained his heart and wanted a day to rest. We'd quite often have breakfast together back in Bombay. We'd talk about anything and everything – Persian poetry, or the letters of Cicero, or some bird he'd seen, or politics. You never knew. That's one of the fascinating things about him. Was, I mean.' He swallowed a few times and went on. 'Would you believe, I was looking forward to it. You'd helped convince me that I'd got myself into a stupid state about the committee. I hadn't told them anything about Griffiths they didn't know already so I didn't have to feel badly about facing him. I even thought I'd tell him how awful some of the members were and we'd have . . . have a good laugh about it.'

He drew a long breath and sat with his hand to his eyes. I took out the Madeira bottle I keep in my desk cupboard for clients and poured him a good glassful. He drank it at a gulp.

'Sorry, Libby. As I said, I was looking forward to seeing him. I was ringing his bell just after eight. I expected Anil to come down and let me in. When he didn't, I thought he was preparing breakfast upstairs and hadn't heard. I tried the door and it was only latched, not locked, so I pushed it open and went upstairs. We never stood on ceremony. I went into that big room with the bookcases and called good morning to him. No reply, and no sign of Anil either. No smell of coffee. I suppose that should have struck me as odd. Then I thought perhaps he'd overslept and Anil was in the bedroom, helping him dress or shave. So I just picked up one of his books, sat down and started reading. I got interested in the book and it was probably ten minutes or so later that it struck me that things were very quiet. No sound of anybody moving. So I thought maybe he'd had to go out early and had taken Anil with him. He might have forgotten he'd invited me, though that wouldn't have been like him. So I stood up to go but I thought I'd take a glance in the bedroom, just in case he happened to be still in there and asleep. I opened the door. Nothing. The bed hadn't been slept in. Then I noticed that the door from the bedroom to the bathroom was half open.'

A long pause. He sat, head lowered, breathing deeply. When he looked up, his expression was dazed, as if living the scene again.

'Have you ever felt as if your mind's split itself in two? As if half of it's saying that of course everything is quite all right, nothing to worry about, while the other half's screaming out that something terrible has happened? That's the way I felt, looking at that door and the sunlight coming through the doorway from the bathroom window. It was just a door, and yet somehow I already knew what I'd see when I went through it.'

'Yes,' I said.

Only I didn't think Tom heard. In any case, it wouldn't have helped him then to tell him why I knew exactly what he meant.

'So I opened the door and went in,' Tom said. 'The sun was bright, even through the curtain, and it was shining in my eyes so I couldn't see properly. He was sitting up in the bath facing me, with his back to the window. I felt embarrassed and started apologizing. I think it was the smell that told me, before anything else. The blood smell, you know, like iron filings.'

'Yes, I know.'

'I looked down and the water was red. It came halfway up his chest. I was thinking, stupidly, "What's he doing sitting there in red water?" I think I'd even taken a step forward to lift him out of it, then I saw his wrist. His left wrist it was, just under the water. It was cut nearly half through, flopping back. His other wrist had got trapped between his body and the side of the bath, but when we got him out that was cut through too.'

'We?'

'Myself and the men from East India House.'

'How did they know?'

'I went and told them. Not immediately. I . . . I had to be sure he . . . really was dead. I knelt down and put my hand on his chest. No heartbeat. I remembered you were meant to try a feather, so I went to the bed and found a feather out of the pillow and held it under his nose. Not a breath. His eyes . . . his eyes were open. All the time, I half expected him to laugh and ask what I was doing. Only . . . oh, Libby.'

I went and sat beside him on the couch and held him. It was a long time before he moved away.

'I must go back. There'll be things to do. They said the coroner's officer will want to speak to me because I found him.'

'He'll wait for a while,' I said.

I got up, poured Madeira for both of us and went back to sit beside Tom.

'So you went and told them at East India House?'

'Yes. It was just round the corner. It was the obvious thing to do. I passed a police constable and thought of telling him, but what would have been the good?'

'How did people react when you told them?'

'Shocked. The first one I told was Mr Jarvis. He's the head of the section where they've put me, not a bad old stick. But before I knew it, the Calcutta men had taken over.'

'You mean, the ones who didn't like Mr Griffiths?'

'Yes. Three of them came back to his rooms with me. They called the porter up from the basement to lift him out of the water and wrapped him in sheets and blankets off the bed. There was blood and water everywhere.'

'They told the police?'

'There was a little crowd outside the house by then. People knew something had happened. A constable came up to them and one of the Calcutta men sent him to tell the coroner. They took his body away in a cart.'

'These Calcutta men, was Alexander McPherson one of them?'

'No, but he'll know by now. I dare say he's gloating.'

A flash of anger went over Tom's face, then he hung his head again.

'If only I could have seen Griffiths over the weekend. I might have persuaded him that things weren't as bad as they seemed.'

'Why are you so sure he killed himself?'

'Libby, haven't you been listening?'

'Just tell me.'

'The old Roman way. If a Roman was facing defeat or dishonour, killing himself was the proper thing to do. Very often, he'd have his servants prepare a warm bath, then slit his wrists and calmly bleed to death.'

'And was the water warm when you found him?'

'Of course not. It was stone cold. It would have gone cold.'

'Those hot water cans in the bathroom, did they look as if they'd been used?'

'For heaven's sake, do you think I was worrying about hot water cans?'

The porter would know, I thought.

'But he wasn't facing death or dishonour,' I said.

'He'd have been in front of that damned committee this afternoon.'

'He didn't seem in the least worried about the committee. I had the impression he was even looking forward to it.'

Tom shook his head.

'That was before what happened on Friday, when McPherson humiliated him in public.'

'But he didn't. I told you what happened.'

'That's not the way the Calcutta men have been putting it

around. In their account, all Griffiths could do was splutter threats and they all laughed at him.'

'He didn't splutter and McPherson seemed quite put out when he was teasing him about things he might say.'

'What things, do you think?'

'His pamphlet, I assumed.'

'The Calcutta men don't say anything about that. In their account, he got the worst of it and slunk away with his tail between his legs.'

'He certainly didn't slink. I thought he seemed quite pleased with himself.'

'He must have been keeping up a front. Then he was alone all the weekend, thinking about it.'

'Not alone all the time, if he had a visitor on Saturday afternoon. Who was it, do you think?'

Tom groaned.

'I don't know. I just don't know. But I must go back.'

'What happened to the pamphlet?'

'It's with his things, I suppose.'

'But we unpacked his things for him. The pamphlet wasn't with them. It was quite a big bundle of manuscript. We wouldn't have missed it.'

'Then he must have kept it with him. It will be in his rooms somewhere.'

'And the servant boy, Anil? Where was he in all this?'

'Nowhere to be seen. The men thought he must have found Griffiths's body, got scared and run off.'

'In a city he doesn't know?'

'It surprised me, I admit. Anil had been in Griffiths's household all his life.'

'But he's only fourteen or so from the look of him.'

'Yes, but his father had been Griffiths's *khitmutgar*. That's how these things go. He was devoted to Griffiths.'

'So he finds him dead and just runs away?'

'Indians see things differently.'

I wasn't so sure about that, but there was no point in arguing. Tom stood up.

'I must go. There'll be so much to see to. Nobody seems to know even who his next of kin is.'

'I'm sure the Calcutta men will see to all that,' I said.

Tom picked up the sarcasm in my voice and nodded.

'Yes, they will if they can. They'll be putting the word round already: "Mad Griffiths couldn't face the committee and killed himself". That's why I want to be back at East India House, to protect his reputation as best I can. I don't want to fail him all over again.'

'Tom, you did not fail him.'

'Didn't I? I give evidence against him, and two days later he kills himself. Doesn't that seem like failure to you?'

I tried to protest but he wouldn't listen and practically ran away downstairs. I think he didn't want me to see him losing control again. I sat and thought about it for a while, then put on my coat and bonnet, walked to Piccadilly and caught a coach to the City.

The crowd had gone from the house where Mr Griffiths had lodged so briefly. The porter was sweeping the front steps and recognized me from three days ago.

'Was he your father, miss?'

'No, just a friend. But I've come to see to his things.'

'The gentlemen locked up his rooms and took away the key. They said they'd be back.'

'What gentlemen?'

'The ones who were here after they found him this morning.'

Calcutta again. Why should they be so careful of the possessions of a man they despised? A small lie seemed justified.

'I think I left my shawl when my brother and I were unpacking the other day,' I said. 'I'd be sorry to lose it.'

I'd come prepared for modest bribery. The half-crown I slipped into his palm prompted him to be kind and remember that there was a service door from the back stairs that had not been locked. He led the way up broad, uncarpeted stairs and through the doorway to the landing. When he opened the door to the main room, a faint metallic tang of blood was still in the air.

'At least he did it tidy enough,' he said. 'Money worries, was it?'

I made as slow a business as I could of looking for my hypothetical shawl, although the tidiness of the room made that difficult. Mr Griffiths seemed to have disturbed very little after the unpacking Tom and I had done, apart from leaving his velvet smoking jacket on the back of the chair by his desk. The desk was open. If his pamphlet were anywhere, it would surely be there. I went over to it and shifted the smoking jacket as if looking underneath. A simple desk, only two shelves and four pigeonholes, all empty. We'd unpacked his blotter, ink bottle and tray of pens and laid them out ready for him. Two sheets of paper lay on the blotter. One of them was a note in what looked like his handwriting, as far as I remembered it from just a glance at his manuscript.

> I trust you are safely settled in. Please do not hesitate to cash and make use of the enclosed as soon as possible. I hope to see you within the next day or two. E.G.

The other smaller sheet was a bank draft in the same handwriting for one hundred pounds, made out to 'Bearer'. Obviously, he'd intended to fold the draft inside the note and address it. The other side of the note was blank. Luckily, the porter hadn't been watching, preoccupied by a rather detailed drawing propped against the wall of what was probably an Indian temple carving. Tom had tried to prevent me from seeing it when we unpacked and left it with its face to the wall. Griffiths, or somebody, must have turned it round. I opened the doors of the cupboard beneath the desk. Empty as an eggshell.

'Did you hear or see anything last night?' I said to the porter.

He turned quickly.

'Not a sound. I'm a good sleeper.'

'I suppose you don't know where his servant went?'

'No. Just scarpered, like they do.'

'Where did he sleep, I wonder?'

I'd meant the servant boy, but the porter nodded towards the main bedroom.

'In there.'

He opened the bedroom door, probably assuming by now that my shawl had been just an excuse for morbid curiosity. The bed was made, not slept in. A small camp bed in a corner answered the question of where the servant slept. An unlit spirit lamp, a jar of coffee beans and a brass coffee grinder stood on a table near the camp bed. Mr Griffiths had been living simply, like a traveller. The only likely place for a pile of manuscript was the chest of drawers. I walked across and opened the top one.

'The gentlemen said they'd send for his things,' the porter said, a little uneasy now.

'Just in case my shawl got put inside,' I said.

We'd left Mr Griffiths to unpack his own clothes. The top drawer contained nothing but clean shirts, underlinen and cravats. The second held two beautifully embroidered silk tunics of the kind a high-born Indian man might wear, carefully folded. The other two drawers were empty. The porter had gone through to the bathroom. I could hear him opening the window. I had a quick look under the mattress, though there was no reason why Mr Griffiths should have hidden his manuscript. Nothing. I went and stood in the doorway of the bathroom. The black and white tiles had been mopped clean but were still damp. The bath had been cleaned too. Mr Griffiths's big yellow sponge was propped on the edge of it, surprisingly unbloodied. As ordinary objects can, it brought home the loss of him more than anything else had done. I looked away from it to the two hot water cans on the floor.

'Did he ask you to bring hot water up to him last night?' I said.

'Not last night, no.'

'Nor very early this morning?'

'He'd have been dead by then, wouldn't he? Why are you asking?'

'I'm not sure. I suppose when somebody you know kills himself, you want to know what he was thinking.'

'Uncle of mine jumped in the canal because he'd lost his taste for beer,' the porter said.

'So no hot water?'

'The only hot water I took up to him was Sunday morning, and he said only half a can, for a wash.'

So Mr Griffiths had not even allowed himself the Roman comfort of a warm bath to die in. I walked over to the window and found myself looking down on the crown of a black top hat.

'It looks as if one of the gentlemen's come back,' I said.

'I might be in trouble if they know I let somebody come up here. You'd better go quick down the back stairs, miss, shawl or no shawl.'

I let him usher me back through the service door, but instead of going downstairs I left it open a crack and waited just behind it, while he went to meet the visitor. I heard their footsteps coming up the main staircase and peered out, getting quite a good view of the gentleman. He wasn't flaunting the diamond hawk today, but the jutting eyebrows and broad broken nose were unmistakeable. Alexander McPherson in person.

'You can go,' he said to the porter. 'I'll call you if you're needed.'

The porter left. McPherson went inside the main room and closed the door. I could hear him moving about inside the room, as if looking for something. Trying to track his steps, I judged that he was standing looking down at the desk. The steps paused there long enough for him to read the note and draft, then went through to the bedroom. He was walking round there longer than you'd expect for a sparsely furnished room. I heard drawers open and close, then what sounded like a wooden lid being lifted up and put down. The only thing in the bedroom with a lid was the commode. I hadn't thought of looking in there. Alexander McPherson was making a thorough search and, judging by the way he went on roving around, not finding what he was looking for. After a while I heard the door slamming and his footsteps stamping downstairs. I ran back into Griffiths's rooms and looked out of the bathroom window as he walked away down the street. He was swinging his arms as he strode along, so not carrying anything. His overcoat was well fitted, with nothing bulging out the pocket – or certainly nothing as heavy as a wadded up manuscript. I waited for him to get well on his way, then went back downstairs and let myself out quietly, so as not to alert the porter again. So Alexander McPherson had not found what he'd come for. Then again, neither had I.

EIGHT

I walked from the City to Fleet Street. At the east end of it, not far from Ludgate Hill, a narrow alleyway leads to a cobbled courtyard within bad-smelling distance of the Thames. The creaking and tapping sounds that came from open doorways around the courtyard in various competing rhythms marked it as one of the communities of small printing shops that cluster behind the larger buildings of Fleet Street. As far as I knew, it was the present working place of my radical printer friend, Tom Huckerby. He and his printing press never stayed in one place long, because of threats from bailiffs and the paid bullies of public men who thought he'd libelled them. He sometimes had, but they deserved it, more often than not. My luck was in. He was at work, leaning over a galley of type. I waited until he straightened up and greeted me by my first name. He was part of a staunch Republican tradition that didn't hold with titles, not even Mr or Miss. After asking after each other's health, I came to business.

'Tom, if you wanted to get quite a large pamphlet printed in a hurry, where would you take it?'

He puffed out his cheeks and spread his arms in a gesture indicating the whole of Fleet Street and probably places beyond.

'Yes, I was afraid of that,' I said.

'Seditious, is it?'

'I haven't read it. At a guess, it will annoy a lot of powerful and wealthy people, but not seditious or treasonable.'

'That makes it harder. Not everyone will print something that might land him in Newgate, but aside from that you could take your pick from several hundred.'

'If it helps at all, the man who wrote it spent most of his life in India and probably doesn't know many people in London. Are there any printers who specialize in Indian affairs?'

He thought about it.

'Probably, back in the City near East India House. But I'd guess those are some of the gentry your friend wants to annoy?'

'Yes.'

'So if he's got any sense, he wouldn't go to any of those, or people might get wind of it and try to stop it.'

'I think he had sense.'

He acknowledged the past tense with a raise of the eyebrow.

'So you can't ask the man himself?'

'No.'

'I'll ask around, if you like. What was his name?'

'Griffiths. The pamphlet was against the opium trade with China. And he'd probably have wanted it done within a few days.'

'Not unusual. Most people want it done the day before yesterday. I'll let you know if I find out anything.'

Then, being a journalist and political to his ink-stained fingertips, he wanted to know what it was all about. If I'd been working for a client I should have been discreet, but as it was I could see no harm in telling him more or less the full story. He knew already about the committee looking into the affairs of the East India Company, but hadn't heard about the confrontation between Mr Griffiths and Alexander McPherson in Westminster Hall.

'I can use it,' he said.

'You'll keep my brother out of it?'

'Of course. Give my regards to young Fraternity.'

He was the only one who still used my brother's radical middle name. I suspected brother Tom himself would like to forget it.

Before I left, Tom Huckerby had already scribbled out the paragraph he intended to put in the next edition of his paper *The Unbound Briton.*

> We hear that the temperature is rising to Indian heights around Leadenhall Street. Recently arrived in town from Calcutta is one Alexander McPherson, a commercial gentleman whose main business is smuggling shiploads of opium into China. Since the ungrateful Chinese have

> seized and burned some of his cargoes, Mr McPherson has arrived at Westminster to demand vengeance and compensation. He has given evidence to the committee of MPs looking into the way John Company is using its vast and chartered powers over millions of our fellow human beings. He recently honoured Westminster Hall with a visit, blazing with looted diamonds. An altercation arose between him and a certain E. Griffiths, a servant of the Company who has greatly annoyed his colleagues. Griffiths's offence was to criticize the policy of using our navy to protect the fortunes of McPherson and his merry smuggler friends. Griffiths had the best of the Westminster Hall debate. Since when he has sadly died in mysterious circumstances, though not before confiding his pamphlet against the opium merchants to the printers. We await its publication with interest.

I made a few objections.

'It was just the one big brooch,' I said. 'Not exactly blazing. And we don't know it was looted.'

'Of course it was. All jewels from India are looted.'

'And you do realize that you're practically accusing McPherson of murdering Mr Griffiths?'

He put on an innocent face.

'Am I really? Where does it say so, exactly?'

'And we don't know the manuscript is with printers. I just hope it is.'

'So if it is, this might flush it out.'

I gave up. The readership of *The Unbound Briton* was devoted, but quite small, and appreciated good political punching rather than slavish sticking to facts. Besides, it wasn't my duty to look after the interests of the Calcutta men.

I thanked Tom Huckerby and turned to go.

'Has Tabby found what she was looking for?' he said.

I turned back.

'Looking for? What do you mean?'

'She turned up here out of the blue four or five days ago, asking where rich bastards went to make money.'

'What!'

I had thought I was managing to clean up her language. She'd developed a liking for Tom Huckerby and his printing friends that was surprising in a girl so determinedly illiterate.

'She had this idea that there were places where rich men congregate, something like pickpockets or beggars all lodging in the same part of town. Not so wrong, after all. She's got a lot of sense, that girl,' Tom said.

'So what did you tell her?'

'I mentioned gentlemen's clubs, but she seemed to know about those.'

'She would. We had a case involving one.'

'It turned out she'd picked up some notion of the stock exchange. I told her about Capel Court, where the stockjobbers trade.'

'Why did she want to know about stockjobbing? Tabby's never had more than a shilling or two in her life.'

'I supposed she was on some kind of errand for you.'

'No. It would have been something specific, not vague like that.'

'Maybe she's setting up on her own,' Tom said.

He meant it as a joke, but I was worried. It looked as if Tabby had taken our difference of opinion on business ethics very much to heart. She surely had too much sense to think that her apprenticeship was over and she could go out and look for cases on her own account. Or did she think she could pick up work the way she once begged halfpennies? I asked Tom to please try and persuade her to get in touch with me if she called on him again, and he promised he would.

I hoped my brother might call in the afternoon, but he didn't. I supposed he was too busy with the formalities of Mr Griffiths's death. That evening, no glint of light from Tabby's cabin, no letters, no clients, no distractions. I drank tea and ate Welsh rarebit for supper with Mrs Martley, spent a conscientious hour doing accounts and went early to bed. In the morning, a shout came up from Mr Grindley, the carriage repairer in the yard.

'Letter for Miss Lane.'

I flew downstairs with a handful of small change to pay the

postman, hoping for news from Athens. The letter he handed over to me was a double disappointment. It was a mere local letter, not a well-travelled one, and was addressed not to me but to Thomas Lane Esquire c/o Abel Yard, Adam's Mews. The address was written in a clerkly hand and the thing had a formal look about it. Probably something from the East India office about Tom's employment, though I was surprised he'd given them my address. When he arrived at last, in mid-afternoon, his exhausted look drove the letter from my mind. His gloves and neckcloth were black. Even his shirt studs were small knobs of jet.

'The inquest?' I said.

He nodded.

'What was the verdict?'

'That he took his own life.'

'Just that?'

He nodded. So no half-consoling addition of 'while the balance of his mind was disturbed'. Mr Griffiths was a suicide, pure and simple.

'Did it take long?'

'No more than half an hour. I had to identify him and give evidence about finding him. Some fat MP who'd been in Westminster Hall gave evidence about that wretched business.'

'Was McPherson there?'

'No, but quite a few of the other Calcutta men were.'

'And nobody argued against suicide?'

'Are you saying I should have? What possible evidence could I have given?'

So I told him about my visit to Mr Griffiths's rooms, about the lack of warm water, the missing pamphlet. Tom looked shocked at first, then downright furious when I came to hiding behind the door to find out what Alexander McPherson was doing.

'Liberty, this is intolerable. What if he'd seen you?'

'Would it have mattered? He wouldn't have known I'm your sister.'

'But you had no right to be there.'

'Nor had he.'

'He might have come to pack up Griffiths's things.'

'On his own? Rather a menial job for him. Anyway, he wasn't packing up anything, he was searching. And I'm sure he was searching for Mr Griffiths's pamphlet.'

'Why do you keep coming back to that?'

'Because it was important to him, and we don't know where it's gone. It definitely wasn't in any of the things we unpacked. That means he kept it with him when he left Richmond for London. What did he do with it after that?'

I hoped Tom might draw the same conclusion as I had: that Mr Griffiths had hurried it straight to a printer. But he was still too occupied in being annoyed with me. That decided me not to tell him about my visit to Tom Huckerby. I was already having some regrets about that paragraph that would be appearing in *The Unbound Briton* and didn't want another cause of war between us.

'I wonder who he meant that bearer bond for,' I said. 'He didn't know many people in London, but here he is intending to send somebody a lot of money.'

'It might not have been for anybody in London,' Tom said. 'They have banks in India too.'

'But it was for somebody he hoped to see in the next day or two. That must mean London, or near it. And why didn't he seal and post it, as he must have intended?'

'Because he'd died,' Tom said, practically grinding his teeth.

'But he was the sort of man who'd want to leave everything in order, wasn't he? So why leave that undone before he killed himself?'

'Liberty, stop it.'

I moved the kettle closer to the fire to boil and rediscovered the letter to Tom, which I'd propped against the tea caddy.

'Something came for you.'

He glanced at the clerkly hand on the wrapper, frowning. I turned away to tidy things on the table, then heard him gasp as if the contents had burned him.

'What is it?'

He said nothing, just held it out for me to see. The thick parchment and bulge of a wax seal through the folds showed it was a legal document. He turned it over. The writing on the outside was also in a clerkly hand, but not the same as the one on the covering wrapper.

LAST WILL AND TESTAMENT OF EDMUND GRIFFITHS ESQUIRE.

'When did this arrive?'

'By the morning post. I'd have rushed it round to you, only I didn't think it was important.'

'Why has he sent me his will?'

Tom stared at me then at the still-folded document, getting no answer from either. I picked up the wrapper. There were two lines of writing on the inside.

> Dear Sir, We have been requested to forward to you the enclosed. A note acknowledging receipt of it is requested. Smith and Danby, Solicitors, London Road, Richmond.

It was dated five days earlier.

'It looks as if he gave it to them just before he left Richmond,' I said.

'But why send it to me?'

'Hadn't you better look at it?'

'It's a legal document, Libby. Shouldn't it be opened in a lawyer's presence?'

'I don't think that's essential. Anyway, why should he have sent it to you if he didn't want you to see it?'

At least Tom still possessed his fair share of curiosity. After thinking about it for a while longer he opened it, read, then passed it to me.

It was a short document, drawn up by an English solicitor in Bombay. It was dated from the autumn of the preceding year and duly witnessed by two men with English-looking names, probably the solicitor's clerks.

> I, Edmund Griffiths, currently resident in Bombay, being of sound mind, do hereby give and bequeath:
>
> The sum of £500 each to the Hindu College in Calcutta and the Sanskrit College in Calcutta, with the wish that it shall be used towards the education of boys who would otherwise be too poor to attend these colleges.

> The sum of £100 to my faithful servant Anil, with the hope that some of it will be used to further his education.
>
> My library, including books, maps, pictures and manuscripts to the Sanskrit College of Calcutta, subject to the provision below.
>
> All the remainder of my estate to the Rani Rukhamini Joshi, of the Red Fort, near Amravati, India in small recognition of the wrong done to her and to her family.
>
> I appoint as my executor Thomas Fraternity Lane and direct that he shall be paid the sum of one hundred guineas from my estate for his trouble, and shall choose what books he likes from my library. I direct him as my executor to see that my body is disposed of according to Hindu rites by the sacred mother Ganges.

Then his signature, and the witnesses. A broad margin had been left below the witness signatures. In it, a line in Griffiths's handwriting in very blue, new-looking ink:

> Or as near to that as he can contrive. E.G.

Tom had been watching as I read.

'Well?' I said.

'This leaves no doubt at all, does it?'

'About what?'

'That he killed himself.'

Relief as well as shock in Tom's voice. I hadn't realized until then how, in his heart, he'd doubted the verdict of suicide.

'Why?'

'Don't be stupid. He leaves the will with a solicitor to forward it, so that it will get to me after his death. He'd planned it all carefully.'

'Had he? Everybody seems to think that he was driven to suicide by that argument with McPherson, but that only happened after he'd moved in to town from Richmond. By then, he'd already left the will with the Richmond solicitors for forwarding. So if he did kill himself, it had nothing to do with your evidence or with the argument.'

Tom said nothing while I made tea and poured it. He was rereading the will, probably several times over.

'What shall I do with it?' he said.

'It will have to go to probate. I should see a solicitor. Ask Daniel to find a good one. He has some legal friends.'

'You don't think I should show it to them at East India House?'

'Of course not. What's it got to do with them?'

'Back in Bombay, Griffiths did say something about naming me as his executor, but I didn't think much about it at the time. Some of the men revise their wills before going on long sea voyages.'

'So who's this Rani who gets the balance of his estate?'

'I have no notion. Literally, 'Rani' means queen, but it's often a term of respect for any high-born Indian lady. Rukhamini is the name of a Hindu goddess. Amravati is in the Maratha. I'll have to find out when I get back to India. But I doubt if there'll be much left over after the bequests to the colleges. I don't think he was a man of means.'

At the time, I didn't give much thought to the clause about Hindu rites and mother Ganges, or Griffiths's footnote to it. There was simply too much to think about. When Tom said goodbye his mind was clearly elsewhere. He surprised me with a last question that seemed to have nothing to do with what we'd been discussing.

'Will Amos Legge be at the stables at this time of day?'

'Yes, they'll be getting ready for evening feeds.'

So at least he was planning to get some exercise.

As I watched him walking away along Adam's Mews, I noticed a member of Tabby's gang standing in the doorway of one of the stables. I'd never sorted out the exact hierarchy of this troop of errand runners, horse-holders and occasional pickpockets, but knew this lad was one of the leaders. His nickname – probably the only name he had – was Plush. He was squat in build, immensely broad of shoulder. Trousers cut off raggedly at the knee showed calves of solid muscle and bare splay-toed feet, very dirty. His body could have been anything from twelve years old to twenty. His face was like some malign gargoyle from the middle ages, his voice as husky as dry leaves shifting in the wind from his habit of pipe smoking. Judging by his yellowed and oddly angled teeth, he'd taken to it as soon as he'd been weaned. He lived for fighting against members of rival gangs and usually carried some recent injury, in this case a left ear so bright and swollen that it looked as if it would glow in the dark. And yet, there was a tentative, almost gentle, air about him.

He shifted his short clay pipe in his mouth and wished me good afternoon. I returned the greeting and asked if he'd seen Tabby recently. He shook his head.

'Not for ten days or more.'

'Do you know where she's gone?'

'Dunno. Just said she was going away for a bit.'

'That's all she said to me. I'm afraid she's annoyed with me.'

'Them little dogs?'

'Yes. It wasn't right, you know.'

He nodded, grave as a churchwarden. I was sure that the business of lapdog kidnapping and ransoming was still being carried on, only transferred for a while out of my orbit. No use saying anything. I asked him if Tabby had given him any idea where she was going.

'Nah. She's been a bit strange the last few weeks, not talking much. Like she's angry about something.'

'She's been like that with me too. I thought it was just on account of the dogs.'

'Something else bothering her, only she won't say what. I said to her when she came for the knife—'

'Knife? What knife?'

'The one she asked me to get for her.'

'Tabby asked you to get her a knife?'

'Good sharp one, with a long blade. Three bob I had to pay for it. She paid me back without turning a hair.'

'What did Tabby want with a knife?'

'That's what I asked her. I said to her if she was expecting trouble from anybody, just let me know and I'd truss him up with his heels round the back of his neck any time she wanted. Wasn't interested.'

I asked him a few more questions, without result, and went back into Abel Yard, badly shaken. Tabby was angry. Tabby had a long sharp knife. Tabby was inquiring about where rich men went. And I could see no way of finding her if she didn't want to be found.

NINE

Amos didn't arrive for our usual ride early next morning, sending a lad on a cob with Rancie instead. The lad explained that Mr Legge had been called away elsewhere. I assumed that he'd gone on some horse-dealing errand, but was sorry because I wanted to talk to him about Tabby. I'd woken in the early hours, worrying about her and the knife and blaming myself. As far as I could see, there were two possibilities. One was that she really had gone out to look for cases of her own and found one more desperate than anything I'd have allowed. The other possibility was even worse: that she intended the knife for attack and not defence. Was this interest in the ways of rich men the start of a crusade? I'd been too pleased with myself for taking Tabby away from the gutter and giving her a chance at better things. In our strange trade, she'd been given a close view of some of the rich and powerful in society. She'd seen things that were admirable, but many that were rotten and hypocritical. Then, in my company and even with my encouragement, she'd met radicals like Tom Huckerby who wanted to sweep away privilege, take from the rich and give to the poor. Shouldn't I have foreseen what a wild and quick-witted girl would make of that? Had I made an assassin of her?

I tried all morning to work, going over domestic accounts with Mrs Martley, drafting a letter to a client who was disputing a bill. In the afternoon, tired of it all, I put on my bonnet and walked across the park to the livery stables in the Bayswater Road. Amos was in the stable yard, informally dressed by his usual smart standards in corduroy leggings, third best boots and felt hat. The leggings looked as if they'd been hastily brushed but there were dried traces of grey mud round the knee buckles. He was inspecting the swingletree of a small carriage drawn up in a quiet part of the yard. He seemed surprised to see me, and not altogether pleased.

'Is that a new one?' I said, looking at the carriage.

It seemed plain and run-of-the-mill in a yard that usually ran to fashionable open landaus and barouches for drives around the park.

'Just borrowed.'

His manner was definitely uneasy, even furtive. Amos could tell lies with the best of them when necessary, but was no good at deceiving me.

'Did my brother Tom find you yesterday?'

A nod. Now he was giving one of the wheels the benefit of his close attention, though there was nothing remarkable about it. I made one of my leaps.

'I suppose you've hired that for Tom.'

His head came up. He looked at me, surprised.

'He told me you weren't to know about it.'

'He did, did he?'

I hate it when men plot against me, especially if it's a brother and a good friend. I left Amos to think it over and went to say hello to Rancie. She was half dozing, with her black cat Lucy comfortably asleep on her back. Something was tucked into the straw at the far corner of the loosebox. I went over and pulled out a pair of boots, covered from soles to tops with dried and encrusted mud, the same grey as the splashes on Amos's leggings. I put them back under the straw, gave Rancie her carrot and strolled back across the yard to him.

'You shouldn't go wading in river mud in your second best boots,' I said.

'River?'

His face was a picture.

'It has to be the river,' I said. 'There's no mud anything like that deep around the park. Besides, there's the colour of it.'

'I told him it was no use trying to keep it from you,' he said.

'Quite right.'

'We had to make sure of it. See how far out you could get when the tide was right.'

He assumed I knew more than I did, and I had no intention of disillusioning him. The picture was becoming much clearer. Amos and my brother had been wading like mudlarks in the

planning. Then I heard Tom's voice, calling softly to somebody, probably whoever was holding the lamp at the bottom of the ladder. He was out of the carriage now and only its bulk separated us. I moved back against the warehouse and watched. The men on the mud were building something, low down near the waterline. A wooden platform, rough planks showing white against the mud. A gangway of single planks led out to it from the bottom of the steps. Amos got down from the carriage and whistled up a boy from the mud to hold the horses.

'Ready?' Tom said.

He held the carriage door open. Amos ducked his head and shoulders inside and straightened up with a white-wrapped bundle across his shoulders. Mr Griffiths had not been a large man and the weight was nothing to Amos. Tom unhitched one of the candle lamps from the carriage and lit the way for Amos to walk with his bundle to the top of the ladder. They disappeared down. Then Amos, still carrying the bundle, appeared again down on the shore, walking steadily along the line of planks, Tom following. I was more and more puzzled. No boat, precious little water. Did they intend to wait on the makeshift platform until the tide came up? It looked as if they did, because they'd built a kind of rough catafalque of logs and driftwood as a temporary resting place for the body. Then, as the shifting silhouettes formed a circle round the platform, shining their lanterns on it, I understood and gasped. Tom was being even more faithful to his instructions than I'd realized.

Since nobody was looking in my direction I went to the jetty then carefully down the ladder, skirt and petticoats bunching up distractingly, and went halfway along the pathway of planks so that I had a good view of what was happening. Amos laid the bundle carefully down on the catafalque. Tom produced a book and read something aloud by candlelight. The only words I caught were in a foreign language so I assumed it was part of the Hindu rite. Then all the men rumbled out the Lord's Prayer. Tom was leaving nothing to chance. With a scrape of flint, somebody lit a torch and the sharp whiff of tar drowned out the mud smell. The torch flowered into a bright orange flame. One of the men was pouring something over Mr Griffiths's body. It was probably raw spirit, because the moment Tom put the torch to the pile of timber, the whole thing flared up. Almost instantly, the body was the dark centre of a tent of flame. After burning fiercely for a while, the flames wavered. The smell of burning flesh hung in the air. I held my breath, trying not to breathe it in, but it was no good. A breeze came up from the river and the flames flared again. The dark centre had crumbled to a shell. I was coughing. Crying too, and not just because of coughing. It had come to me suddenly that Tom had been away in India when our father died, so hadn't been there to observe his funeral rites. I thought that in doing all this for Mr Griffiths, who perhaps had come to be a kind of father to him, he was performing a duty that he'd missed then.

The plank I was standing on quivered on its base of mud. Somebody was walking softly along the planks behind me, coming from the jetty. I turned and saw a figure all in white, standing out against the darkness. It was a man, in loose trousers and tunic. I couldn't make out much of his features except that he wore a turban as white and neat as a bandage. He was walking quickly and so purposefully that I went to step aside for him, until I realized that would land me knee-deep in mud. Without hesitating he nodded to me and solved the problem by stepping on to the mud himself. Now he was knee-deep, but he kept on walking towards the group standing by the pyre, more slowly but unperturbed. Tom turned and saw him and seemed startled. The man in white said something that I couldn't hear. If it was an explanation, Tom must have accepted it because the man moved closer to the fire. The flames were dying down now, but it must still have been hot where he was standing. His unmoving silhouette gave no more sign of discomfort than when he'd been wading in mud. He spoke in a rising and falling rhythm, facing outward to the pyre and the dark river so I couldn't hear the words. I doubt if I'd have understood them in any case. Then everything went quiet and we all stood looking at the sinking flames with a small glowing core in the centre, where the body had been.

Small rippling sounds in the channels flowing through the mud showed that the tide had turned and the river was beginning to rise again. The man in white turned and came walking back. As he passed me, he was looking towards the shore. I watched as he climbed easily up the iron ladder and, on an impulse, turned to follow. When I got to the jetty there was no sign of him. If he'd walked away up the street, he'd be screened by Tom's carriage beside the warehouse. I squeezed past the carriage and found myself looking at the back of another one, at the top of the short street. The man was a few steps away from it. As I watched, a door of the second carriage was opened from the inside and the man in white got in. It started to move, but slowly because it had to turn a sharp corner. When it came sideways on to me I had a glimpse through the window and saw the man in white. There were other people in there with him, in darker clothes, two of them I thought. Before I could see more, a hand in a white glove pulled down the blind over the window. It wasn't the man's hand. He hadn't been wearing gloves. This was a long glove, a woman's, and the hand inside it was small and slim.

I watched as the carriage rolled slowly away.

'They'll be needing a farrier,' a voice said from behind me.

I turned.

'Amos Legge. What are you doing here?'

'Saw you following the Indian and thought I'd better keep an eye on what was happening.'

'Are they with your party?'

'No. Never seen the man before. Your brother hadn't either.'

'There was a woman too, in the coach. Probably more than one. Who are they and how did they know?'

'Goodness knows. Your brother wasn't exactly sending out invitations.'

'Not even to me.'

'He thought you wouldn't approve.'

I thought Tom still didn't know me very well. The carriage had disappeared into the darkness. If Tabby had been with me, I could have got her to do her trick of clinging to the back of it and tracing it to a destination.

'We'd better go back,' I said.

Amos went first down the ladder and helped me on to the planks. This time I went all the way to where the men were standing, around the glowing ashes of the fire. The river had come up quickly while Amos and I had been away and was creeping towards the edge of the makeshift platform.

'What are you doing here?' Tom said.

'Paying my respects, like you are.'

For once he didn't argue. Just perceptibly, the platform was being to move up and down under our feet from the rising water. One of the men, speaking with a strong Cockney accent, said we'd better get back. Amos went first, then Tom and I. As the gang of men retreated, they brought the planks that had made up the pathway with them and piled them at the top of the ladder. I think Tom must have paid them for their night's work because I heard coins clinking, then they disappeared into a dark alleyway by the warehouse. Out by the river, the funeral platform was almost afloat now, the glowing heart of the fire rocking on the swell. I stood beside Tom on the jetty until it was afloat entirely. Slowly, it began to move upriver on the tide. By the time it came to Westminster Bridge the fire would be nothing but red embers, much smaller than the glow from a steamboat's fire. When the tide turned in the morning, the river would carry the grey ashes that remained of Mr Griffiths out to the estuary and beyond. Not Mother Ganges, but Father Thames. *Or as near to that as he can contrive.*

'You did well,' I said to Tom.

He nodded.

When we couldn't see the red glow any more we turned and went back to the carriage. At first there was no sign of Amos, then the glow of the candle lamp came from the end of the street, with him behind it. Tom didn't object when Amos held the door open for me to get into the carriage. After all, he could hardly leave me stranded on the river bank. The inside of the carriage was full of smells, old leather from the seats, the faint sickly smell of human corruption mostly masked by spices and, I thought, jasmine or tuberoses. Tom glanced at me but I decided not to tell him I'd seen too much to be squeamish. When he'd seen us settled, Amos gave a tip to the boy who'd been holding the horses all this time and we drove back to the bridge and across to the north side. We stopped in Adam's Mews and Tom escorted me to the bottom of the stairs, still subdued and quiet. Amos stayed on the driver's seat and called out cheerfully that he'd see me in the morning.

Mrs Martley had gone to bed early, leaving cold cuts on the table for my supper. I stirred up the fire and made tea, ate a little. The ceremony by the river, especially the sudden appearance of the Indian gentleman, had changed something inside my brain. I thought I'd been looking at the question of Griffiths's death from the wrong direction entirely, as if the answer lay somewhere between the Palace of Westminster and the City of London. Wrong. Whatever had caused the killing of Mr Griffiths – and I was certain that he had been killed – came from five thousand miles and many months away in Calcutta and I couldn't see how I could even get a foothold on understanding it.

TEN

'Just appeared out of nowhere, like the genie in a pantomime,' Amos said.

The flighty chestnut he was riding thought of shying at a man walking a wolfhound. The slightest pressure of Amos's leg decided him against it. It was the morning after Mr Griffiths's funeral and we were discussing the Indian gentleman.

'Did Tom say anything to you about him after you left me?'

'Not a word. But he was puzzled, I know that.'

As well he might be. If the man had been one of Mr Griffiths's friends in London, surely he'd have mentioned him to Tom. Then there was the question of how he'd known about the ceremony.

'Nearly left it too late, though,' Amos said.

'Yes. As if he hadn't known until the last minute.'

'Or followed us.'

'How would he have known to follow you?'

'We tried not to attract notice when we put the old gentleman's body in the carriage, but anybody watching his lodgings might have seen.'

'But why would he be watching Mr Griffiths's lodgings unless he knew something like that was going on anyway?' I said. 'And you'd have noticed somebody following, wouldn't you?'

'Not necessarily with the traffic like it is. South of the river you'd be more likely to notice, but perhaps he hung back then.'

We cantered for a good stretch, but it didn't clear my mind.

'I'd give a lot to talk to him,' I said.

'I'll see what I can do, then.'

I laughed.

'Amos, even you couldn't track a perfectly ordinary carriage you'd seen just once on a dark night. It could have come from anywhere in London.'

But when I glanced across at him he had that expression which signalled something up his sleeve.

'One of their bays had a shoe loose,' he said. 'You could hear it clinking on the cobbles. Then when they turned the corner, it wasn't clinking any more.' Amos tapped three beats on the pommel of his saddle, the fourth one softer than the others. 'So it had been cast.'

On these matters, Amos was as accurate as a musician. But still . . .

'We can't go hunting all over London for a horse with only three shoes. Besides, they'll have it at the farrier's by now,' I said.

'That's the whole point.'

He glanced across at me, grinning.

'Well?'

'I went up the street and found the shoe he'd cast. Not difficult. They wouldn't see many horses in a little street like that.'

'So you're planning to take the shoe all over London until you find a horse it fits, like Prince Charming and Cinderella?'

'That fellow could have saved himself a deal of trouble if he'd thought of asking the cobblers.'

I gave in and asked him to explain.

'Take a shoe to any shoemaker and he'll tell you who made it,' Amos said. 'Just the same with horseshoes. Every farrier's got his own little tricks of the trade. Show him a shoe and ten to one he'll recognize it. Maybe something as simple as the spacing of the nail holes, the chamfering of the edge, even the colour of the iron it's made out of. They're all different.'

'Are you telling me you can look at that cast shoe and know where the horse was shod?'

He shook his head. For a minute I'd hoped. Then I saw he was still grinning.

'I can't, but I've got a friend who can. A farrier I have a drink with now and then. He reckons he can tell where any horseshoe came from within a five-mile radius of Charing Cross. Never known him wrong.'

I thought he was being too confident. Amos never liked admitting that there might be things he couldn't find out. Still,

I wished him luck. I wanted to meet the Indian gentleman and, almost as much, the possessor of that small gloved hand that had pulled down the carriage blind so smartly. On our way back, I turned the conversation to Tabby. Amos had seen her courage and recklessness at close hand, and took the business about the knife as seriously as I did.

'If that one was after me with a knife, I'd be careful where I walked.'

Since Tabby was a foot and a half shorter than Amos and probably less than half his weight, that was a tribute of a kind.

'Did she ever talk to you about hating rich men?' I said.

'I've seen her spit in the gutter once or twice, when somebody tried to come high-handed, but nothing particular.'

'Or traders in stocks and shares?'

'Didn't even know she knew about them.'

I could tell he was turning it over in his mind and before we parted he delivered an opinion.

'She's not stupid, that girl. She'd know you couldn't change who's rich and who's poor just by stabbing one man.'

'As a gesture, perhaps?'

He shook his head. Perhaps he was thinking of the kind of gestures Tabby sometimes made at men who shouted remarks at her.

'If she's thinking of putting a knife into somebody, it'll be somebody particular she's got in her mind,' Amos said. 'Somebody intending harm to you.'

This wasn't reassuring.

'But she's angry with me.'

'She'd be a good sight angrier with anybody wanting to hurt you.'

'I don't know of anybody intending harm to me,' I said. Then thought again. 'No more than usual, at any rate.'

'See what I mean? The things you find out, there's bound to be some people wanting to even the score. If that girl heard that one of them was planning mischief, that might explain it.'

'But why wouldn't she tell me?'

He shrugged.

'Maybe she didn't want to worry you.'

Or maybe, I thought, she'd been too annoyed with me about the wretched dog kidnapping business. Too annoyed to take me into her confidence but still risking her life to protect me. That would be just like Tabby. For once, talking things over with Amos had made me feel no better.

Tom didn't visit that evening, so I had too much time to think over what Amos had said. I went over all our cases – the list was not so very long – and made a mental list of people we might have left desiring vengeance. For practical purposes, it came to no more than half a dozen. True, that left some pretty big omissions. Quite recently we'd been involved in a case that had spoiled the plans of a major European power. I still wasn't quite sure which, though I had my suspicions. But governments and their secret agents tend to be practical. If a scheme fails, they don't waste time in personal vengeance, and soon move on to another one. There had been a mad old baronet who would have liked to spill my blood, and Tabby's as well, but I knew on good authority that he'd died in a private asylum a few months before, to the relief of his family.

Some of our smaller cases had offended people in society. There were several ladies who'd cut me socially at a reception, but would probably draw the line at cutting throats in an alley. In two cases, our investigations into missing jewellery had proved that a family member was responsible. A son had been sent into the army, a female cousin packed off to live abroad. It was just possible that either had returned to plague us, but not likely. There was only one likely case I could think of that left somebody vengeful enough to be a threat. A man had tried to trick me into giving false evidence so that he could divorce his wife but keep her money. I'd discovered something so foul about him that I'd gone over to the wife's side and provided her with evidence that allowed her to separate from him, keep her children and not give him a penny. I knew that the husband would gladly have seen me dead, if he'd had the nerve for it. The objection to that theory was that Tabby had known very little about the case and, to the best of my knowledge, never met the man involved. Once I'd seen the direction things were taking, I'd been determined to shield her from it. I decided that Amos was wrong for once and looked out to the yard, hoping against hope to see a light in Tabby's cabin. Nothing.

Early next morning, Tom Huckerby arrived.

'Found your printer, I think.'

'Wonderful. Where?'

'Not so far from me, it turned out. Just round the corner from Ludgate Hill. Elderly gentleman arrived three days ago and asked him to print a pamphlet in a hurry. Paid in advance, of course, otherwise the printer wouldn't have accepted the work, not knowing him. Title: "Some Observations on the Trading Practices of the East India Company and Related Matters". Does that sound like your man?'

'Yes. Was there an author's name?'

'The Griff.'

'Did you get a copy?'

'No. It was still being proofread, then they had to get it stitched together. He wanted five hundred copies done.'

Tom suggested we should go to the printer and see if a copy was ready. He took it for granted that we'd walk there. He resented spending money on coach fares and about the only time he travelled in a horse-drawn vehicle was when police or duns were arresting him. He knew every street, alleyway and short cut from Hyde Park corner to St Paul's and had a story to tell about all of them – usually of some injustice or brutality suffered. I suppose we looked an odd couple, Tom Huckerby in his unbuttoned jacket and shapeless felt hat, striding along, talking nineteen to the dozen and flinging his arms around for emphasis, I in my blue cloak and bonnet trying to keep up. We attracted some amused and curious looks, but Tom was unconscious of them and I tried to be too. Still, it was a relief when we arrived in the street off Ludgate Hill. Tom pointed to a large sign hanging over a doorway: SETH ROBINSON, PRINTER.

'You'd told me your man was new to London, so I thought I'd take a walk round and look for the printers with the biggest signboards out. I reckoned that was what he might have done.'

Seth Robinson was a small man, his printer's paper cap perched on a totally bald head, his hands large and capacious in proportion to the rest of him, as if made for handling heavy galleys of type. A smell of warm glue as well as ink hung over the workshop. Several apprentices were working at the back of the shop, half-screened by sheets of copy hung on lines for the ink to dry.

'I told you, not till tomorrow,' the printer said, as soon as he set eyes on Tom.

'What about a proof copy?' Tom suggested.

Seth Robinson gestured towards the drying pages.

'Since it's set in type now, could we please take Mr Griffiths's manuscript back?' I said.

I was guessing that the printer wouldn't have heard that his client was dead. He considered for a while.

'Don't see why not.'

He opened a cupboard and took out a pile of manuscript. The title page was now dog-eared and ink spattered, but the handwriting was undoubtedly Mr Griffiths's. The printer found some newspaper and string to wrap it and, still at Tom Huckerby's fast pace, we carried it in triumph back to Abel Yard.

By then, I was gasping for tea. I asked Mrs Martley to make it while Tom Huckerby and I sat at the parlour table and started reading.

'He's giving it to them good and strong,' Tom said, after the first few pages.

He certainly was. It began:

> For the past two hundred years, the stewardship of the great land that we call India has been entrusted to the East India Company. The result of that stewardship has been, largely, to convert the wealth and labour of India into profits for the City of London. It has been a process of greed, short-sightedness and corruption. Recent attempts by our Parliament to restrain the Company's activities have led only to the continuation of the old abuses in new forms, mostly carried out by those same men whose rapacity led to the demands for reform. The purpose of this summary is to give examples of that rapacity, in the hope that they will arouse indignation in

> Parliament and public that even the opium-dulled consciences of our Indian traders cannot ignore.

After a while, Tom Huckerby had to leave to attend a meeting, but obviously found it hard to tear himself away from the manuscript.

'Since your man's paid for having it printed, it would be a pity not to circulate it. I'll talk to a few booksellers, if you like,' he said.

'Why not. And he wanted to send it to MPs.'

Properly speaking, it should have been a decision for my brother, as Mr Griffiths's executor, but I decided to spare him the worry. After all, he was a Company servant. Come to think of it, Mr Griffiths had been as well. He surely couldn't have expected to remain one once his pamphlet was published. I said goodbye to Tom Huckerby and settled down to read more. There was no doubt that Mr Griffiths's heart, as well as his considerable brain, was deeply involved. The first part of the manuscript concentrated mostly on land transactions and in some cases outright land theft, ranging over twenty years or so. It made the blood boil to read some of the examples and learn what had been done in our name. I wondered how much my brother knew about all this and resolved to ask him. But the blood can't keep on boiling and I was very weary from a fast walk to Ludgate Hill and back. I turned over a few more pages of manuscript, hoping to come across the name of McPherson, but my eyes rebelled against reading so much by lamplight and kept shutting. I marked my place in the pile of manuscript, stacked it up tidily and went to bed.

Around mid-afternoon next day, Tom Huckerby was at the bottom of my stairs, hat in hand, hair disordered.

'It's gone. Somebody just rolled up and took the lot of it, every single copy.'

He was red-faced with hurry and anger. I fetched him a glass of water and made him drink before he started explaining, though I'd guessed almost as soon as I saw him.

'You know you'd agreed I could approach some booksellers? I found three that were willing to take it and put it in their windows, all of them in Fleet Street, so it would make a stir.

So I borrowed a handcart and went round to the printer to load up. Too late, he told me. A man had come in a carriage and collected all of them an hour ago.'

'What man?'

'Didn't know the name. Middle-aged, clerk type.'

'Useless. So he just handed them over?'

'Yes. The apprentices carried them out and piled them on the carriage floor and seats. The man was most insistent that they shouldn't miss a copy and was not at all pleased when Robinson told him he didn't have the original manuscript any more.'

'So what did he say?'

'That a young lady who said she was a friend of the man who wrote the pamphlet had come the day before and taken it away with her. The man rolls away with the pamphlets, then a couple of hours later he's back, saying the woman must have been an imposter and wanting a full description.'

'Which Robinson gave him?'

'Yes. He's not pleased with either of us. Robinson says we put him in the wrong and we're to give the manuscript back.'

'When it snows in Hades, I will.'

Tom nodded. I sat beside him on the edge of the water trough in the yard. We were both downcast, Tom Huckerby because he'd lost a chance to take another tilt at the rich and privileged, I at a loss.

'What I don't understand is why that pamphlet's so important,' I said.

'Obvious, isn't it? The robber merchants don't want people to know the truth about what they're doing.'

'But it's not the first time people have criticized the Company. Besides, rich men are thick-skinned. Accusing them of being corrupt and greedy is about as much use as trying to shame a jackal by calling it a carnivore.'

Tom kicked at a loose stone. We sat in silence for a while.

'So Robinson's told the man he'll try to get the manuscript back,' I said.

'The fellow's threatening him with trouble if it's not back by midday tomorrow.'

'I don't suppose he left an address for sending it?'

'No. He said he'd call at the print shop on the stroke of twelve and Robinson had better have it there, or else.'

If I could be somewhere near the print shop at twelve, I might recognize the man. A faint chance, because it sounded as if he was acting on somebody else's instructions, but better than nothing. I said nothing of that to Tom Huckerby. He'd done enough.

That evening, before it got dark, that other Tom, my brother, arrived. I poured Madeira for both of us and told him how much I respected him for organizing Mr Griffiths's funeral rites. I think that pleased him a little.

'I've just been talking to an old friend of Griffiths's,' he said. 'He told me he thought it was exactly what Griffiths would have wanted in the circumstances.'

'An old friend? Was it the Indian gentleman?'

'No. An Englishman named Tillington with a house in Holborn. He knew Griffiths in India a long way back. He's a Sanskrit scholar, like Griffiths. Rather an invalid. He left a note for me at East India House this morning. I went round to call on him this afternoon.'

'How did he know about you?'

'Griffiths had mentioned me to him. Tillington has been following proceedings of the Indian committee, very much from the same point of view as Griffiths. He has no love for McPherson and his kind.'

'Was he surprised by Mr Griffiths's death?'

'He hinted that he doesn't think he killed himself.'

'You see!'

'Liberty, don't start on this again. I'd only just met Tillington. I wasn't going to interrogate him. It was only a hint.'

I thought that if I'd been present, I shouldn't have let it stop at hinting. I'd have liked to meet Mr Griffiths's friend, but knew there was no hope of an introduction from Tom.

'So have you found out anything about the Indian gentleman?' I said.

'I haven't tried. I don't think I should. It was Griffiths's business.'

'And you didn't recognize him, from back in India?'

I was afraid he'd snap me up, but he didn't.

'Not the man, no. But the type.'

'Type?'

'He was a Brahmin, I'm almost sure. That's the highest caste for Hindus, their ancient priesthood.'

'What makes you think so?'

'By the river there, he was reciting something from the Sanskrit scriptures. I knew just enough classical Sanskrit to recognize it. It was more than that, though. There was a dignity about him.'

I nodded. I'd felt that, even as he passed me barefoot in the mud.

'There was a woman with him,' I said.

He sat bolt upright.

'Where?'

'Waiting in the carriage. I saw her hand drawing down the blind.'

'Liberty, I told you to stop it. It was bad enough that you followed us to the river . . .'

'So I'm not allowed to follow you to the Thames, but I'm supposed to follow you all the way out to India?'

We bickered for a while, until I backed down enough to say I was sorry I'd annoyed him. Unusual, but there was something about my brother that worried me more than ever. He was keeping something from me. You might think that was fair enough, because I was keeping quite a lot from him, like Griffiths's pamphlets and their disappearance. I might have told him, if it hadn't been for the argument. Truce again. We drank the wine and talked about other things. He said he must go, but didn't move from his chair by the fire. I took the risk of asking him what was worrying him.

'Nothing.' Then he sighed and said, 'Nothing really.'

So then it came out. Tom was sure that his room in the lodging house for junior Company employees had been searched.

'I'm almost certain it happened while I was away doing what had to be done for Griffiths.'

'Cleaners move things sometimes,' I said.

'Do cleaners work in the evenings? Do they go through piles of paper in a document case? I found out when I was looking for something this morning. They'd been taken out and put back in a different order.'

'Sure of that?'

He nodded. I asked him if he had any idea who and why.

'As to whom, I've no idea. With so many of us lodging there, the house isn't locked till late at night. Dozens of people come and go.'

'What about why?'

'It must have something to do with Griffiths. There's nothing of mine that would interest anybody.'

'Was Mr Griffiths's will in the document case?'

'I left the original with the solicitor, but I'd made a copy of the main points. That was in there, yes.'

'Have you been talking to anybody at East India House about the will?'

'No.'

'Or anybody—'

'Leave it, Libby, or I'll be sorry I mentioned it. I was probably mistaken.'

We both knew he hadn't been mistaken. I left it, not wanting to start another argument, but was more worried than I could admit to him.

'Tom, do you have to stay in that house? Why not come to us here? You could have my study for yourself and sleep on the daybed.'

I watched his face, thinking how good it would be to have my brother under my roof, even for a short time. The idea attracted him, I could see that, but he shook his head.

'They'll think I'm running away from them.'

It was no good trying to persuade him. I watched him go with a heavy heart and a nagging fear that I couldn't protect him.

ELEVEN

In the evening, I went on reading Mr Griffiths's manuscript. It was fine, fighting stuff most of the way, but towards the end it took on an almost confessional quality.

> It has been well said that for evil to triumph it is only necessary that good men should do nothing. There is one story I must tell, even though the writing of it may cost me more pain than any of the preceding pages. It is the story of a great wrong done twenty years ago. To follow it from its roots, we must go further back than that. Let me call it, in a spirit of confession rather than of vainglory, the tale of The Griff.

It was midnight by then. I read with only the rustle of pages and the hissing of my lamp breaking the silence.

> Griff is a word the British in India have for a young man newly come out from the home country, an unlicked cub, wet behind the ears. Since it happened to be close to my name as well, I came in for some quizzing on that account. All three of us were originally Griffs together, coming out from England on the same boat, nearly 35 years ago. None of us had reached the age of 17. We were entering on careers as servants of the East India Company. Servants of the Company, you note, not employees. All the men who work for the Company, from the lowliest clerks, called writers, up to the governor general himself are known as its servants. It is an affectation of humility in a body of men who are collectively as proud as Lucifer.
>
> At the start we were set to work side by side in the Writers' House in Calcutta. The time it takes a new man to slough off his Griffishness varies. Some achieve it almost at once and within months are talking and

behaving like old India hands. That was the case with the first of our trio. He was helped by the fact that an elder brother, his senior by five years or so, was already well advanced on what was to become a very successful career as a Company servant. I do not mean to imply that this man, whom I shall from now on call The Merchant, received any special favours. Simply he learned from his brother and was quick at understanding the country and its possibilities for advancement. .

The second Griff took a little longer to lose his wetness behind the ears. After a while he decided that a clerk's life was not for him and was allowed to transfer as an officer into the Company's army. Let us from now on call him The Soldier. His choice proved a wise one and in a few years he was a lieutenant in a good regiment, with no trace at all about him of the Griff.

As for the third it must be admitted that he never lost that shameful label of a newcomer at all. Griff he remained. Why was that? He was as able as his fellow writers, diligent at his work, reasonably ambitious to rise in the Company. So what happened to him? In a word: India. From the first sight, even the first smell from the ship's rail, India got into his heart. Every step, every breath of his first weeks there brought some new wonder. It is the mark of a newcomer to be continually surprised and curious about the life going on around him. It was this man's fortune or misfortune never to lose that curiosity. Which is why the author of these pages must subscribe himself, for better or worse, as the Griff of the title. An eternal Griff.

Our Griff nearly committed that worst sin of the Company man in India: going native. It's all very well, of course, for a man to take a decent interest in the welfare of his servants or, in the army, the native soldiers. It's a commendable thing to learn a little of the native languages, Hindi, Hindustani, Persian, from a munshi or teacher, enough to pass the official examinations. It's an altogether different matter for a man to seek out the society of the natives and immerse himself in their languages and customs. Our Griff's seniors in the

Company looked askance, but occasionally found his knowledge of language and customs useful. Increasingly, he was sent on missions away from Calcutta, acting as a translator for other men. It suited him well.

It was on these sorties that he first became aware of the importance of the poppy. He knew in theory about the constant tide of opium flowing from India to China. Now he found himself riding through a lilac and purple sea of poppy flowers. It seemed that the amount of land they covered increased with every month that passed. One day he and his small caravan of servants were resting at a serai and he got into conversation with a local ryot, or peasant farmer.

> *Griff*: Is there much profit in opium?
> *Ryot*: Not enough, sahib. It's greedy for water and manure, much more than other crops. And my children can't eat poppy. I'd rather grow corn, the way I used to.
> *Griff*: Then why do you grow poppy?
> *Ryot*: Sahib, I owe so much money to the man who sold me the seed, I must grow it to pay him back.
> *Griff*: And if you'd told him you'd rather grow corn than poppy?
> *Ryot*: I did, sahib. The next night, men came and trampled and pulled up my corn crop.
> *Griff (Heated):* Who did this?

A very Griffish question of course. He got no more answer than a shrug.

Still, it set the young man thinking. He was indignant on behalf of the small farmers. A few weeks later, he had a chance to put his indignation into practice. He came across another ryot, being attacked by several men who seemed intent on burning down his hovel. The young man and his servants went to the rescue, scattered the attackers and captured two of them. Again, it turned out that refusal to grow the poppy was the cause. He carried the two prisoners back in triumph and delivered them to the courthouse for justice. He was rather pleased with himself and perhaps expected praise for his prompt action. He certainly did not expect what he got, in the British quarters that evening. We were four of us, all Company men, sitting round a table drinking imported whisky. The conversation went much on these lines.

> *Senior Man*: Well, young Griff, you've caused me a deal of trouble today.
> *Griff*: How so, sir?
> *Senior*: Letting your servants attack those two fellows. They were bleating to me for an hour about their wrongs. You owe me eight rupees by the way.
> *Griff*: Eight rupees, sir?
> *Senior*: What I had to give them in compensation to keep them quiet.
> *Griff*: Compensation? But they were making an entirely unprovoked attack on—
> *Senior*: How do you know it was unprovoked? When you've been out here a good few years longer, you might learn not to intervene in quarrels between natives that are no concern of yours. If you want to be the village beadle you'd better get yourself back to England and apply to some damned parish council.

I don't suppose that the sun rising over the Ganges was as red as the cheeks of that young man. When he raised the poppy question later with a more sympathetic senior, the man was good enough to explain to him.

'It's a simple question of exchange. The Company buys tea in China and sells it in England. We pay for the tea by selling opium to the Chinese. The Government in Westminster puts a tax on the tea and that pays for our army and navy. So if we didn't grow poppies the Government wouldn't have anything to tax and couldn't pay the army and navy, and that wouldn't do, would it?'

A conclusive argument. At that time, we were at war with Napoleon. The very freedom of Europe, it seemed, depended on the poppy. So the young man tried not to worry about the tide of poppy and got on with his work.

Of the two companions who had travelled out with him, he lost touch with The Soldier. The other one, The Merchant, to nobody's great surprise, decided to leave the Company and join an importing and exporting business, trading mostly in the Far East. He rose rapidly to be a partner. The Soldier became a captain, The Merchant flourished and The Griff was promoted. It was not a promotion that many men coveted because it involved going a long way from Calcutta to a small princedom in the Maratha or central region of India. The area was disorderly, under constant attack from local warlords. For some years the soldiers of the Company had been waging campaigns against those warlords in support of the various princes. For the princes, that support proved expensive. The Company would send in groups of advisers who had to be paid from the royal treasury. The Griff was sent to join one such group. The name of the princedom is of no matter. It does not exist any more.

Even at the height of its powers it was no larger than a moderately sized English county. Its religion was Hinduism, its ruler a maharajah who entertained his Company advisers with tiger hunts, music and dancing girls, presents of jewels. He was a shrewd and jovial man, inclined to laziness, but that was no great matter because his country was fertile and rich from the spoils his ancestors had won. Like all the native princes he kept his own army, but his was largely for show. Their ceremonial drill, involving lines of elephants, magnificent horses, foot soldiers in silk tunics as bright as orchids, was something to be seen. So were the womenfolk. They were permitted quite a degree of freedom and were said to be some of the most beautiful in India, a claim the present writer would not dispute.

While the clever old man lived, all was well, but he

died and was succeeded by his only son, a weak and pleasure-loving young man in his early twenties. He wanted to be a greater man than his father and was easily flattered into thinking that could be achieved by show and extravagance. Most of the flattery came from his British advisers. The young prince was persuaded into importing frivolous luxuries from Europe: gold and silver plate, Wedgewood china dinner services, English boots and saddlery. Little of what he bought was as fine as what he could have had from India, but it was foreign, so to him desirable. After a while, his supply of ready money began to run short. No matter. His advisers had English merchant friends who were happy to advance him loans. After a while, when they began to hint that repayment might be convenient, the prince was embarrassed. Again, his advisers had a solution: the opium poppy.

Up to that point, it had been little cultivated in the principality. Now the lilac and purple tide flowed over it. It flowed over the prince too. It paid for his fripperies from Europe, but after a time he wasn't concerned about those so much because he'd become a slave to the poppy and wanted only his silk cushions and his opium pipe. He took little interest in the affairs of his realm, but that was all right because the kind Englishmen from the Company were quite prepared to take care of them. The Griff looked, but did nothing. He had grown older, learned cynicism and taken it for wisdom. Then something happened that catapulted him back to being The Griff of many years before. The poppy prince was going to war. His slightly larger neighbour had defied and insulted him by invading an area of border land and there was nothing for it but to fight. I knew that piece of land. It was wretchedly rocky and unproductive. You could ride across it in ten minutes and hardly notice it. I went to the senior man among our team of advisers.

Griff: This is madness. The prince can't care about the bit of land.

> *(In fact, we both knew our prince didn't care much about anything apart from his pipe and his nautch girls.)*
> *Senior*: Then it's just as well we're looking after his interests for him.
> *Griff*: His army's useless.
> *Senior*: Ours isn't.
> *Griff*: The land's not worth a dog's life, let alone a man's.
> *Senior*: If we tolerate one encroachment, the neighbour will take the whole thing and we can't have that, can we?

No, we couldn't have that. Because the neighbour didn't take the whole country. We did. On the verge of war, the prince came out of his opium dreams long enough to beg his English advisers for help. Obligingly, they sent in their army. The battle lasted one and a half days. By the end of it, five Indians had died and one of our officers had suffered a sword slash in the arm. Conclusive and glorious victory for the prince – until the bill for the Company's help was presented. The use of an army does not come cheap, and there were other debts. The only way out was for the prince to sign away his country to the Company's care, with full powers to make laws and levy taxes. The prince kept his title and castle, with full complement of servants, nautch girls, elephants and horses.

Then there were the jewels. The old maharajah, with his shrewd eye, had amassed one of the finest collections in India. Diamonds and rubies, mostly, with a few good emeralds and sapphires. Some of them set in fantastic shapes of tigers, peacocks, horses, others kept in their purity in fine muslin bags, only brought out to dazzle visitors. It would be hard to put a price on them because, even in this country of jewels, there weren't many comparable. I've heard men suck their teeth and mention hundreds of thousands. Pounds, that is, not rupees.

The jewels went. Where did they go? But I'm getting

ahead of my story. For our Griff – almost mad with frustration at not being able to prevent this unnecessary war – there was another consequence of it. He met again his two old . . . should we say friends? That was how the world saw it at any rate. Three men, now in their thirties, who'd travelled out to India as youths on the same boat.

'Amazing coincidence . . .'

'All new men together . . .'

'Had desks side by side in the Writers' House at Calcutta . . .'

'Heard you'd become a sadhu, Griff. Joking of course. Dashed good to see you again.'

Not so amazing. With men travelling as much as we did, India was a country of coincidences. So it wasn't very surprising that my old colleague, The Soldier, had turned up as an officer in the regiment of the Company's army that saved the prince's strip of useless land for him. Slightly more surprising, perhaps, that The Merchant – on some never quite explained mercantile sortie into this part of the country – happened to run into his old friend The Soldier on the eve of the campaign and stayed to cheer on his victory. But these things happen. One certain thing is that they were not dashed pleased, or pleased in even the slightest way, to encounter their so-called friend, The Griff. The way their faces fell on meeting him gave him his first smile for weeks. Still, some of the more senior advisers turned out to be good friends of The Merchant so the victory celebrations went on for some time.

By now, my lamp was guttering, empty of oil. I waited in the dark for it to cool enough for refilling. It was past one o'clock and cold, the fire almost out. I lit a candle from the embers to give enough light to fill and relight the lamp, wrapped myself in my cloak and went on reading. It looked as if Mr Griffiths might have paused in his writing at the same point, because from then on the writing was still legible but looked more hurried, as if writing against time. 'The Griff' became simply 'I'. Perhaps he would have changed it if he'd had more time, or perhaps not.

Fountains of diamonds, emeralds, rubies arced into the night. Fireworks, brought all the way from China. The military band, made up of native soldiers, played British marches with an oriental touch that turned them to a strangely wistful sound. The air was popping with firecrackers and rifle shots. In the occasional lull, loud British laughter came from the open windows of the prince's rooms.

'I wish they were all in hell,' the princess said.

Her room was almost in darkness, with only a few small lamps glowing, but washed at intervals by the rainbow flares of the fireworks. The air smelled of jasmine, from the white flowers framing her window or from her perfume. Both perhaps. She sat on a heap of big silk cushions, her legs folded under her like a cat's. At least, that's how he imagined they'd be. He couldn't tell for sure because the folds of her sari spread round her, silk on silk. She'd pushed back her scarf and let her hair down in a loose plait, twined with a rope of gold and small pearls. The princess must, by then, have been in her thirties. Still beautiful, a fool might have added. There was no 'still' about it though. Just beautiful. She'd been married at fifteen years old to a much older man. By her twenties she was a childless widow, come back to live with her brother. All very proper and pious – except piety was not one of her virtues.

'Not a very Indian wish,' The Griff remarked.

He was sitting by the window on another heap of cushions. She'd sent her servants away some time before. She made her own rules and had nobody to accuse her of impropriety.

'Hell is one of the better Christian ideas. There should be a place to send one's enemies.'

Her voice was low and quiet. They were speaking English because the princess preferred it.

'Are they all your enemies?' The Griff asked, gesturing towards the bright windows of the prince's wing.

'Not my brother, I suppose. He can't help being a fool.'

'But the rest?'

'Your Company. Jan Company – the noble company, that's what we used to call it. Noble! Boxwallahs and badmashes. Travelling salesmen and ruffians. And thieves.'

The Griff said nothing.

'You're not denying it, then? Thieves?'

'I'm not denying it.'

'They're stealing my country.' Another silence. 'You're not denying that either?'

'I'm not denying it.'

'But you don't do anything about it. You watch and do nothing.'

'I tried to persuade them.'

'Persuade!'

More silence, then whooshes of shooting stars.

'So what do you want me to do,' the Griff said at last.

'I want you to persuade them to set aside my brother and make me ruler.'

'But he's the lawful ruler . . .'

'He's not the ruler any more, not in any way that matters. He never had much brain and what he had has been eaten away by opium.'

'But if the English really rule the country, what's the point in any case?'

'They might not always rule. The Grand Moghuls ruled once and where are they now?'

'Why would the English want to depose your brother? They like things as they are.'

'They might not like things so much if my own army rose in support of me.'

'What!'

'Why not? The commander of our own soldiers is on my side. At a nod from me, he'd bring his men out in support and put my brother under house arrest.'

'And he and his men would instantly be shot down by the Company soldiers.'

The princess smiled, adjusting the end of her pigtail where the string of pearls was coming loose.

'The Company's soldiers are Indian after all. Suppose they refused to fire on my men?'

'They wouldn't.'

'Quite sure of that, are you?'

No, The Griff wasn't quite sure. He knew little about the army, but he did know how deep the fear of a mutiny went. The whole of British India depended on the Company's native soldiers obeying orders. The princess stood up and, apparently casually, moved to a pile of cushions closer to him. The perfume was hers, not the jasmine's.

'There need be no firing, no fighting. My army comes out in my support. Your officers do nothing, waiting for orders.'

'They wouldn't do nothing.'

'A day's hesitation, that's all it needs. The Company has time to think and decide that rather than fight, they'll accept me as ruler. What does it matter, after all? The ruler is nothing but a bird on the elephant's back. And a woman is easier to control than a man, even a fool of a man.'

Her smile softened the bitterness of the words. The Griff looked at her with more thoughts running through his head than he could manage. Among them was the idea that she'd been thinking about this for some time. He believed her claim that her country's not very effective army was on her side; half believed in her influence with the Company's army as well. Deeper than anything was the guilt at what his people were doing to hers. One man can't put right a wrong done to a whole country. Perhaps – just now and then – he can do it for one person in that country. And there would be justice, of a kind, in replacing the all-too-compliant brother with a woman who might be more than a match for the Company schemers. His thoughts weren't logical, he sees that now. But he wasn't an old man then.

'What do you want me to do?' he said.

And she told him. Over the next few weeks, he should prepare the minds of the other Company advisers, impress on them the princess's friendship to the British, the increasing imbecility of the prince. Sooner or later, the prince would be overthrown, perhaps by somebody less tractable. Wouldn't it be better to get it over now, by a mere woman who could so easily be controlled?

'Even conveniently married off, perhaps,' she said.

His heart lurched.

'Married to some neighbouring princeling? Would you want that?'

'Not necessarily.'

That was all her voice said, but her eyes were looking into his, so close that he could feel her breath on his face, and what her great dark eyes said was something else altogether.

Once in his life, every man should be in love and plotting a palace coup. An eagle must feel like that, high up above the mountains with senses that can pick out the shift of a single pebble on a scree slope. I spoke my words in some receptive ears. They sounded good sense to me and seemed to make sense to others. I became more sociable with my own kind, even seeking out the company of my old friends, The Soldier and The Merchant. Of course, I said nothing to them about the plot, but from the occasional remark they let out, I could tell that the princess had been doing her work well. She kept mostly to her own wing and did not come out in society much, but everybody seemed impressed by her. One night The Soldier remarked that it was a pity her brother didn't have more of her intelligence and The Merchant agreed with him, adding that she seemed to have a surprisingly good grasp of business, for a woman. Later, The Griff reported to the princess.

'You should be careful,' I told her. 'If they think you're too clever, they won't want you.'

She only laughed, touched my neck with her light fingers in the way she had. Only much later, when it was all over, did I start wondering how The Merchant and The Soldier had developed their good opinions of her.

We failed. After all those weeks of preparation, the thing was over in a matter of hours. One damp dawn, her soldiers in their bright clothes with their pretty horses, surrounded the quarters where the British were staying, calling for independence and the princess. The officers of the Company's army didn't hesitate. They lined up their soldiers and gave the order to fire over the rebels' heads. The order was obeyed. That was all it needed. Nobody died. A couple of men were injured when bullets ricocheted. The rebels were marched away, technically under arrest. They were released later when the prince agreed to pay a fine to the Company for their extra trouble. The Griff ran to the princess.

'I have two good horses waiting downstairs. We must hurry. No luggage.'

She looked at him, not a trace in her expression of the tension of the last few hours.

'Hurry? Why? And where?'

'Before the officers come to arrest you. If we get to Bombay before the news of this does, we can embark on a fast ship and be in England by the time . . .'

Her smile was tolerant, as to an excited child.

'What would I do in England? Of course they won't arrest me.'

She was right. It was never even discussed. As far as the princess's part in the regrettable incident was mentioned at all, it was as a figurehead for overambitious officers in her brother's army. Her friend the old commander was sent into comfortable internal exile. And The Griff? He was sent back to Calcutta. No blame attached to him, at least not officially. Since the princess was not to be blamed for the incident, a Company servant could hardly be accused of conspiring with her. Still, they all knew. For the rest of his career in India, The Griff was to be kept on a short lead. No advisory missions to remote princedoms. No politics. A desk life was all he was given and – largely – all he wanted. It took him some time to recover from those few weeks of being an eagle. When he did, his consolation was his Indian studies. If he couldn't help the country, at least he could try to understand it a little.

The Princedom disappeared a few years later. Or, to put it more officially, the growing incapacity of the prince made it desirable, for administrative reasons, to amalgamate judicial and fiscal functions with those of the neighbouring principality. (That same principality, by the by, that had gone to war over a strip of useless land.) All done in a calm and gentlemanly manner, but as arrant a piece of robbery as ever committed by any highwayman on Hounslow Heath. The Company ran everything. The prince stayed in his palace, not knowing or caring. The Griff asked a man he could trust, more or less, about the princess.

'They've given her an estate of her own with an old castle, quite comfortable, usual complement of servants, elephants, peacocks and so on. Doesn't go out and about much, I gather.'

If she'd summoned him, The Griff would have left his desk and gone, no doubt about that. But she didn't.

And the jewels went, those glittering tigers, ruby and emerald snakes, great diamonds, and to this day nobody knows where. They were not part of the Company's official booty. They never figured in the accounts in Calcutta. The prince – or more likely his Indian friends – believed they had gone to Calcutta and petitioned now and then to have them back. On one of those occasions, a worried adviser to the governor came to my desk and asked if I had any idea what had become of them. I told him, in all honesty, that I had not. By that time The Merchant was in Canton, becoming one of the biggest men in the opium trade. The Soldier had been brought low by one of those liver ailments that so often follow fevers and been invalided home to England. It remains a mystery. There is little now that can be done to put much of this right, but if the foregoing helps my countrymen to see what is being done in their names, so that at least such things may not happen in the future, then this life has not been entirely wasted. Perhaps, even now, some small part of the injustice may be put right at last. That is the devout wish of the writer who signs himself The Griff.

TWELVE

Next morning, at a quarter to midday, I waited in an alleyway opposite Robinson's printing shop at Ludgate Hill. The man had said he'd be at Robinson's for the manuscript copy on the stroke of twelve. My intention was to see him and follow him, without being seen myself. I wasn't confident. Tabby was better at this kind of thing. In her street urchin clothes she'd have loitered without being conspicuous, following him through a maze of streets like a ferret down a rabbit hole. I'd dressed as plainly as possible, but was still out of place in this commercial part of town where there weren't many women around. I'd already been pestered by two beggars, a crossing sweeper and a man handing out Biblical tracts.

A boy went into the print shop and came out loaded with papers. A flock of pigeons skirmished over oats dropped from a horse's nosebag. A dog was chased out of the bookseller's next door. The man was punctual. At one minute to twelve, a cab drew up and a middle-aged clerkly-looking man stepped out. Nobody I recognized. His face was pasty, lips pursed. He opened them just enough to issue one word to the cabby: 'Wait.' Then he crossed the pavement and went inside the shop the instant the clocks all round began striking twelve. I knew his business wouldn't take long. There'd be an admission from Robinson that he had not recovered the manuscript then an angry exit. I turned over the waistband of my skirt, lifting the hem to ankle-height to help me walk fast. Not respectable but nor was following an unknown man. The cab looked quite new, the horse fresh and brisk. I couldn't keep up with them for long. My best hope was that they'd be delayed in the traffic, but as bad luck would have it there seemed less than usual.

Then my luck turned. Another cab came round the corner. It was old and the horse unenthusiastic, but the great thing, it was empty. I rushed out of my hiding place, hoping that the man was still giving Robinson a piece of his mind, and called up to the driver to wait.

'Where to, ma'am?'

'Wait until a man comes out and gets into that cab there, then follow them.'

'Where're they going then?'

'Not far.' (I hoped.)

I passed up half a crown into his hand to silence further questions, opened the doors at the front of the cab and settled myself in, pulling my bonnet down to shade my face and sitting well back in the seat. Almost at once the man came striding out of the print shop empty-handed, mouth clamped even more tightly. He snapped something at his driver and practically threw himself into the cab. It went off at a brisk walk, had to halt briefly at the turning into Ludgate Hill, then turned left towards the Mansion House and the commercial heart of the City. My cab got off to an annoyingly slow start but caught up at the Ludgate Hill junction, then stayed within twenty yards or so of the one in front. If the angry gentleman had happened to look behind him, he'd see nothing suspicious about it. The City was as full of cabs as an old dog of fleas. Into Threadneedle Street, still close together. I'd hoped that the cab might confirm my suspicions by making for East India House, but instead it turned into narrow Bartholomew Lane.

Capel Court, the stock exchange, was in Bartholomew Lane. I was too occupied with watching the cab in front to wonder why that nagged at my memory. It stopped, and we stopped too, our horse's nose almost nudging the back of the man's cab. I watched as he got out and started stumping up the steps of the stock exchange then threw myself out and went to follow him.

'Oy, ma'am, one shilling and threepence.'

My cabby's bellow from the top of his box. Over the odds, especially considering the money I'd already given him, but I didn't want to draw attention by arguing. I was uneasily conscious that I'd forgotten to turn my waist band over and lower my skirt, so my ankles were showing. Nothing to be done about that now. Reluctantly, I handed up the coins and hurried up the steps. The man had disappeared by now. A broad-shouldered doorman with a face like a section of brick wall, wearing some kind of uniform and a top hat was standing at the top of the steps. He stretched out a meaty palm.

'Can't come in here, ma'am.'

I started saying that I only wanted to ask the identity of the man who'd just gone in. He didn't listen, just stood there repeating the same phrase. I was getting angry by then, wondering why the trading of bits of paper with numbers on them was too sacred for profane or female eyes. I might have wasted my breath in saying so, only something happened that changed the scene entirely. Some vegetable – I think it might have been a rotten turnip – came like comet out of nowhere and struck the doorman's hat so hard that it shot off his head and went rolling down the steps.

He stood amazed for a moment, gap-toothed mouth wide open, then yelled and ran down the steps after his hat. Jeers and laughter came from a group of ragged boys opposite. I guessed the vegetable had come from them, then glimpsed one that didn't look quite like the rest of them. The figure was slightly less ragged than the others, booted rather than barefoot, and was moving rapidly out of sight round a corner. A glimpse was enough. I knew from the way she walked, from the whole determined look of her. Tabby. There was a choice to make: run after her and find out what she was doing or use the opportunity she'd made for me. Almost without thinking about it, I did what she expected, even though it hadn't been in my mind before. While the doorman was chasing his hat and shouting threats at the urchins I walked in through the doors of Capel Court. Tabby and I were a team. Sometimes her wildness gave me a push when I needed it, just as my common-sense pulled her back from the brink of some excess. Head up, look as if you have a right to be there.

It was loud inside, like a cattle market without the cow smells. It had a smell of its own, though, that was just as animal in its way, of a lot of men at close quarters being competitive. They were all dressed in formal blacks, whites and greys and the convention of the place seemed to be that top hats remained on heads, even inside. A blue haze of cigar smoke hovered just above the top hats. They were mostly formed in loose groups of three or four but were in constant motion as men broke away from their own groups to join others, like a disorderly country dance. The room was crowded and I guessed my man must be on the outskirts of it. Almost at once, I saw him talking to a stoop-shouldered man who was standing with his back to me. He was probably reporting his failure to get the manuscript. As I came nearer, the other man snapped some remark at him and turned away, his face petulant and impatient. It was an oddly shaped face, low and broad across the forehead then curving inwards to a narrow chin above a thin stalk of neck, like an inverted pear. I'd seen that face before, several times and at close quarters. On the last occasion the expression had been worse than petulant. The man had been literally spluttering in my face with fury. I was doing something I'd hoped never to have to do in my life again – breathing the same air as my ex-client, Cyril Eckington-Smith MP. I decided to leave before he saw me so turned towards the door. But in my surprise at recognizing him, I'd hardly noticed what was happening round me. The noise of conversation was fading like a wave receding. Men were nudging each other, eyes turning in my direction. If a camel had strolled into the cattle market, the ranks of gaping farmers' faces would have looked much like these gentlemen. Naturally, Eckington-Smith turned too, to see the source of the excitement. He saw me.

By now, a tide of gentlemen was slowly advancing. I don't suppose they'd have thrown me out bodily, but I'd no intention of waiting to see. I turned and walked out, briskly but not too hurriedly. The doorkeeper, hat back on head, face shiny from anger and exertion, took a step towards me.

'I told you, you couldn't go in there.'

'Yes, I heard.'

I walked past him and across the road. The great thing now was to find Tabby. The urchins had run away from the doorman's wrath, but not very far. I found them loitering round the next corner, dispensed a few pennies and got some answers. Yes, they'd seen the girl before. Only in the past couple of weeks, though. She was an odd one. Sometimes she dressed and talked like them, other times she'd be dressed more like you, miss, then she'd pretend not to know them. They supposed she must be on the game, only she wasn't quite like the others. She had a good aim, for a girl.

'Do you think she'll come back today?' I said.

A collective shrug.

'Might. Might not. Can't tell with her.'

For a while I roamed the streets around Bartholomew Lane, but without success. I hadn't much hope. Tabby wouldn't be found if she didn't want to be. Obviously, she didn't want to be – at least not by me. My appearance must have come as a surprise to her. There was no possibility that she could have expected me at Capel Court. She'd decided I needed help and immediately given it, then gone away without waiting to see what happened. I gave up the search and committed the extravagance of another cab home, because something must be done urgently about Griffiths's manuscript. Eckington-Smith knew where I lived. I decided to take it straight round to my friends in Bloomsbury, Daniel and Jenny Suter, for safe keeping. None of the people in the present case would know them and Daniel's only connection with India had been composing incidental music for a play about the Great Moghul.

It was only on the way home from Bloomsbury, on foot, that a worrying thought came to me. Trying to account for Tabby's strange behaviour, Amos had suggested that she might be trying to deal with some threat to me. Was it a coincidence that she should be outside the stock exchange when Eckington-Smith was inside? In the end, I decided that it was time to call on some inside information and delivered a note to 1 Grosvenor Gate.

THIRTEEN

'Eckington-Smith is a parliamentary hippopotamus. There's a whole herd of them,' Mr Disraeli said.

His sixteen-hand dark bay thoroughbred tossed its head against the bit. Mr Disraeli had a tendency to raise his bridle hand when eloquent. I'd noticed that he was riding some expensive-looking new horses since his marriage to Mary Anne.

'Hippopotamus?'

'They keep their bodies safely under water, their stumpy legs firmly rooted in the mud and only their nostrils poking out, to sniff anything to their own advantage. Every now and then the whips will rouse them up enough to make them splodge through the division lobby and occasionally throw one of them some minor ministerial post.'

In spite of everything, I laughed, with that feeling of flying above the rest of the world that came from Mr Disraeli's company. It was common knowledge that Disraeli himself was disappointed at not being offered a ministerial post, but his worst enemy couldn't have likened him to a hippopotamus. Too clever for his own good, most of them said. I tried to be sparing of the times I asked for his help, especially when it came to getting up early to join me on my early morning rides in the park on my mare, Rancie. It was much more enjoyable than 'At Homes', and I suspected he thought so too, but on the dangerous edge of respectability. Still, I couldn't think of anyone more likely to tell me what I needed to know.

'Somebody remarked that if there were half a sovereign to be picked up on the floor of hell the demons would have to move quickly to get there before Eckington-Smith,' Disraeli said. 'Still, I don't suppose he's any worse in that than the rest of the herd.'

I had my own reasons for thinking him quite a lot worse, but kept quiet from confidentiality towards Eckington-Smith's wife. It seemed even Disraeli's network had not found out that connection.

'I suppose I can guess your interest in the fellow,' Disraeli said. 'The same matter that we were talking about last time we met?'

'Does he have any connection with McDruggy McPherson?'

'Oh there are a lot of them adrift on the same raft. At present they'll work together to keep it afloat, but they'll be at his throat if it looks like sinking.'

'Raft?'

'Eckington-Smith and his like are investors in McPherson's opium operations. They're facing ruinous losses since the Chinese decided not to play their game. That's why there's so much urgency about getting the Government to pay them compensation.'

'And will it?'

Disraeli shook his head.

'No. At least, not until we've won the war against China.'

'So there will be a war?'

'The gunboats are already steaming towards Canton. Nice sharp little campaign, total capitulation by the Chinese and payment of compensation. After that McPherson and the rest of them might get their money, but that could be a year or more away. Still, they've got no choice but to hang together.'

'Can they hold out for a year or more?'

'Rumour on the stock exchange says they can't. Not many people's credit holds up so long without something to support it. Which is where McPherson's jewel collection comes into the picture.'

He looked at me sidelong and must have noticed my change of expression.

'You knew about that, of course.'

'The jewels that weren't stolen when his assistant was killed?'

'Fortunate, wasn't it?'

'I've heard that they once belonged to a maharajah,' I said.

I was taking a leap, associating those with the jewels in Griffiths's story, but Disraeli nodded again.

'So I gather. He was flaunting an example of his stock in Westminster Hall. To reassure the creditors, I suppose. Vulgar, though.'

This from Disraeli, whose own taste in rings and neck chains had raised many eyebrows.

'So McPherson's credit depends on the jewels?' I said.

'Yes, and if he crashes he'll take a lot of other men along with him.'

I looked towards Rancie's ears, thinking that explained why Eckington-Smith and others were prepared to run errands for McPherson. It might also explain why they were so determined that any doubts about McPherson's right to them should not be made public.

'Did you and your brother have anything to do with that story suggesting that McPherson had Griffiths killed?'

The question came from Disraeli in a conversational tone, as if it weren't anything of great note. I almost jumped out of my saddle.

'My brother had nothing to do with it.'

'But you did?'

'Are we talking about a news-sheet called *The Unbound Briton*?'

'Some such scandal rag. I can't remember the title. I hear it was causing quite a stir in the committee yesterday.'

I said nothing, wishing I hadn't been carried away by Tom Huckerby's journalistic enthusiasm. My brother would be furious.

'So did he?' Disraeli said, still conversational.

'Have Griffiths killed? I can't prove it.'

'And did Griffiths kill McPherson's assistant?'

'I don't know. I simply don't know.'

My own voice sounded desperate in my ears. Perhaps it sounded that way to Mr Disraeli too because he said nothing until we'd turned and were riding back towards Grosvenor Gate. When he did speak, he was unusually serious.

'Miss Lane, I think you should be careful.'

'Why?'

I knew, but wanted him to spell it out.

'There are big issues involved, and not very scrupulous men.

If you or your brother were obstacles to their plans, I think they'd do something about it.'

'It really is nothing to do with Tom. He's sure Mr Griffiths killed himself. He doesn't want me to have anything to do with it.'

It mattered more than anything to me to convince him of that.

'Then maybe you should take your brother's advice.'

I glanced at him and saw what looked like genuine concern on his face. My heart lurched. I didn't even know if it was from fear or from surprise that he should care. He raised his hat to me, wished me good morning and cantered away towards the gate. It was one of the conventions of our park rides that we should meet like acquaintances by chance, then go our own ways.

As soon as he'd gone, Amos Legge came up to ride beside me. When Mr Disraeli was with us, he kept respectfully back, pretending to be any other groom.

'My farrier friend, he's not getting anywhere so far with that horseshoe. Reckons it wasn't made by any of the men he knows.'

I was less disappointed than Amos sounded, not having counted very much on the horseshoe in any case.

'He'll keep on trying though,' Amos said. 'It's annoying him, not knowing.'

I told him about seeing Tabby. He was as much at a loss as I was about how to find her.

'Do you remember a member of parliament named Eckington-Smith?' I said.

Amos looked as if he was on the point of spitting and only just restraining himself.

'Reckon his backside still remembers the nails in my boot.'

'You kicked him, then?'

I knew there'd been a rough-house towards the end of that unlovely story, when Eckington-Smith had been lying in wait for me, intending violence, but had met Amos instead. I'd never been told the details of it.

'Should have done worse,' Amos said.

'I saw him at Capel Court yesterday, the stock exchange.

It was just after I'd seen Tabby there. It's in my mind that she might be following him.'

'If she thinks he's threatening any mischief to you, that would account for the knife,' Amos said.

His matter-of-fact tone only increased my worry.

'If that's it, we've got to find her and stop her,' I said.

'Or give her a bit of a hand.'

'No, for pity's sake. Do you want to see her hanged for trying to protect me? If that really is what she's doing.'

'If she heard he was threatening you, she should have come to me,' Amos said.

'Of course she should. Or to me. But that's not Tabby's way. She doesn't talk about things, just goes off and tries to do something about them.'

Sometimes effectively, occasionally disastrously, as we both knew.

'What I can't understand is how she'd have heard about it,' I said. 'I don't think she ever met Eckington-Smith while I was working on the case. Saw him a few times, but that was all.'

'Unless she found him hanging about waiting for you.'

'No. Eckington-Smith wouldn't be standing outside my door with a knife or pistol, once you'd scared him away. He'd hire somebody.'

'Same thing. She might have followed whoever it was and found out.'

Talking about it like this made it seem all too likely. Amos saw how worried it had made me.

'Do you want me to see what I can find out?'

'Would you, Amos?'

'I'll have a word with Eckington-Smith's groom or driver, see if they've noticed anything. He still lives in the big place in St John's Wood, I suppose?'

'I don't know. He may have moved somewhere smaller after he had to give up his wife's money.'

Amos said he'd see what he could do, which was comforting. I was all too aware that concentrating on my brother's problems had made me less attentive than I should have been to Tabby.

Later that day I raised my spirits by visiting one of my best friends Beattie Talbot. The excuse for the visit, as far as it needed one, was giving music lessons to her children. It kept my hand in, just in case the investigating business failed and I had to go back to teaching, but was a pleasure in any case. George's and Beattie's comfortable and unobtrusively well-run home in Belgravia was always an oasis in dark times. Beattie probably knew more about me than anybody else, though I didn't burden her with the details of my cases. She'd been totally sympathetic in the matter of my brother's return and his disapproval of me and had been racking her brains to find a way of helping. Over tea after the music lessons, she shared one of the results.

'We'll give an Indian dinner party for your brother. You know how George loves to meet new people. It will help convince Tom that you're highly thought of and have some more-or-less respectable friends.'

That was understating it. George, newly knighted, was a Yorkshireman who'd become one of the most respected businessmen in London and a generous philanthropist. He had an insatiable interest in politics but refused to belong to any party. Their hospitality was well known and many plans and new friendships had been launched at one of Beattie's dinner parties. George fancied himself, with some justice, as a picker-out of talent and liked doing what he could to help his friends' careers with suitable introductions.

'George was just saying to me the other day that he thought he should be better informed about India,' Beattie said. 'He'll find the right people to invite. You must ask your brother for the names of any of his friends he wants to be there.'

'I don't think he's been in London long enough to have many.'

'There must be some. Perhaps I can find some Indian musicians with those curious instruments they play. Would your musical friends know anything about that? And I never know about – what is it? – *nautch* girls. Are they respectable dancers or the other thing?'

I promised to ask Daniel about Indian musicians but couldn't give an opinion one way or the other on *nautch* girls, so Beattie decided we'd do without dancers. As usual, an hour in her company was such a lift to the spirits that we were soon giggling together like fourteen-year-old girls.

'Cook and I shall have such fun experimenting with recipes,' she said.

She knew some ladies on her charity committees – widows mostly – who'd lived in India while their husbands were serving there and would ask them for recipes.

'I dare say that means we'll have to invite them, but it will help balance the table. We'll ask the younger ladies, like you, to wear muslins and Indian shawls. I wonder about drinks? In the novels, the men are always calling for whiskies and sodas, but you can hardly serve that with dinner, can you? And what's a *chota peg*?'

We moved on to the guest list. No more than sixteen, she thought, or twenty at the very most.

'And we must invite Mr Calloway. I don't think he has any connection with India, but he's so good at putting people at ease and getting them to talk to each other.'

A sidelong glance at me. Beattie had not yet abandoned her hope of pairing me up with young Mr Calloway from the Foreign Office, though neither of us had encouraged her. I probably looked embarrassed, remembering that the last time Mr Calloway and I had seen each other was when I'd been carried off by a brother in a bad temper. Beattie was apologetic.

'My dear, I'm sorry. You don't want him?'

'Not the case, I promise you. By all means invite Mr Calloway.'

She was quiet for a while, wondering how to interpret that. Then: 'The man who's travelling, have you heard from him?'

I shook my head. Her hand came lightly over mine.

'Oh my dear, I'm so sorry. Letters can get terribly delayed, you know.'

I nodded, not trusting myself to speak.

'Have you thought of asking his brothers if they've heard from him?'

I shook my head. But I had thought of it several times, and not done it. For one thing, his half brothers didn't know how things stood between Robert and me. For another, I dreaded hearing that, yes, he was writing to them regularly, in which case he'd chosen not to write to me. Tactfully, Beattie changed the subject back to her Indian dinner.

'Tell your brother I'm relying on him to propose at least two more young men for the guest list,' she said as we parted.

I had my chance sooner than expected because Tom was waiting for me back at Abel Yard. Mrs Martley had made him comfortable in the parlour, even to the extent of pouring my Madeira. He smiled and stood up to greet me when I came into the room. I'd been apprehensive when I heard his voice, certain we were heading for another argument, this time about Tom Huckerby's piece. He didn't mention it. Perhaps he didn't know about it, because he'd spent most of the last two days with a solicitor in his capacity of executor of Mr Griffiths's will. I breathed a sigh of relief for an argument postponed at least and asked him if he'd made any progress in tracing the lady who was the residuary beneficiary.

'No. I think that will have to wait until I get back to India. Whoever she is, it should come as quite a pleasant surprise to her.'

'We didn't think there'd be much left after his other bequests.'

'We were wrong. The solicitor and I have been going through his papers and it turns out he was quite a wealthy man. A brother had died a few years ago and left Griffiths all his estate. The Rani should get about forty thousand pounds. Quite substantial compensation for whatever the wrong was.'

'We can't know that until we find out what it was.'

For once, he didn't pick me up on not interfering. Something had lightened his mood.

'I've had another talk with Tillington. You should see his rooms – a museum in themselves, hundreds of Sanskrit books, pictures, carvings; like Griffiths's rooms back in India, even more so. He's convinced me I shouldn't blame myself over what happened to Griffiths.'

I felt annoyed that Tom gave more weight to this new friend's opinion than to mine, but didn't say so.

'The two of them had an arrangement to meet again, the day after Griffiths . . . died.'

I looked at Tom. I'd deliberately not raised the question, knowing what reaction I could expect, but here he was doing it himself. He'd hesitated before the last word. I waited.

'That's one of the things that makes him believe Griffiths didn't kill himself,' Tom said.

'What about the suggestion that Mr Griffiths was unbalanced by the scene in Westminster Hall?'

'Impossible, Tillington says. Griffiths despised McPherson and the whole opium crew too much to lose a night's sleep over them, let alone kill himself. Tillington feels the same about them. You should hear him on the subject.'

'I'd like to.'

I meant it. I was already wondering how to contrive a meeting. Tom ignored the hint.

'So if he thinks Mr Griffiths didn't kill himself, then it must follow that he was murdered,' I said.

'Tillington thinks so.'

'Does he have a culprit in mind?'

'McPherson and his cronies wouldn't have done it themselves, of course.'

'So they paid somebody?'

'That's what Tillington thinks.'

'And what do you think?'

The glance my brother gave me was a familiar one from a long way back, the desperate look of a boy puzzled and exasperated by the adult world, looking to his elder sister for an explanation.

'I don't know. I just don't know.' Then, as in the past, the guard instantly went up again and he was annoyed with me. 'Anyway, there's no point in asking because I don't see what we're supposed to do about it.'

The words 'Look for evidence' were on my tongue, but I didn't let them out. In the family, the secret of winning arguments is to know when not to say anything. I asked something else instead.

'Did he have any idea who the Indian gentleman at the funeral might have been?'

'No. It interested him. He said there were a few Indian Brahmin scholars in London and he thought he knew most of them. He'd make inquiries.'

Before he went, I told him about Beattie Talbot's plan for an Indian dinner party, provisionally arranged for the coming Saturday. He seemed more pleased than not. I suspected that he'd been making enquiries about the Talbots and been impressed. Her instructions to nominate two young friends with Indian connections were a problem, as I expected.

'I hardly know any of them, and those I do know, I don't trust.'

'You could suggest Mr Tillington, if he's well enough to go out. He sounds a gentlemanly sort of person.'

'Do you think I could?'

I thought Beattie could always sit him next to one of her Indian-service widows, with me on his other side.

'I don't see why not. I'll ask her.'

So Tom and I parted on surprisingly good terms. I only hoped it might last.

FOURTEEN

When we rode out on Friday morning, Amos had the look of a man with news to tell. As so often, he teased me by waiting for me to ask.

'Your farrier friend?' I said.

He nodded. 'He got there in the end, only it wasn't London, that's why it took him so long. He reckons that horse was shod right out at Richmond. Farrier named Lisday with a forge near the Green.'

'Richmond, now there's a coincidence.'

It hadn't surprised me that Mr Griffiths should rent a cottage at Richmond. It was a pleasant, quite fashionable place. But it was a surprise that the carriage bearing the mysterious Indian gentleman should come from there as well. Had there been some reason why Mr Griffiths should have chosen the place for his English lodging?

'Next step would be to ask him what carriages he deals with. He'd remember an Indian,' Amos said.

'If it was the gentleman's own carriage. It might not be.'

'I'll ride over there and make inquiries if you like. Only we're short-handed and I can't get there before next week.'

'Let's leave it for a day or two. Tom has a friend who's trying to find the man as well. If he can't, we might go out to Richmond together.'

I asked if he'd had any success in the other hunt for Tabby, but he'd drawn a blank.

'The Eckington-Smith fellow's moved away. The new people there don't know anything about him.'

I didn't think Tabby had ever known his old address, and would have no way of discovering a new one. That would account for her haunting the stock exchange. Then again, her absence might have nothing to do with the man at all.

There was still no news of her by the time I went to the Talbots' house on Saturday morning. Beattie had appealed for my help in the preparations for her Indian dinner party, so I went in a cab with my evening clothes packed into a travelling bag. Almost at once I was whirled into the kitchen where Beattie, cook and two kitchen maids were surrounded with wafts of steam and exotic smells from saucepans on the big cooking range. The temperature was hot enough for India itself. Beattie handed me a small ladle and told me to taste.

'The recipe says three heaped tablespoonfuls of mild curry powder, but the grocer only had one kind and I don't know if it's mild or not. What do you think?'

'Hot,' I said, when I'd stopped coughing.

'Oh dear. It's vegetable mulligatawny. The recipe says to add cayenne pepper if it's not hot enough. So no cayenne, you think? Does it seem rather salty to you?'

'A little, yes.'

About as salty as the Channel. Beattie's forehead wrinkled.

'We thought a tablespoon of salt was a lot, but that's what the recipe says. Do you think arrowroot would help?'

She and cook went into intense consultation, while I roved round the kitchen looking at the assembled ingredients: a small sack of rice, a basket of hothouse tomatoes, coconuts drained and halved, chickens, beef steaks, prawns still in their shells, pineapples, eggs, almonds, pistachios, ginger root, jars of coriander seeds, cloves, sticks of cinnamon, jugs of buttermilk, several trays of what looked like small uncooked pancakes.

'Chapattis,' Beattie said. 'You fry them.'

'There looks enough for an army here.'

'We'll be twenty-two altogether. George has insisted on adding two men he met for the first time yesterday. You know what he's like when he's getting up a new subject. Your brother's friend Mr Tillington sent such a kind acceptance note.'

She seized a pineapple and a chopping block, cleared a space beside one of the maids and started peeling it.

'Libby, you might start on the lemons. We need the juice of eight of them for this and the rind of two, in thin strips.'

'What is it?'

'Indian milk punch. I found the recipe in a magazine. It sounds just right for people who aren't drinking wine.'

I pared and squeezed lemons, while Beattie sliced and cubed the pineapple then pounded it to a paste in a pestle and mortar. Considering the price of pineapples out of season, champagne would have come cheaper, but Beattie never did things by halves. She scraped pineapple pulp into an earthenware bowl large enough to bath a baby in, added the lemon juice, sugar and a breakfast cup of cold green tea. One of the maids, Prudence, was set to counting in twenty coriander seeds, six cloves and a cinnamon stick.

'Is it looking right, do you think?' Beattie said doubtfully.

'I've no idea what it's supposed to look like,' I said.

'Oh dear, nor have I. Perhaps it will look better with the drinks in.'

Prudence was sent to the dining room and came back with three bottles on a tray. Beattie picked up a pewter measuring jug and consulted the recipe.

'A pint of brandy, it says. Perhaps another splash for luck. A pint of rum. Give it a good stir, Libby.'

By now the fumes rising from the bowl would have flattened a sailor. I remembered that this was supposed to be a concoction for people who weren't drinking wine, but decided not to interfere. Beattie studied the label on a small green bottle.

'Rack. George had to order it especially from his wine merchant. Just a gill of that.'

A strong smell of aniseed rose from the mixture. Beattie wrinkled her nose.

'A quart of boiling water next. That should tone it down a little.'

Prudence brought a big kettle over from the range and poured while I stirred. If anything, it made the smell stronger.

'What now?' I said. I was becoming horribly fascinated by the process.

'It has to stand for six hours. What is the time? Oh heavens, that's only just enough. Then it has to be filtered through muslin, mixed with a quart of hot milk and more lemon juice, strained again, cooled and iced.'

I resolved privately to stick to wine and water.

The afternoon passed in a haze of steam and exotic smells.

Around six o'clock, Beattie left the final preparations under the command of cook – who looked understandably nervous – and we went upstairs to change. Alone in the guest bedroom, I doused my hair with rose water to drive away the kitchen smells. A maid knocked on the door with cans of hot and cold water. Trust Beattie, even in the throes of dinner party preparation, to care for her guest's comfort. A hip bath behind a screen, a fluffy white towel on a stand beside it and a cake of lemon-geranium scented soap completed the kindness. I washed and dried myself, enjoying the feel of thick Turkish carpet under my bare feet. I didn't envy Beattie's well-ordered life, but it was wonderful to drop into it occasionally. Altogether, I felt better than I had for weeks. My brother couldn't fail to respond to the warmth and kindness of the Talbots. When he saw me happy and confident with my friends, he'd realize what nonsense it was to talk about carrying me off to India. In obedience to Beattie's theme, I'd brought a simple dinner dress of white muslin with puffed sleeves and tucked bodice and an ivory silk sash. Over it I wore a glorious Indian shawl in gold and green that Tom had sent me as a Christmas present. I put my hair up in a pleat, secured with a mother-of-pearl comb. When I looked at myself in the mirror I hoped I was a sister that a man would not be ashamed to own.

George Talbot was in the dining room, supervising the decanting of wine. He kissed me on the cheek, like one of the family, and said how much he was looking forward to meeting my brother.

'We've invited some people I know he'll be interested to meet. Most of them are older than he is, but they have India in common. I'm sure I'll learn a lot tonight.'

Soon afterwards, the first guests arrived with remorseless punctuality on the stroke of seven. Beattie, alerted by the doorbell, emerged from the kitchen just in time to stand beside her husband to greet them. She looked beautiful, in cream muslin embroidered with flowers round neck and hem, but her face was flushed and I detected a faint smell of aniseed. The early arrivals were her two Indian-service widow friends. One was small and bird-like, who said little but had eyes that seemed to miss nothing, the other plump, colourful and talkative. Their names were Mrs Dulas and Mrs Glass. Doing my social duty, I went with them to the drawing room and made conversation over glasses of sherry, but most of my attention was on the hall, waiting for my brother's arrival.

He timed it well, at the same instant as that paragon of diplomatic manners, Mr Calloway. My fear that there might be some embarrassment after the circumstances of their last meeting was unfounded, because they seemed to have decided to behave as if only just introduced. As they came into the room together, I felt a surge of pride in Tom. He had lost some weight since his arrival in London and looked tall and elegant in his evening dress. After properly greeting the two older women, he came straight across the room to me.

'Liberty, you're looking very well.'

I hoped he might kiss me on the cheek, as George had done, but either he couldn't bring himself to do that in company or I wasn't quite forgiven. In any case, there was no time to do anything about it because other guests were arriving thick and fast and George was now on duty in the drawing room, making sure everybody was introduced to each other. Tom was soon whirled away from me. I stood by a bookcase, watching him smiling at other people, talking animatedly. It was good to see, but there was a little ache in my heart. I kept looking at the door, wondering if I'd identify Tom's friend Mr Tillington when he arrived. Beattie had promised to sit me beside him at dinner.

'So glad you could get here,' George said to somebody just outside the door. He moved forward to meet whoever was coming in. Tom must have noticed, because his eyes went to the door too. For a moment George's back was blocking my view of the new arrival, then he stood back and in walked the last person I wanted to see there. A tall man, with jutting eyebrows, broad nose and an air of important hurry about him, even walking into a drawing room. Apart from the absence of the diamond hawk from his coat lapel, Mr McPherson was just as I'd seen him in Westminster Hall. A silence fell. I didn't know if it was one of those natural gaps in conversation or because some of those present knew an embarrassing situation was developing. I could see Calloway's face and knew that he understood. George, oblivious, was leading McPherson straight towards Tom.

'Mr McPherson, may I introduce my young friend Thomas Lane. Like you, he's quite recently arrived from India. Mr Lane, Alexander McPherson.'

'We have met.'

I was proud that Tom was the one who managed to get those words out first. McPherson echoed them in a bass rumble. Both were too glacial to leave any doubt about how each felt about the other.

George instantly picked up the signal and understood that his broad trawl in the way of guest invitations had netted two fighting fish. Hastily, he moved Mr McPherson on towards Calloway. My attention was caught by the plump lady, Mrs Glass. Up to that point she'd been sitting in an armchair, chattering happily to a gentleman beside her. Now her jaw had dropped open, her forehead was puckered, and she was making frenzied fanning movements with her hand. The gentleman she'd been talking to looked alarmed. As much from curiosity as humanity, I went over to her and asked if she needed any help. She gulped and blinked her round blue eyes.

'Thank you. Just a shock. Didn't expect to see him of all people.'

Her hand closed on her sherry glass. She drained it and blinked again. It struck me that she too had been unpleasantly surprised by the appearance of McPherson. She and he seemed much of an age. Could there have been some romantic involvement in their past? The gentleman beside her remarked on the heat. It wasn't particularly warm, but she seized the excuse gladly. She was quite all right, she said. Sorry to have alarmed us.

My attention went back to Tom. I was relieved to see him in easy conversation with a gentleman who looked to be about sixty. He must have come in just behind McPherson, unnoticed in the general embarrassment. He was tall and very thin, leaning on an ebony cane with white hair worn rather long, a scholarly stoop to the shoulders and a faint yellow tinge to the complexion. His evening clothes were old-fashioned in cut. From Tom's relaxed air and his obvious interest in what the gentleman was saying, I guessed it must be Mr Tillington and moved towards them. I wanted Tom to introduce us and it was almost time to go in to dinner. George was glancing towards the front door, clearly waiting for last arrivals. The doorbell sounded and he hurried out to the hall. I touched Tom on the shoulder and smiled at Mr Tillington.

'Tom, will you kindly . . .'

And got no further, because George had returned triumphantly escorting his two tardy guests. They were a gentleman with dark, amused eyes and long flowing locks and a middle-aged woman dressed at least ten years too young for her age in white muslin frills and ringlets twined with jasmine. Just the very two people in London that, from my point of view, an unkind fate had sent to make an already problematic dinner party ten times worse. George was hastily making introductions but they were hardly needed because the gentleman was quite well known and it was probably a coup for the Talbots to secure the couple.

'Of course, you know Mr and Mrs Disraeli.'

We went in to dinner. Mr Tillington was sitting on my right, Mr Calloway on my left (Beatrice hopefully matchmaking, as usual). Tom was half a table's length away from me, on Beattie's right, with Mary Anne Disraeli on his other side. McPherson was at the far end of the table, which was either good luck or deft manipulation of place cards by Beattie when she saw which way the wind was blowing. The quieter of the two widows, Mrs Dulas, was on one side of him and a middle-aged woman I didn't recognize on the other. Mrs Glass was near the head of the table, opposite Tom. I thought she still looked ill at ease, but at least she too was separated by some distance from McPherson. Mr Disraeli was sitting opposite McPherson. With anybody else, that might have been inconvenient placing too, because Disraeli had been sarcastic in print about the men who'd made their fortunes from opium, but he'd probably find it amusing. Both he and McPherson were capable of looking after themselves. Still, there was an atmosphere, no doubt about it, though things thawed to some extent with the circulation of the food and wine. I wish I could give a better account of the dinner, since Beattie had taken such trouble with it, but beyond noting that the vegetable mulligatawny hadn't been tamed much by the addition of arrowroot and the chapattis tasted better than they looked, I didn't give it much attention. Tom had contrived to introduce Mr Tillington to me between drawing room and dining room and most of my attention was on him.

He was courtly and pleasantly old-fashioned in his manner, but what made me like him was his willingness to talk about Tom. He said almost at once how pleased he was to have made his acquaintance.

'I was afraid he might have thought me importunate in writing to him. I'm sure Griffiths would have introduced us if he'd lived. He'd mentioned your brother in letters as a great support to him in Bombay.'

'I'm sure Mr Griffiths was a great support to Tom as well,' I said.

'Griffiths did give the impression that your brother wasn't a fervent admirer of some of the Company's policies and might feel isolated from the other men. In fact, he was worried that associating with him might damage Tom's career.'

'He said that in his letters?'

'Yes, and when we met in London. He also said India needed young men like your brother. I do hope he won't be deterred by this . . . unpleasantness.'

A hesitation, and the slightest nod of the head down the table towards where McPherson was sitting. As far as I could see, Disraeli was happily holding forth as usual. McPherson looked glum. A waiter appeared at our shoulders, offering hock or milk punch. I chose hock. So did Mr Tillington and Mr Calloway. Still, the punch looked better than I expected, sparkling with crushed ice in a crystal decanter. I glanced up the table and saw Mrs Glass and Mary Anne Disraeli drinking it with obvious enjoyment.

As the plates were changed for the next course, I turned to talk to Mr Calloway. He grinned at me and spoke softly.

'Poor George.'

'I don't think he realized he was bringing civil war under

his roof,' I said. 'He admitted he didn't know a lot about Indian affairs. Still, at least McPherson is outnumbered.'

Calloway was forking up chicken curry with an enthusiasm that might have been real or diplomatic. He swallowed and took a hasty gulp of water.

'Outnumbered? I'm not sure about that. At least two of the other men are four star shareholders in the East India Company, which probably puts them on McPherson's side.'

'Four star?'

'Four asterisks against their names in the list of shareholders. That means they have ten thousand or more invested.'

'Oh dear.'

'Don't worry, they can hardly start shouting at each other at their hosts' table. It's quite amusing in its way.'

I said I was glad he found it so, and turned back to Mr Tillington as the next course of curry arrived. Since he must be as aware of the undercurrents as anybody, I risked a question.

'Did you know Mr McPherson in India?'

'Our paths crossed when we were much younger. I didn't stay in India long enough to know him well. I have many regrets about leaving the country, but that is not one of them.'

For so polite a man, his tone was emphatic.

'I have the impression that Mrs Glass shares your opinion,' I said. 'She seemed shocked to find he'd been invited.'

'Mrs Glass?'

He followed my glance and saw her taking a hearty gulp of the punch.

'I can't recall her. She was in India?'

'With her husband. Some time ago, I think.'

The ill-assorted party was relaxing now, conversation flowing. I tried another question, more direct.

'Tom tells me you don't believe Mr Griffiths killed himself. Is that right?'

'I'm sure he didn't and I intend to prove it.'

Mr Tillington spoke quite loudly and drew his shoulders back so that he was looking straight into my eyes. His eyes were bright grey, with chalky rings round the pupils.

'How?'

My question was too blunt. His eyes left mine and his voice dropped.

'Forgive me for being carried away, Miss Lane. Mine is hardly suitable conversation for a charming young woman at a dinner party. I hope you will excuse me, but the memory of my friend . . .'

It was my fault for raising the subject, I said, and I was the one who should be asking for forgiveness. I meant it, and was glad of the arrival of dessert – pineapple creams, pistachio cake, mangoes in brandy – as a signal to turn back to Mr Calloway.

He'd been amusing himself observing the polite hostilities further down the table.

'Disraeli's stopped talking and started listening. That's when he's dangerous.'

'Dangerous?'

'Politically speaking. Have you noticed what an instinct he has for people's weaknesses?'

It hadn't struck me until then, but I could see he was right.

'McPherson is looking quite heated,' Calloway said. 'I dare say Disraeli's managed to say something to get under his skin.'

On my other side, Mr Tillington had gone quiet, refusing dessert and not attempting conversation with his neighbour. It was something of a relief when Beattie stood up, the signal for the ladies to withdraw and leave the gentlemen to their port and cigars. We trooped into the drawing room for coffee and sweets of almond paste. Milk punch was still being served to the ladies who wanted it, and several did. Mrs Glass had become bright eyed and even more talkative.

'So delicious, so good for the digestion. You must let me have the recipe.'

Beattie promised that she would and, ever generous, offered to have some bottled and sent round to Mrs Glass's address. After cheerfully circulating round her other guests she came over to me, letting her anxiety show.

'It's not a success, is it Libby?'

I tried to comfort her. The curries had clearly been appreciated – give or take a few outbreaks of coughing – and most of her guests looked happy. She was too experienced a hostess to believe me.

'There's an atmosphere, isn't there? George likes to invite people with different views, but this is more than that. Some of them just can't stand each other.'

'I'm afraid that's true.'

'Maybe George and Mr Calloway will be able to reconcile them over the port. Do you think they might?'

Unlikely, I thought, but didn't depress her further by saying so. She went to talk to Mrs Dulas, who was sitting on her own. Immediately, Mary Anne Disraeli moved on to the sofa beside me.

'Miss Lane, isn't it? So good to meet you again.'

Not pausing for breath, she launched into a series of questions about me, my family, my political views with the efficiency of a butterfly sucking up nectar. Since she'd shown very little interest when we'd met at her 'At Homes' I guessed Disraeli had been talking about me and wondered what he'd said. When she ran out of questions at last she turned to the subject of her husband: how unjust it was that he hadn't been given ministerial office, when he was clearly so much more brilliant, well informed, influential than any other young politician.

'Jealousy, that's all it is, pure jealousy. One day they'll see how much they need him.'

Her opinion of Disraeli was clearly even higher than his own of himself. Luckily, after some more of this, she decided that she'd extracted as much as she needed from me and took herself off rather abruptly.

That left me free to do something I'd been hoping to do all evening: have a few words with Mrs Glass on her own. I moved to a footstool beside her chair and remarked that it was hot in here.

'Nothing compared to India,' she said. 'There were afternoons in Calcutta so hot you couldn't bear to put a foot to the ground. Too hot to breathe, almost. Of course, it killed poor Humphrey in the end.'

Her late husband, I assumed. I listened for a while as she talked about the impossibility of comfort in India, then made my move.

'You've recovered, I hope,' I said.

'You never recover from India.'

'I meant earlier this evening, before dinner. I thought you seemed a little indisposed.'

'Oh that.' She seemed embarrassed. 'A gentleman had come in that I never wanted to see again. Of course Mrs Talbot couldn't have known poor thing or I'm sure she'd never have invited him. It was such a long time ago, you see.'

I'm sure I could have persuaded her to tell me more, but there was a general stir as the gentlemen came to join us and somehow the room rearranged itself so that I had to abandon my place by Mrs Glass.

It was clear almost at once that the rearrangement was on battle lines, or rather the lines of a battle that had just taken place. On one side of the room McPherson, and two others that I was sure fitted Mr Calloway's category of being major shareholders in the East India Company. On the other side my brother, George, Mr Calloway and Mr Tillington. Mr Tillington looked agitated, his face pale yellowish, making jerky hand movements as he spoke. Mr Calloway was listening to him, making the occasional remark and nodding his head in what was evidently meant to be a soothing way. Disraeli had gone straight to talk to Mary Anne, but soon afterwards he came over to me with the glint of devilment in his eye.

'Livelier than most debates in the House of Commons.'

'What happened?' I said.

'Our elderly friend went for McPherson like a terrier against a bulldog.'

He nodded towards Mr Tillington.

'Why?'

'I didn't hear the very start of it, but McPherson suddenly produced a newspaper cutting from his pocket, waved it under Tillington's nose and asked if he had anything to do with it.'

'Oh no!'

Disraeli nodded, probably assuming shock at such bad manners at somebody else's dinner table. In fact, I was thinking I could guess the source of the cutting.

'It was the one from that scandal rag, practically accusing McPherson of killing Griffiths,' Disraeli said. 'Tillington said no, he wasn't responsible for the piece, but he agreed with every word of it. McPherson said: "You think I'm a murderer and a thief then?" and Tillington said, "One of the two, at any rate." If Tillington weren't so obviously an invalid, I think it would have been pistols at dawn.'

Disraeli was clearly enjoying himself. Given his love of drama and gossip, a highly coloured account of all this would be round London by lunchtime.

'What did everybody else say?'

'They were pretty well struck dumb. Then our host and the young man from the Foreign Office jumped in and tried to change the conversation to politics. Unfortunately, somebody mentioned the Chinese war and the whole table were at it hammer and tongs. Still, at least it took some of the attention off Tillington.'

'Did my brother take part?'

'Not a large part. He was mostly looking after Tillington. The poor old man was pretty shaken.'

I glanced towards Tom, standing on his own and looking miserable. George had settled Mr Tillington in an armchair and was standing beside it as if to protect him from further dramas. The Talbots' well-intentioned efforts seemed to have ended in disaster. Tom might assume that this happened at every dinner party I attended.

Disraeli was tugged away by Mary Anne. A musician was playing a sitar in a corner of the room but nobody was taking any notice of him. I stood for a while then, in a spirit of pure contrariness since so many boats were burned, crossed the invisible dividing line on the drawing room carpet and went up to McPherson. He'd drawn a little apart from his friends and was looking stormy and sipping brandy. He had no reason to know who I was and would certainly not have noticed me in the background at Westminster Hall. The large number of people at dinner meant I hadn't been formally introduced to him and he struck me as a man who didn't waste much time being sociable with women.

'Mr McPherson, isn't it? I believe we have an acquaintance in common.'

'Have we?'

His tone was barely civil. Beyond a routine attempt to glance down my bodice, defeated by my demure muslin, he wasn't interested.

'He's a member of parliament, Mr Cyril Eckington-Smith,' I said.

It was an experiment. If Eckington-Smith had indeed been acting as McPherson's messenger boy in the matter of the pamphlets and found out who I was, surely he'd have reported back. There was no recognition in McPherson's eyes, no change in his bored tone.

'I'm afraid you must be mistaken. I don't know the man.'

I said I was sorry and crossed back to my own side, aware of eyes on me, including Tom's. Another black mark.

Soon afterwards, the party broke up in the usual mild confusion of people looking for their cloaks and overcoats, waiting in the hall for carriages and cabs. Determined to salvage something from the wreck of the evening, I helped Mrs Glass on with her wrap.

'I was interested in what you had to say about India,' I said. 'I'd be so pleased if you'd let me call on you to hear more about it.'

She was surprised, but only mildly so. As far as I could tell, she was one of the few who'd enjoyed the evening, after that first shock of seeing the man she'd never wanted to see again.

'Call as soon as you like, dear. Monday if it suits you. Perhaps I can get you interested in a bazaar we're planning for the Calcutta orphanage.'

She gave me an address in Kensington. Beattie arrived beside us and put an arm round Mrs Glass.

'So kind of you to come,' Beattie told her. 'I'm having cook put up a bottle of the milk punch. I'll send it round to you with the recipe.'

Mrs Glass's driver arrived and she went out into the night, uttering thank yous. Most of the guests were still there, but dispersed over the next ten minutes or so until only the Talbots, Tom and I were left.

'I'll take Mrs Glass's punch if you like. I'm seeing her on Monday,' I said.

The Talbots insisted on calling out their carriage to take Tom, myself and Mr Tillington home. They stopped at the gateway to Abel Yard to drop me off first. Tom walked with me to the bottom of my stairs. He hadn't said a word on the journey. I could feel the anger radiating from him.

'That piece in the paper, was it anything to do with you?'

I couldn't lie to him. I said nothing and he drew the right conclusion.

'I don't know what you're doing. I don't know what you're thinking.'

He didn't add: I don't know what you've turned into, but it was there in his tone. There was no point in telling him that I didn't know what I was doing either, so I wished him good-night and went upstairs.

FIFTEEN

On Monday morning I walked across the park to Kensington, carrying the bag with Beattie's bottle of milk punch. Tom's remark was very much in my mind. I did not know what I was doing, except following a stubborn belief that Mr Griffiths's death had its explanation in what had happened in India a long time ago. Tom's new friend Mr Tillington could have told me more. It was annoying that I'd made progress in getting him to talk about it, then cut off the flow with too blunt a question. If I tried again, Tom would hear about it and be angry. Apart from Amos's horseshoe clue, that left only Mrs Glass. She was of the same generation as Griffiths and McPherson and clearly had a story to tell. The question was, could she be persuaded to tell it to me? It was worth a try, at least.

Mrs Glass's little house in Kensington High Street proved that the late Humphrey, who died of India, had left his widow well provided for. Its sash windows gleamed in the sun, with velvet curtains looped up inside. Rows of red-and-white tulips stood on parade in the window boxes and two closely clipped bay trees in tubs guarded the front door. A maid in a white frilly cap opened the front door and showed me into a ground-floor drawing room. Mrs Glass was sitting in a chair by the window, in a loose gown of brocade, her feet in embroidered slippers and a kind of turban round her head.

'You'll excuse my not getting up, Miss Lane. The fact is, I'm not quite myself this morning.'

Indeed, her face had a greyish tinge, and her eyes were bloodshot, as if she'd slept badly. Her breath had a faint odour of garlic. I asked if I should go and call another time, but she said no, it was nice to have company. We exchanged a few remarks of no importance about the Talbots' dinner party. I produced the bottle of milk punch from my bag, explaining that I'd offered to bring it over to save Beattie the trouble of sending a servant. Her reaction was unexpected.

'She's already sent it.'

'When?'

'First thing on Sunday morning. Just after eight o'clock it was. I was still in bed. My maid Jane answered the door and said a boy had come with a bottle for me from Mrs Talbot.'

I stared at her. Beattie wouldn't have forgotten that I was delivering it. In any case, her household would have been too busy first thing on Sunday morning cleaning up after the dinner party to have anybody to spare for running errands.

'Are you sure it was from her?' I said.

'Of course. I had a touch of indigestion all day yesterday – no reflection on Mrs Talbot's dinner – so I told Jane to pour me a little glassful yesterday evening, thinking it would put me right.'

She made a face.

'It didn't?' I said.

'It did not. I think it must have gone off overnight. In fact it made me . . .' She put a hand on her stomach and mimed, as genteelly as could be done, violent vomiting. 'It left a metallic sort of taste, like eating sugar off a cheap spoon. Only I wouldn't want Mrs Talbot to know.'

'Might I see the bottle?' I said.

She looked surprised, but rang the bell for Jane and the bottle was brought. It was ordinary green glass, full to within a few inches of the neck. I eased out the cork and sniffed. The aniseed smell from the rack was much stronger than I remembered from Beatrice's brew. I put the bottle I'd brought beside it for comparison. That one was clear glass. When I opened the bottle, the aniseed smell was indeed less pronounced.

'Beattie will be very sorry about that,' I said. 'I'll take both bottles away with me, if I may.'

'You won't let her think I'm complaining?'

'Of course not, no.'

I tried to follow my plan of questioning Mrs Glass about McPherson but to no effect, partly because my mind was on the bottles and partly because she made it clear that she was allowing no trespassing in that quarter. Even a gentle reference to her moment of uneasiness the evening before was batted firmly away.

'Don't let's talk about it, dear. I was being silly and that's that. I'd hate Mrs Talbot to think I'd been upset in any way.'

She was willing enough to talk about other aspects of her life in India. She'd been sent out at the age of eighteen, to act as a companion for an aunt who'd married a government official.

'Up to then, I'd never even crossed the Channel, been no further away from home than Bath, then there I was sailing halfway round the world. Oh, it was such a life – the jewels, the elephants, all those handsome men in their uniforms. I didn't mind the heat then. You don't feel it so much when you're young. We'd dance all night, then go out on breakfast picnics at dawn with real champagne imported from France. Would you believe, I had three proposals of marriage in my first season?'

Her eyes were sparkling and the pink coming back into her complexion at the thought of it. I resisted the temptation to ask if one of those proposals had been from McPherson.

'Then there were our concerts and plays. We had to make our own entertainment as a rule, but some of the gentlemen were as good as Garrick. Too good, some might say. Amateur dramatics can be very dangerous to the feelings in sultry climates. Then I married poor Humphrey. I'm not saying a word against him, but it's a different thing being a wife from being a girl. Different anywhere, I dare say, but more so in India. I buried three children in four years. None of them lived beyond three months. Fever, you see.'

'You had children who lived too?'

'Yes, two sons. And they're both in India, one a colonel already and the other with the Company. It's in your blood, you see. If you're there any time, it's in your blood.'

At least we got on well enough for Mrs Glass to say she enjoyed talking to me and I must call again. Back home, I put the two bottles on the table in my study, dipped my finger into the liquid from the green bottle and licked it. Since a spat-out mouthful had not killed Mrs Glass, it seemed no great risk. The flavour was mostly aniseed. There might have been the faintest metallic aftertaste, but then perhaps I imagined that because I was expecting it. I knew about arsenic. There was a reliable test for it now. A few months ago, I'd stood in a London laboratory and made notes while it was done. I took my casebook from the cupboard to refresh my memory. The experimenter had mixed a sample of the suspect cold coffee with sulphuric acid and zinc to produce a gas that left a silvery black deposit on a glass test tube. Metallic arsenic. My client had been standing beside me at the time, solemn faced.

'As I feared. It looks very much as if my poor wife is trying to poison me.'

Not enough to kill him, he'd insisted. She only wanted to make him ill. In her poor, confused brain she saw him as her enemy. My client wanted me to keep watch on his wife and produce firm evidence, then he could decide what must be done. He was a liar. I'd suspected it from the first consultation, but it was several weeks before I'd proved it. The aim had been to consign his entirely innocent wife to an insane asylum. The name of my then client had been Cyril Eckington-Smith MP. And here we were, with Eckington-Smith crossing my path again and the presence of arsenic. Coincidence?

Possibly, yes. For one thing, it wasn't conclusively proved that it was arsenic in the false bottle. I could go to the trouble and expense of sending it to a laboratory. At less expense, I might have asked one of the urchins in the mews to catch me a live rat for experiment, but couldn't have brought myself to kill even a rat that way. For the moment, let it stand as arsenic. I wrote out a note giving the date and circumstances, tied it round the false bottle and locked it away in a cupboard and went on trying to sort out my ideas. Eckington-Smith had not been at the dinner party. Only a very small group of people knew that Mrs Glass was expecting the delivery of a bottle of milk punch – Beattie's dinner guests and their servants. I ruled out the servants. They'd all been with the Talbots for some time and could have no possible motive for poisoning their dinner guest. I cast my mind back to that scene in the hall where Beattie had made the promise, trying to remember who might have overheard. No help. As far as I could remember, it could have been any of the guests. Even ruling out the

Disraelis, Tom and Mr Tillington, Mr Calloway and myself, that still left fourteen. Of those, who had heard me making an appointment to call on Mrs Glass? A smaller number, certainly, but I couldn't remember clearly enough to narrow it down. Again, who could have noticed that I'd been deep in conversation with Mrs Glass? The women mainly, because it had mostly happened while the men were still at table. I'd still been sitting on the footstool at her feet when they all came back into the drawing room, but it would have taken a very quick eye to notice that or draw any conclusions from it.

A quick eye, or the eye of a man with reason to be worried about what Mrs Glass might say. A man who had figured so unhappily in her past that, many years later, she was shocked when he walked into a room. McPherson. Because of my prejudice against the man, I'd been trying not to rush to the conclusion, but he was the obvious one from the start. He'd noticed me talking to Mrs Glass. Soon afterwards, I'd accosted him about Eckington-Smith and put him on the alert. I was sorry about that now, but couldn't have foreseen how things would develop. Then he'd overheard me making that appointment to visit Mrs Glass and drawn the right conclusion: I knew Mrs Glass had a secret involving him and was hoping to root it out. What I hadn't expected was this immediate and ruthless action. He'd taken ten hours or less to concoct something resembling the punch and deliver it. Almost certainly, he wouldn't have attended to the details himself. He seemed to have plenty of cronies to do his dirty work for him. Did he intend the drink to kill her or just make her too ill to receive visitors? No way of telling. I worried at it all day until my head was splitting. All paths seemed to lead back to McPherson but there was no sure proof against him. Eckington-Smith was possibly his only weak point.

In the afternoon, Mrs Martley and I took a walk across the park to the livery stables, to give a carrot or two to Rancie. Amos was in the yard.

'I've got a horse to see out Richmond way tomorrow. That mare of yours could do with a proper bit of exercise.'

Trust Amos. If I'd had an errand at the court of the Emperor of China he'd have probably known a horse in Peking he wanted to see. Instead of our usual ride in the park, we set out westwards and were on Richmond Green by mid morning. We dealt with Amos's business first, going to a private stables to see a carriage horse that might do for one of his clients. He watched, giving nothing away, as it was trotted out in the head collar and harnessed to a phaeton, then made his offer to the head groom. The man shook his head.

'They won't let him go for that.'

Amos wished him good morning, cheerful as ever.

'Waste of your time, then?' I said as we rode away.

'Not a bit of it. He'll come down five guineas, I'll go up five. Nice little horse. I'll be bringing him back with me this time next week. That's the farrier over there.'

We had to wait – loosening the girths and letting our horses graze – while the farrier finished shoeing a carthorse. As soon as it was led away, Amos got into conversation with him. The farrier was friendly enough, but didn't waste words. He had bristly grey hair and looked sixty or older, but had handled the big horse as easily as a child with a doll. They'd never met before but had acquaintances in common and the horse world has its own freemasonry. Pretty soon, Amos had turned the conversation to a carriage owned or hired by an Indian gentleman.

'Hired,' the farrier said. 'From over there.' He nodded his head in what was probably the direction of a local livery stables. 'Taken it and the horses and driver for three months.'

'Staying a while, then?'

'Seems so.'

'See much of him?'

'Not a lot. Keep to themselves.'

'More than one of them, then?'

'Him and the two ladies.'

'Indian ladies?'

A nod.

'Wonder what brings them here?'

A shrug.

'Staying near here?'

A nod towards the other side of the green. I joined in the conversation for the first time.

'That cottage over there?'

'S'right.'

We said good day to the farrier and led the horses away.

'It's the same cottage,' I said. 'The one that Mr Griffiths stayed in. That can't be a coincidence. And there were two women with the gentleman in the carriage that night by the river, I'm sure of it.'

'We paying a call then?'

'Yes.'

It wasn't worth remounting for that short distance so we led the horses across the green. The cottage looked much the same as the first time I'd seen it, except that red geraniums had replaced the forget-me-nots in the border. I left Amos holding both horses, walked up the brick path to the front door and knocked. For a minute or so nothing happened and I wondered whether to knock again. Then suddenly, without any sound from inside, the door opened. Standing inside was the same Indian lad in turban, tunic and white trousers who'd opened the door to Tom and myself when we came calling on Mr Griffiths. At first I thought I must be mistaken, and they only looked alike to me because both boys were Indian. On second glance, I was sure it was the very same lad. What's more, there was a glint of recognition in his eyes, as if he'd seen me before. Surprise made me stumble over the words I'd prepared.

'Please tell your master that I knew a friend of his and I should be very grateful for a chance to speak with him.'

I gave him my card. He stared down at it, then at me. The recognition had faded from his eyes. They were blank.

'Sorry, not understand.'

He began to close the door.

'Please, at least give my card to him. Tell him I'm a friend of Mr Griffiths and . . .'

I spoke deliberately loudly, sure that in so small a cottage somebody inside must be hearing. Before I could finish the sentence I found myself staring at a closed door.

I walked slowly back to Amos.

'No good?'

'Something's badly wrong.'

I took Rancie's reins from him and moved so that we had a view of the back of the cottage. Surely somebody inside must be curious about us. Curtains were firmly closed over the downstairs windows but above them, in what was probably a bedroom, they were parted and the window was half open. As I looked up, a flash of red and gold caught my eye. It looked very like the silk shawl an Indian woman might wear over her head, then it was gone.

'Being watched from two sides we are,' Amos said. He nodded across the green. 'See the gentleman on the grey?'

A man on a grey was walking unhurriedly away from us.

'He was taking a good look at you when you were waiting at the door,' Amos said. 'Stopped his horse until you started walking back, then he went.'

'What did he look like?'

'Elderly, quite upright, like an old soldier on parade.'

'Soldier?'

'Just how he struck me, like.'

After all, Richmond was probably full of retired officers with nothing better to do with their time than observe their neighbours' affairs. The presence of an Indian family would arouse curiosity. If the horseman had been closer, I might have tried to get into conversation with him, but you need a good reason for cantering after strange men. We remounted and turned for home.

'So they weren't feeling sociable,' Amos said.

'They might have good reason. That lad who came to the door was Mr Griffiths's servant. He was almost certainly the last person to see him alive. I thought he must have run off scared.'

'Perhaps he did, to these people.'

'All the way out to Richmond? And how would he know where to find them? Another thing, when he was with Mr Griffiths he understood English perfectly well. I remember Mr Griffiths giving him instructions about the coffee. Now he's pretending not to.'

'Because he was told to?'

'Yes. The question is why?'

'To put off strangers asking questions?'

All strangers I wondered, or me in particular? If the Indian gentleman renting the cottage was the same man who'd attended Mr Griffiths's funeral rites it was just possible he'd looked out and recognized me. I'd assumed from his presence that night that he'd been Mr Griffiths's friend. He might be quite the reverse.

'So what do we do now?' Amos said.

'I want to speak to that boy, but I don't know how. Perhaps they're even holding him prisoner.'

'Maybe somebody was pointing a gun on him from inside when he opened the door to you.'

'I wish there were some way of keeping watch on that cottage.'

We couldn't think of one. The position on the edge of the green would make concealment almost impossible. My presence would be noticed at once and Amos's as well, even if he had the time to spend long days out at Richmond, which he didn't. The only person who might have managed it was Tabby. If only I could find her, I'd set her on it. It might at least be a distraction from whatever she was doing in London.

It was evening before we got back to Abel Yard. I said goodbye to Amos and Rancie at the gate and went upstairs. My brother was sitting in the parlour. He raised an eyebrow at my dusty riding costume.

'Where have you been?'

'Richmond.'

I was determined to talk to him about it, even if it meant an argument. But he had something he wanted to say to me.

'I came to let you know that I'm moving in with Tillington.'

'Why? You know I wanted you to come to us.'

'That's not the point. I'm moving in with him to protect him. He was attacked in the early hours of Sunday morning.'

'What happened?'

'He's a light sleeper. I suppose he'd been upset by that confounded dinner party. About three o'clock in the morning he heard somebody on the stairs. He called out but whoever it was didn't go away. He thinks there were two of them. He could hear them breathing through the door. So he got up and went out. There was a scuffle on the staircase, in the dark of course. He seems to have given a good account of himself for an old man, threshing out with his cane, and they ran off.'

'Was he hurt?'

'Tender place on the back of his head and grazed elbow, but very shaken of course.'

'Didn't anyone come to help him?'

'His landlady sleeps in the basement and drinks too much. Apart from that, he's on his own in the house. That's why I'm moving in with him. I didn't protect Griffiths and I'm damned if I'm going to have the same thing happen to his friend.'

I was so shocked by the story that it took a while for what he'd said to penetrate my mind.

'The same thing?'

He sighed. There was worry in his face, also the dragging regret of a stubborn man conceding that he's lost an argument.

'This has convinced me, Libby.'

'That Mr Griffiths was murdered?'

A nod was the nearest he could bring himself to admitting I'd been right all along. I told him then all I knew, including the day's events in Richmond. At first he interrupted with a string of reproaches and objections, but by the end was just listening with a stupefied expression on his face.

'This is beyond anything we can cope with,' he said.

'We have to. Who else is going to do anything? Is there anything in this we could put before a magistrate as proof?'

He shook his head.

'And how would your seniors in the Company react if you told them a good friend of theirs had killed one person and probably tried to kill two others?'

'You mean McPherson?'

'Who else? I'm not saying he did all this with his own hand, but every trail leads back to him.'

We talked for a long time, always coming back to this problem of no proof.

'There are two people who know more,' I said.

'The Indian gentleman who came to the funeral?'

'Yes, and the servant boy.'

'Anil. Yes, and you're right about that at any rate, Libby. He speaks excellent English. But you're sure it's the same boy?'

'Certain. What's more, he recognized me.'

'I wonder if I were to go out to Richmond . . .'

'Not without me.'

I got a promise from him that if he did go to the cottage, Amos and I should go with him.

'I want very much to speak to them,' I said. 'It struck me today that this whole thing hinges on what happened in India, but apart from a few words with the lad, I haven't spoken to a single Indian person.'

'Is that so surprising? Whatever's happening, it's among the British.'

'But it started in India.'

'Burton's murder, you mean?'

'More than that. Whatever caused the quarrel between McPherson and Griffiths happened when you and I were still in the nursery. Can you go over to Daniel's tomorrow and read that manuscript?'

'Yes, and I could take it back and show Tillington. He might have some more idea on how it all connects together, if it does.'

'Better leave it with Daniel and just tell him about it. It might be what those two men who broke into his house were looking for.'

'You think so?'

'Somebody's been going to great lengths to suppress it. It's safer with Daniel.'

He agreed with that as well. The attack on Tillington had shocked him into a remarkably cooperative mood. I took advantage of it.

'I suppose they keep a lot of records at East India House.'

'Of course, going back nearly two hundred years. They've always set a lot of store by putting things in writing.'

'Do you have access to them?'

'Yes. They're in the library. I dare say they keep back all the confidential stuff, but the ordinary records should be there.'

'So you could consult them without attracting attention?'

‘Where is this leading?’

‘We know from the pamphlet that Griffiths served for some time in a small state in Maratha. Twenty years ago there was a very short war there. It would be interesting to know what Europeans were there at the time, particularly army captains.’

Unreasonably, the elderly man with the riding style of a soldier was in my mind. Of the three main characters in the story, we knew who The Griff was and there was precious little doubt about The Merchant. That left The Soldier unaccounted for. Since he’d been invalided home, he’d probably died twenty years before, but even the remotest chance of another witness to what happened was worth following. Tom was sceptical, but for the third time in succession agreed to do what I wanted – probably a happening without precedent.

SIXTEEN

It was tantalizing to think there were probably only two people in the world who knew what had happened on the night Mr Griffiths died, and I'd been standing the width of a doorstep away from one of them. There must be some way of speaking to Anil, but I couldn't think of one. By next morning I'd decided to forget that approach for a while and try some other way. I walked to Piccadilly and took the omnibus to the City of London. The house where Mr Griffiths had lived so briefly looked just the same, with no sign of any new tenant. Perhaps the men from the Company were still keeping it locked up. I walked past and glanced down into the basement. The porter was outside, filling a coal scuttle with his back to me. I was glad about that, because I wasn't sure whether I believed his story about sleeping too deeply to have heard anything on the night of Mr Griffiths's death. If he'd been bribed to say nothing, he was in the enemy camp and would certainly be suspicious of a second visit from me. The house on the left looked a long time empty, with shutters over the windows. The one on the other side was inhabited, with a maid in a mob-cap cleaning the downstairs windows. She gave me a long look as I passed, glad of any distraction from her work. The place had a buttoned-up look about it that was useless for my purpose. I needed to find somebody who might talk to a stranger.

Then the gods sent me just what I needed in the shape of two Dandie Dinmont terriers. They came down the steps of a house opposite, along with a Dalmatian, the leads of all three of them in the hands of a middle-aged woman. Just stepping out of her front door on a calm spring day, she managed somehow to look windswept. You could tell she was a country and not a city person. She wore a cape of rusty-looking black wool, a plain bonnet with the ribbons tied unevenly and ankle-length black boots. I liked the look of her, and the dogs even more. When she turned right and walked briskly along the pavement, I fell in behind them, not close enough to be obtrusive but keeping them easily in view. They seemed to be making for a small square with a few plane trees. I was relying on one of the great laws of the natural world: that two terriers of any breed can't go more than four hundred yards without causing trouble. I was wrong. By my reckoning it was closer to five hundred yards before it happened.

They'd almost reached an open gateway into the square when a manservant with a spaniel approached from the opposite direction. The well-trained Dalmatian pretended they didn't exist, but the two terriers set up a barking like stones rattling into a tin bath. The manservant can't have been concentrating because the spaniel twitched the lead out of his hand and made straight for the terriers. By now they were racing in circles on their leads, spinning their owner like a top and tangling with the Dalmatian. She almost fell and, in saving herself, dropped one of the leads. The spaniel and the liberated terrier turned into one sphere of fur that whirled and growled while the other terrier yelped blue murder, struggling to join in the fight, and the Dalmatian started barking. Both the woman and the manservant were yelling at their dogs without effect. As soon as I saw how things were developing, I'd started unfastening my cloak. I hurried up to the spinning dogs and dropped it over them. It brought them to a halt just long enough for the manservant to grab the larger dog. He lifted the spaniel, still swaddled in my cloak. The terrier, clinging with its teeth to the hem of it, was snatched off its feet. I moved in and caught it. It came away, still snarling, with part of my cloak lining in its teeth. One of its ears was bleeding.

'Crispin, you worm,' the woman said to it.

I untangled the lead from round the terrier's legs and restored it to her.

'I don't think he's badly hurt,' I said.

She inspected the ear. 'Nothing that can't be cured.'

The manservant, standing at a safe distance, had unwrapped the spaniel which also seemed largely undamaged. He held out my cloak. I fetched it and walked back to the woman.

'Oh dear,' she said. 'Your poor cloak.'

I told her not to worry about it, though part of the hem and lining were torn. I only hoped it would be worth the sacrifice.

'It really was uncommonly resourceful of you,' she said. 'How lucky you came to be there. I'm so sorry. It's London, you see. They're not used to it.'

So I'd guessed right. By the time we were back at her doorstep, with me leading the combatant terrier and she the other two dogs, I'd learned that her name was Miss Sand, she was from Kent, spending time in London nursing her sick brother, a lawyer, that he was on the road to recovery and not a moment too soon for her. She'd learned from me my name and the fact – which was true – that I had a friend who bred Dandie Dinmonts.

'You positively must come in for a sherry,' she said. 'It's the least I can do.'

The maid who opened the door to us was sent for sherry, dilute carbolic and cotton gauze. They arrived on a tray together and the girl went away with my cloak to brush.

Miss Sand poured generous glasses of what turned out to be good dry sherry, tucked the terrier under her arm and efficiently bathed its ear. I asked if she liked this part of London. As much as she liked any of it, she said. It was quiet at least.

'A relative of mine knew the gentleman opposite,' I said. 'The one who died.'

I liked her and had decided not to lie to her.

'How dreadful. The man who killed himself? Did you know him?'

'I met him twice. Did you see him at all?'

'No, but then he'd only just moved in, hadn't he? Somebody said he'd come over from India.'

'Yes.'

'He was lonely perhaps, poor man. If my brother had been well, I'm sure he'd have gone across and left his card. Not that it would have helped much, I suppose.'

'Did he get many visitors?'

'Not that I saw, but then our sitting room and my brother's bedroom are out at the back.'

So I'd sacrificed my cloak in vain. Then she sipped her sherry and thought about it.

'Except for the Indian man.'

I nearly spilled my sherry.

'Indian man?'

'Yes. It was quite extraordinary. A brougham drew up and this Indian got out, quite like any gentleman paying a visit, except he was dressed all in white and had this – what is it you call it? – turban round his head.'

'And he went into the house opposite?'

'Yes. Another Indian, only a boy, opened the door to him. It looked as if the Indian man was giving the boy a card in quite the normal way. Then he waited on the step for a few minutes and the boy opened the door again and let him in.'

'When was this?'

'The Saturday night. It was on the Monday morning that we heard the poor gentleman was dead.'

'Late at night?'

'No. It can't have been late because it was still quite light. Half light at any rate.'

'Did he stay long?'

'I don't know. I looked out about half an hour later and the brougham was still there, but my brother wanted to play cards so I didn't see when it went. My brother said if the gentleman opposite came from India, he might have an Indian butler. Are there Indian butlers?'

'Did you see the man again?'

'No. Of course, there were a lot of comings and goings from the house once they'd found the poor gentleman, but I never saw the Indian man again.'

'Nor the boy?'

'No.'

Miss Sand was looking surprised at my questioning. Not wanting to be trapped in explanations, I turned the conversation back to dogs and escaped as soon as politely possible. She thanked me again and urged me to call on her if I was ever near her village in Kent.

I took the omnibus back, wondering what to do with this unexpected piece of information. There was no reasonable doubt that the Indian man who'd called on Mr Griffiths and the unexpected arrival at his funeral pyre were one and the same man. A second Indian gentleman, living in the cottage once occupied by Mr Griffiths and employing his servant boy, would be too much of a coincidence, so the same man again. And a man who had a great deal of explaining to do. The certainty that McPherson, or one of his agents, was responsible for Mr Griffiths's death was beginning to crumble. Above all, I needed to know more about that household out at Richmond and couldn't see how to set about it. With nobody else available, it looked as if I'd have to do the job of observing it myself. I walked into Abel Yard turning over various desperate ideas, like disguising myself as an elderly woman selling apples, wishing heartily that Tabby were there to take on a task she did so much better. Then, for the second time in the day, the gods were good. There she was, standing just inside the gateway talking to the urchin leader, Plush.

Goodness knows what the conversation was about. Both looked guilty when they saw me and Tabby was a hair's breadth from bolting.

'I need you,' I told her. 'I have a job for you.'

She followed me reluctantly to the bottom of my stairs. I guessed that if I started questioning her about where she'd been, she'd be away as quickly as a cat. The best hope was to hold her interest.

'There's a young Indian boy I think may have been kidnapped. He's in a house out at Richmond with an Indian gentleman. We need to find a way of speaking to him on his own.'

A glimmer of interest in her eyes, though her face was still sullen. She was wearing her respectable grey dress but her standards of cleanliness had slumped; hair dull and dirty, shoes scuffed.

'We'll get the next coach out to Richmond and I'll show you what's to be done,' I said.

We stayed long enough for her to wolf down the cold beef sandwich I brought her and to collect her cloak from her cabin. That was my suggestion, because her appearance meant we'd be riding on the outside of the coach. When we got down at Richmond the sullen expression was still in place.

'That's the cottage over there,' I said. 'I don't want to go any closer, because they might recognize me. If you . . .'

A carriage went past at a walk. It was an ordinary brougham of the sort that might come from a livery stables. Nothing remarkable about it at all, except for the flash of white from inside. A white turban.

'Oh confound it.'

I turned away as quickly as I could, hoping the person inside hadn't noticed us. We watched as it went on then passed out of sight near the cottage.

'He's going home,' I said. 'I wonder where he's been.'

'That the man what's kidnapped the boy?'

'Probably, yes.'

Her grammar had slipped too, but at least she was showing some interest. I explained the nearest thing I had to a plan.

'We need to know if he has a regular routine for going out and coming back, and whether the boy ever goes with him. There's at least one Indian woman in the house, probably two. Do they ever go out and are there any servants apart from the boy? Once we know that, we can work how to approach him.'

She nodded. I seldom had to explain anything to Tabby twice.

'So we'll go home and I'll book a place on the first coach back here for you tomorrow morning,' I said. 'The sooner you start, the better.'

She gave me a cool look.

'What do I need to go back for? It's here I'm supposed to be, isn't it?'

'But you've got nowhere to stay.'

Looking as she did, there'd be no room at an inn for the likes of Tabby.

'I'll find somewhere. Any road, I'll be watching all night as well, won't I?'

'The day should do. They must sleep sometimes.'

'No point if I don't.'

I was going to protest and insist on taking her back with me, but it struck me that this would be the certain way of losing her again. By the look of her, she'd gone back to her old habits, sleeping in whatever nooks or crannies she could find. At least this way I knew approximately where she was and what she was doing.

'Very well, but I want you to come back and report to me tomorrow evening. Will you do that?'

A brief nod.

'And whatever you do, don't approach any of them directly and try not to be noticed.'

Another nod. I put a couple of half-crowns into her hand for food and the fare and began walking back to the inn for the coach to town. After a few dozen yards I turned to look back at her, but she'd already disappeared.

My brother arrived the following evening, heavy-eyed. He'd spent his spare time at the Suters' house, reading Mr Griffiths's manuscript.

'I can hardly believe it, Libby. It's not the man I knew.'

'You knew an old man. He was younger then.'

'Not so very young with that business of the princess. About twenty years ago.'

'He was thirty or so. That's not so old for a man to fall in love,' I said.

'It would have been treason, encouraging mutiny in the Company's army.'

'Would it, legally speaking? It's not the same as the British army.'

'Pretty much the same thing. At the very least, gross disloyalty.'

'To a Company that had behaved very badly.'

'They were hard times, Libby, not like now.'

'I wonder. In his place, would you have behaved very differently?'

He stared at the fire. I waited, dreading his answer would widen the distance between us. It came as a relief.

'Probably not, in some ways. I hope I'd have tried to stop the war, as he did.'

'Good.'

'But it's the business with the woman that's surprising. I can't believe he let himself be led by the nose like that.'

'She was beautiful and wronged. That's a powerful combination.'

'Even so.'

I looked at him while he went on frowning at the fire. So my little brother hadn't fallen in love yet. He'd learn.

'That aside, what did you make of the business of The Merchant and The Soldier?' I said.

'The Merchant's Alexander McPherson, that's obvious.'

'And The Soldier?'

'I don't know.'

'That's why it might be interesting to look through the Company army records. Have you had a chance yet?'

'When I've almost worn my eyes out on Griffiths's pamphlet? There's a whole shelf of army records. It will take weeks. Does it matter?'

An impression of a soldierly-looking man on a grey horse seemed too shadowy to mention.

'Mr Griffiths seems to imply that The Merchant and The Soldier may have been in some sort of conspiracy,' I said. 'At least, there's a hint that it might have been more than coincidence that they were in the principality at the same time.'

'Griffiths was as good as accusing them of stealing the prince's jewel collection.'

'The collection that the thieves missed in Bombay and that McPherson has probably brought with him to sell in London.'

'We don't know it's one and the same. A man like McPherson would pick up jewels all over the place.'

'What about that hawk? We know some of the prince's pieces were in animal shapes.'

'There are a lot of jewels in India.'

But Tom said it without much conviction.

'I have it on good authority that McPherson is depending on those jewels for his financial survival,' I said. Tom opened his mouth to ask how I knew so I pressed on quickly. 'Any hint that they're not legally his to dispose of might have a disastrous effect on his credit. No wonder he and his cronies wanted to stop Mr Griffiths's pamphlet going into circulation.'

'To the extent of killing him?' Tom said.

He didn't sound so sceptical about it now. It was ironical

that he was working himself round to a position just as I was close to abandoning it.

'Except I'm not sure now that McPherson and his friends did kill him,' I said.

'So suicide after all?' Tom said.

He started running his fingers through his hair, then clamped them together on the top of his head as if he feared his brain might explode. I told him about the visit of the Indian man the evening before Mr Griffiths died.

'It's the same man we saw by the river, it must be,' I said. 'And he's got Anil with him.'

'Anil wouldn't have left Griffiths willingly,' Tom said. 'The boy was devoted to him. I can't believe he'd see Griffiths killed and go away with his murderer.'

'So did this man take him away by force?'

'I don't see any other way. If you're sure it was Anil . . .'

'I am.'

'. . . then I'd better go out to Richmond tomorrow and insist on talking to him. At the very least, he's a beneficiary under Griffiths's will and I should speak to him about that.'

'I don't think you should do that until we know more,' I said.

I was about to explain about keeping the cottage under observation when several thunderous knocks sounded on the door at the bottom of the stairs and feet came clumping up. Tabby arriving to report. I wished I'd had a chance to prepare Tom beforehand. After another perfunctory knock on my study door she stamped into the middle of the room, oblivious of Tom.

'I think he might of killed him.'

Even I was stunned. Tom stared at her, mouth open. She was even more dishevelled than when I'd left her the day before, the hem of her skirt trailing, hair flopping down with wisps of hay clinging to it.

'Who?'

'The boy. The Indian boy you wanted to talk to. I reckon they killed him last night, after they seen us together.'

'Explain, Tabby,' I said, trying to keep my voice level. 'In order, please.'

I dared not look at Tom. Tabby took a deep breath.

'I did like you said. By the time I got near the house, the Indian man had gone in and the carriage had gone off somewhere. There's a tree near their garden. You can see the side window from there. The man was inside. I could see him from the white things he was wearing. He was walking up and down and looked as if he was talking to somebody. When it started getting dark, a woman inside lit a lamp. Foreign, she was. Dark, like the man.'

'Young or old?'

'Old. Before it got really dark, the man came out and walked round the house, as if he was making sure nobody was watching. I saw him first and got behind the tree. Then the boy opened the front door to him and he went inside.'

Tom, leaning forward, snapped a question.

'The Indian boy, you mean?'

She gave him one of her stares, then looked at me to see whether she should answer.

'He's my brother,' I said. 'So was it the Indian boy?'

'He looked Indian and he was wearing one of them things on his head, like the man.'

'Did the man say or do anything to him?'

'Not that I saw.'

'Did the boy look scared?'

She shook her head. 'Just ordinary.'

'What happened then?'

'They drew the curtains so I couldn't see inside no more. I seen there was a woodshed at the back of the house, and I thought if I had to stay somewhere for the night, I might as well stay there. So I pushed the logs about to make a space to sit and left the door a bit open so I could see out. I'd see anybody if they came out the back door. If anybody came out of the front door, I'd hear it open. Anyway, quite a bit after that I heard them quarrelling inside.'

'Who was quarrelling?'

'The man and the woman. She was the one you could hear most of, but she was talking foreign. She sounded annoyed. He was answering but his voice was lower.'

'And the boy, could you hear him?' Tom said.

This time she condescended to answer him.

'He never said anything. Not the whole time.'

'So why do you say you think he was killed?'

'After they'd been arguing for a bit, there was this sort of wooden-sounding crash, as if somebody had been knocked downstairs. Then everything went quiet. A bit after that, they put the lamps out. In the morning, as soon as it was light, the man came out and walked all round the house again, looking out for something. The woman was inside, standing at the window. No sign of the boy. The man had to open the door for himself.'

'And on that evidence, you conclude that the boy's been killed.'

Relief at this unconvincing conclusion had turned Tom sarcastic and pompous again. She glared at him.

'You should wait for the end of it. I went on watching, then I heard the front door open and a carriage drawing up outside. Still early, it was, nobody about. The Indian man goes up the path and says something to the driver, then they both go inside. A bit later, the driver and the Indian come out and they're carrying a big wooden box between them. They push it in on the floor of the carriage, then the Indian man gets in with it, the driver gets back up and they drive off.' She turned to me. 'I left it too late to get up on the back, so I don't know where they went to.'

'Big?' said Tom. 'How big?'

He didn't sound sarcastic any more.

'Big enough to put the boy in easy,' Tabby said. Then, as an afterthought, 'If they folded him up a bit that is.'

Tom looked at me, simple appeal on his face. I couldn't think of anything to console him.

'I'm afraid she's sometimes right,' I said.

SEVENTEEN

Next morning, my brother was waiting at the gate to the yard, as arranged, when Amos and I came in from our ride, and the three of us held a hasty conference. Amos already knew from me about the latest turn of events so there wasn't a great deal to discuss.

'I'll be able to find out where the carriage went,' Amos said. 'The odds are it's the one he's already got hired from the livery stables. He'd have been hard put to get another one short notice at that time in the morning.'

'Would normal hire terms include carrying dead bodies?' I said.

'Normal hire is carrying pretty near anything and not making a song and dance about it. If the lass is right, it was just a chest and the driver had no call to know what was inside it.'

'How soon can you find out?' Tom said.

His eyes were feverishly bright and he looked as if he hadn't slept. He hadn't said anything this time about it being my fault, but we both knew that if the boy Anil had been killed, it might have been because his kidnappers had noticed me making a second visit and guessed that I wanted to speak to him.

'I'll get straight over to Richmond as soon as I've arranged things at the stables,' Amos said. 'If I strike lucky, we might know by this evening.'

He'd have to pay a man to take over his day's work, but he didn't mention that.

Tom asked if we should be keeping a watch on the cottage. I said I didn't see much point in it, and if our suspicions were right, the household would be on the alert. In fact, we had nobody to keep watch because Tabby had disappeared again. After her report the evening before, I'd brought her down a supper of bread, mutton and pickles and assumed she'd spend the night in her cabin. By the time I'd come down for my ride at first light, there was no sign of her and the cabin was empty.

'But you might let me know if you see that elderly man on the grey again,' I said to Amos.

'What man?' Tom said.

'Probably nothing. He just seemed curious when we were there last.'

Tom left for his work at East India House. By six in the evening he was back in my study at Abel Yard, wanting to know if there was any news from Amos. I said to give him time and it was a long ride back from Richmond. Tom sat on the daybed under my glass mermaid, fidgeting out tunes on my guitar, so that by the time Amos's shout came up from the yard, just as it was getting dark, my nerves were frayed as well. Riding boots sounded on the stairs and Amos ducked his head and shoulders under the low lintel of my room.

'Got him right enough.'

I asked him to sit down and raised a finger at Tom, cautioning him not to rush in with questions and let Amos tell the story in his own time.

'I was right first one out of the bag. It was the hired carriage. The driver had just come back from London when I got there and didn't object to sitting down and chatting over a beer or two. The Indian gentleman has taken the carriage with driver, sole use, until further notice, two weeks' money paid up front. The driver has instructions to come round early every morning first thing. Sometimes he's needed, sometimes he isn't. He helped the gentleman carry the chest out to the carriage yesterday morning and the gentleman gave him the order to drive to St Paul's Cathedral.'

Tom couldn't keep back a sound of disbelief.

'I know,' said Amos. 'Doesn't sound likely, does it? For one thing it will take them all morning to get there. The driver wasn't expecting that. He hadn't much call to drive to London in the usual course of things, so he wasn't used to finding his way round. Any road, St Paul's is big enough not to miss. So he stops the carriage there, gets down and asks the Indian man what he's supposed to be doing now. The man gets up on the box with him, calm as you like, and gives him directions.'

'Where to?' Tom was getting impatient.

'Well, the driver doesn't know that part of the world at all and I'd had to put three pints of beer inside him to keep him talking, so after that it gets a touch confused, look. One thing he's sure about is that they went downhill towards the river.'

A movement from Tom. I guessed he was thinking of his own journey to the river with Griffiths's body.

'I couldn't get him much clearer than that, except there were yards and wharves down by the river and some big carts coming and going. Timber carts for sure, and lime he thinks. The Indian man tells him to stop outside one of the yards. There's a smell of horse dung, stronger than you normally get, he reckoned. That and mud.'

Another sudden movement from Tom, but he waved to Amos to go on.

'The Indian man gets down off the box and comes back with two workmen. They look a bit surprised, but one of them's clinking coins in his pocket, so the driver reckons the Indian's tipped them well. They unload the chest from the carriage, carry it across the yard, put it in a little skiff and row it out to a boat on the river. Then the Indian man comes back and tells the driver to go, just like that.'

'Did the Indian man go with him?' Tom said.

'No. He stayed where he was.'

'The driver couldn't get all the way back to Richmond in one day,' I said.

Amos nodded. 'That's what he said to the man. The horse was worn out as it was. The man doesn't argue. He gives the driver a sovereign and says to find lodgings for himself and stabling for the horse and to go back to Richmond in the morning. So that's what he did. He'd just got back when I saw him.'

We all said nothing for a while, Tom and I absorbing it.

'It's a pity the driver didn't know London,' I said. 'There must be any number of wharves.'

'Timber Wharf, Iron Wharf, Lime Wharf, Dung Wharf.'

Tom came out with the list suddenly, like a child reciting its tables. We stared at him.

'As you're going down the river,' Tom said. 'They're the wharves on the north bank beside Puddle Dock.'

Amazing the things boys remember. As children, we'd gone on that boat journey down the river several times when our father was travelling, then once more to see Tom off to India from Gravesend, but the names of those wharves hadn't stuck in my mind as they had in his. Amos was looking impressed.

'Sounds as if you've hit it, Mr Lane.'

'I don't think there's a doubt of it. Puddle Dock is downhill from St Paul's and not far away.'

It struck me that it wasn't far either from the heart of the City, including East India House and the lodgings where Mr Griffiths had died. Tom was looking thoroughly fired-up.

'So the driver saw them rowing the chest out to a boat on the river,' he said. 'Did he see it sail away?'

'No. I asked him that. He didn't stay long enough to see what happened. He was too annoyed at having to stay in London overnight and bothered about finding lodgings.'

'There was a mud smell,' I said. 'That means the tide was out. They'd have to wait for the tide to go anywhere.'

'If the Indian man stayed there by the wharf, that must mean he was intending to go out with the boat,' Tom said. 'Otherwise he'd have gone back with the carriage.'

Silence again. I was sure Tom was thinking, as I was, that if the man did go out with the boat, it would be to make sure that Anil's body was dumped quietly over the side.

'What sort of boat was it?' Tom said.

'I asked him that. He was a coachman not a sailor, he said. Just an ordinary boat with two masts. The only thing about it was that it had a green and gold painted figurehead in the shape of a sea horse. It struck him that the figurehead was coming it a bit grand for the size of boat it was, but that was all he noticed.'

Tom slapped his hands down on his knees.

'Well done, Amos. I think we've got him.'

I didn't want to spoil Tom's optimism, but it seemed to me that we were very far from getting him.

'A man can't come out of the blue and hire a boat just like that,' Tom said. 'It's a different matter from tipping a couple of workmen to carry a chest. Either he owns the boat himself and they'll know him around the wharves, or the boat owner will know who he is.'

'Then we'll go to Puddle Dock first thing tomorrow,' I said.

'No point in hurrying now,' Tom said. 'They'll have dropped off the poor lad's body as soon as the tide was right. The thing is to find out who the boat's owner is without raising suspicions. Anyway, I can't get away from East India House before lunchtime. Can you be free tomorrow afternoon, Amos?'

Amos nodded. 'I'll borrow the clarence and meet you in Leadenhall Street, if you like.'

'And you can pick me up here on the way,' I said.

'Oh no he can't.'

Tom said it in his most dogmatic voice. I glared at him.

'And why can't he?'

'Because you're not coming. We don't need you and wharves can be rough places.'

'I probably know more about rough places than you do. In any case, you wouldn't even have known about the chest if I hadn't sent Tabby to watch.'

'Yes, I acknowledge that.' Tom was trying to sound reasonable. It only made him more infuriating. 'I promise you that I'll come back here afterwards and let you know what happened and you can tell me what you think.'

'You won't need to, because I'll be there to do the thinking on the spot.'

'So you're suggesting now that I'm incapable of thinking for myself?'

'It's taken you long enough to start.'

Tom turned from me to Amos.

'Kindly ignore my sister. Will it suit you, then, if we meet in Leadenhall Street at two o'clock?'

Amos looked from Tom to me and back again, face so full of doubt that it seemed painful. Doubt was unlike him. I could hardly breathe. If he took my brother's part in a masculine league against me, something in our friendship would be broken forever. It seemed a long time before he replied to Tom.

'Miss Lane looks at things a different way from most folk. Why run a horse in blinkers if it's got no need of them?'

I understood what he was saying and breathed again, but Tom took some time to work it out. When he did, he wasn't pleased.

'You're saying she should come with us?'

Amos nodded. At least Tom had the sense to realize that opposing him would be like trying to nudge Stonehenge aside, and he needed his help.

Saturday afternoon found us travelling to Puddle Dock in the livery stable's work-a-day clarence, Tom and I sitting opposite each other inside, Amos driving the cob from the box. We'd agreed that if anybody wanted to know why Tom was interested in the boat with the sea horse figurehead, he'd pretend to be acting for a merchant with goods to ship. Amos brought us to a halt halfway down Puddle Dock Hill, with a view of the river. A dozen or so ships were anchored off the wharves, rocking on the outgoing tide. Five of them were two-masters but from that distance you couldn't tell if they had figureheads. We rolled on, and stopped outside the gateway of a timber yard close to the river. There wasn't much work going on, just a man sawing a plank and another one smoking a clay pipe and watching him. Amos gave a whistle and a wave and the man with the pipe strolled over. A coin changed hands. There was always somebody willing to earn a shilling by dozing on his feet alongside a horse doing the same.

'Stay here,' Tom said to me, preparing to get down.

I didn't bother to reply. We'd decided that he and Amos should go together to find somebody who knew about the boat. I'd agreed, but only because the presence of a woman might have drawn unnecessary attention to them.

I waited until they were out of sight, then got out. The man holding the horse seemed only faintly surprised to see me. We agreed that it was a nice day, but with a bit of a cold breeze up the river.

'Left you to wait for them, have they, miss?'

I agreed that they had, in the martyred tones of a woman who did a lot of waiting for her men folk.

'I can't even see the ships from here,' I said.

'They're not much in the way of ships, but if you want to look at them, you could take a stroll between those stacks there. Only watch out for the rats.'

The stroll brought me to the river. Our two-master was one of the closest boats, gilding on the edge of the sea horse scales glinting in the sun as it rocked. No sign of anybody on board. I strolled back to the clarence and the man guarding it.

'Whose is the one with the pretty sea horse?'

It would have been amusing to steal a march on Tom, but the man said he didn't know, with weary tolerance of the female taste for glittering things.

'I suppose it goes out to sea a lot,' I said.

He grinned. 'About as much as this horse we're standing by.'

'You mean it doesn't?'

'Hasn't moved from here in two weeks or more. Lads were only talking about it yesterday.'

'Hadn't it been out the day before yesterday?'

By now he was too convinced of my simplicity to find anything odd in the question.

'I told you, not for a fortnight or more. Have birds nesting in the ropes this rate.'

I stood with him for a while then got back inside the clarence. It was an hour before Tom and Amos reappeared. Tom came and sat opposite me while Amos leaned at the open door.

'Well?' I said.

Tom seemed downcast. 'There weren't many people around to ask. All anybody seems to know is that it's owned or chartered by an Indian man.'

'Is that all? We knew that anyway.'

'The name of the boat is *Calypso*. If she's insured at Lloyds we should be able to trace the owner that way.'

'*Calypso* doesn't travel very much,' I said. 'She hasn't moved from here for two weeks or more.'

They both stared at me.

'She must have,' Tom said. 'What about the day before yesterday?'

'She didn't move. If you don't believe me, ask the man who was holding the horse.'

Amos chuckled, then stopped abruptly when he saw Tom's face.

'I thought I told you not to go round asking questions.'

'You did nothing of the kind. You see what that means?'

I watched the change in his face as annoyance gave way to something more serious.

'That the chest is still on board.'

'Yes.'

He thought for a while, then: 'Amos, can we keep the clarence out?'

'All night, if you like, as long as the horse gets a rest.'

'It shouldn't take that long. It gets dark around eight. If we're back here at nine there shouldn't be many people around.'

'Not down here on a Saturday night,' Amos agreed.

I didn't interrupt because Tom was proposing exactly what I should have done. Also he'd said nothing this time about leaving me behind. Amos got back on the box and we all went together to a decent-looking inn with a stable yard not far from St Paul's. Amos arranged stabling and a feed for the cob, and Tom a private parlour for me to wait.

'So where are you going?' I said.

'To hire a rowing boat.'

'Easier to borrow one,' Amos suggested from the corridor. 'Nobody will know that time of evening.'

But Tom preferred to do things legally. He was back in about an hour, looking embarrassed.

'Isn't it strange how people always assume the worst?'

On questioning, it turned out that the owner of the rowing boat had thought Tom wanted it for some amorous adventure and probably increased the price accordingly. Unable to explain, Tom had to let him go on thinking it. What was really strange, I thought, was that Tom should be concerned about that, but apparently quite cool about boarding a boat that almost certainly contained a murdered boy. I was still learning things about my brother. The three of us dined together in the private parlour, not saying much. At quarter to nine we went out to the stable yard, where a groom had the clarence ready with the cob looking well rested. In darkness, without even our carriage lamps lit, we rolled back down the hill to Puddle Dock.

The timber yard was deserted. With the moon not up yet, everything was in almost total darkness so it was difficult not to crash into woodpiles.

'Should have brought a lantern,' Tom said.

I produced one I'd brought from Abel Yard and tucked away in the carriage until needed, along with a flint lighter. It was the kind with a metal shutter you could turn to give only a thin beam of light.

'Burglar's lantern,' Tom commented, sounding quite amused about it.

'Yes, and very useful they are too.'

As with our children's adventures long ago, I could sense the excitement in him, as well as the finely strung nerves. I let him lead the way with the lantern, to where a rowing boat was tied up at the foot of steps down from the jetty. He went first, I followed, then the boat rocked under Amos's weight. The boat was too narrow for both of them at the oars, so they settled it that Amos should row, with Tom in the stern to untie us and push off, myself in the bow as a lookout. Amos's rowing was powerful but splashy. I was afraid that somebody might hear us and call out from the boats we passed, but they stayed dark and silent. Probably they weren't valuable enough to have a man on board when at anchor, especially on a Saturday night. Now and then, when Amos rested on the oars, sounds of music and laughter drifted across to us from taverns near the water. Tom whispered the occasional instruction from the stern. We'd taken note by daylight of the approximate position of the Calypso.

The lamp beam fell on a curve of scaly tail then shot away as Amos pulled on the oars.

'Hold steady,' Tom said.

I angled the beam upwards, picking out the name: *Calypso*. From the shore, it had seemed a simple matter to climb on board but we were rocking alongside an outward curving cliff of wood. Amos rowed as delicately as he could manage along the port side, but his oar kept striking against the planks. If there'd been anybody on board the noise would have brought them out. There was no sound. Towards the stern, Tom told me to shine the beam up again. It picked out what looked like a coiled up rope ladder.

'Should have brought a boat hook,' Tom said.

This time I couldn't oblige. Tom stood up in the boat, took one of the oars and tried to hook the rope ladder with the blade. It was just out of reach. Amos handed the other oar to me.

'Get hold of it halfway down. Try and use it like a paddle and keep us steady.'

I did my best as Amos hunkered down in the middle of the rowing boat and made a back for Tom to stand on. The arrangement seemed desperately precarious, with Tom reaching up to the point of overbalancing, the oar thumping against the boat in several failed attempts. Then: 'Got it.'

Tom and the end of the rope ladder fell back into the boat together, tangling with Amos. It took us a while to sort ourselves out, but at the end of it the ladder made the steep hypotenuse of the triangle between the *Calypso* and our rowing boat.

'I'll go up first,' Tom said. 'There should be a rope up there. I'll throw it down for you to tie up the boat.'

He was doing well, I thought, but spoiled the effect by trying to take the lantern in his teeth. In the scenes we'd acted out as children, pirates had made nothing of doing that with cutlasses and pistols. In real life, all Tom got was exasperation and a burned lip, so he made the climb with no more light than the glimmer from the water.

It seemed a long time before a rope thumped into the water beside us. Amos picked it out and tied it through a ring on the bows of the rowing boat.

'Right then. Up we go.'

He steadied the ladder as I climbed. I'd expected something like this and, learning from experience, had put on my plainest and least bunchy petticoat. It wasn't easy getting off the rope ladder and over the gunnel but Tom was there to help me, although grudgingly.

'I should have told you to stay down in the rowing boat.'

Amos came up next. The ladder swung alarmingly with nobody to steady it at the bottom, but he still managed to bring the lamp up with him. We clustered round the main mast, keeping low so that our silhouettes in the faint lamplight shouldn't attract attention if anybody happened to be watching from the shore. The deck was bare, with nothing in the way of superstructure except a shelter round the wheel. Behind the main mast, two hatch covers meeting in a low peak were the only way below decks. They were just secured by cabin hooks. Tom and Amos opened them while I held the lamp, revealing a flight of wooden steps down to what looked like an empty hold. Tom took the lamp from me.

'Stay on deck, Libby. Call down to us if you see anybody rowing out.'

It wasn't likely. We'd have known by now if there were anybody following us. Still, I didn't argue. I waited until their steps were echoing in the hold, then went halfway down the flight of steps and sat there. I knew that Tom wanted to spare me the sight of what they expected to find in the chest and was grateful.

'In the corner here.'

Amos's voice. The lamp shone on the back of the chest, plain wood. Tabby had been horribly right about the size of it: just big enough. Tom and Amos were staring at the other side. They seemed puzzled. Perhaps it was locked and they'd need to break it open. Then Tom bent down and pulled at something. The sound was unexpectedly domestic, like a dressing table drawer being opened. I stood up and went down the steps to join them. It was a drawer, and they were staring at something inside it. The whole thing was a rough-looking two-drawer chest, with lettering in Chinese characters painted over it. The drawer Tom had pulled open was divided into ten compartments. Each compartment contained something round and pale, about the size of a large cooking apple. At first I thought they might be cannon balls, until Tom lifted one out and it was obviously much lighter. He seemed to recognize it. A scale fell off it and settled on the floor.

'Opium.'

His voice echoed round the hold. Absently, I picked up the scale. It was a petal, withered and silvery.

'Poppy petal,' Tom said. 'It's what they wrap it in.'

'That whole ball, opium?'

'All twenty of them.'

He put it back in its compartment, shut the drawer and slid open the lower one. Just the same, ten petal-wrapped spheres each nestling snugly in its own compartment.

'It's how they export it from India to China,' Tom said. 'It's sold by the chest, like this, hundreds of chests to a shipment.'

Amos picked up one of the spheres and turned it gently in his hand, as if he expected it to hatch into something.

'How much would this lot be worth then?'

Tom considered. 'Five hundred pounds. Perhaps more. I'm not an expert.'

'So this came from India?'

'Certainly. Look, there's the Company's mark. It means the contents of the chest are guaranteed pure.'

'But why bring it here? And why take it all the way out to Richmond and back?' I said.

Amos, replacing the ball of opium, said they'd want to look after it at that price, but Tom seemed almost as puzzled as I was.

'I agree, Libby. The Chinese may have banned opium but it's perfectly legal in this country. Anybody could bring in a hundred chests like this, if he wanted to. But why send it here when it's nearer and more profitable to run it into China?'

'But would they have to pay duty to bring it in?' I said. 'Suppose somebody's trying to set up an English smuggling trade in case China is closed to them.'

Tom considered. 'You might even be right, Libby. But would the likes of McPherson risk whatever reputation they have here? They're smugglers half a world away, but gentlemen in England.'

'It might not be anything to do with him. Suppose your Brahmin and his friends are acting on their own account.'

'So have they smuggled in a whole shipload?'

We all three of us considered the chest.

'This might be by way of a tradesman's case of samples,' Amos commented.

We looked round the rest of the hold before we left, but it was as empty as the inside of a cello. Going down the rope ladder was considerably worse than going up, but we made it safely to the timber jetty. Tom tied up the hired boat there, as promised, and we went back to the clarence. With nobody to hold the horse at this time of night, Amos had hitched the reins to the fence. It had bothered him, but the cob had scarcely moved. We'd been travelling for some time before Tom spoke.

'If you're right about the opium smuggling, Griffiths would have been furious if he found out.'

'Even if it was Indians doing it? He might see it as appropriate revenge for the British foisting the poppy on India.'

'I'm sure he wouldn't have seen it that way.'

'So if Mr Griffiths found out somehow and tried to stop it, that might have been a reason for killing him?'

Tom didn't answer, but I knew he must be thinking, as I was, about that late-night visit by the Indian gentleman. We dropped him off at Mr Tillington's house, where he was staying. The attack on the old man hadn't been repeated, but Tom said he was still shaken. He was sorry to have left him alone so long. Tom promised to come to Abel Yard in the morning. There were no lights showing in the house, so Amos and I said we'd wait while he made sure that all was well inside. He was to signify it by waving a candle at the window of his room on the first floor. He let himself in with his key. A few minutes later the candle moved from side to side and we went slowly on our way, the horse as tired as we were. I'd asked Amos to draw up outside the gateway to Abel Yard, so as not to wake anybody inside. It was nearly midnight by then. He got off the box to help me down.

'Excuse me.'

Even Amos jumped with surprise, a thing I should not have credited if I hadn't been standing so close to him. The white figure seemed to have materialized out of nowhere.

'Have I the honour of speaking to Miss Lane?'

The pronunciation of the words was correct and precise, only the rhythm distinguishing him from a native English speaker. It was the Indian gentleman. Amos stepped between us.

'What do you think you're doing?'

The man's words were muffled by the bulk of Amos, but he went on speaking to me as if Amos weren't there.

'I should very much appreciate an opportunity to talk to you and your brother.'

Although my heart was thumping, I knew we couldn't miss this chance.

'And we should very much appreciate a chance to talk to you,' I said, trying to keep my voice calm. 'Only, not now.'

'Indeed. When do you suggest?'

'There's a reservoir pond in the park, near Grosvenor Gate. Do you know it?'

'Yes, I know it.'

'We'll be there at midday tomorrow.'

'Very well. Thank you.'

Then he was gone as suddenly as he'd arrived.

'Well, that's a turn-up,' Amos said, restored to his usual calm. He walked with me to the foot of my staircase. 'I'll wait out there till I'm sure that one's out of the way.'

I wondered how the man had known where I lived, or that Tom was my brother. I told Amos there was no need to worry, but it was comforting to look down from my room at his dark shape standing at the horse's head. I was more than half asleep by the time the clarence rolled away.

EIGHTEEN

He was waiting for us, an upright figure in pale clothes beside the reservoir pond, apparently oblivious of curious glances from Sunday morning strollers in the park. When we came near him he put the palms of his hands together and bowed his head, a gesture mirrored by Tom. I'd agreed that Tom should do the talking. He knew India, after all.

'It seems you know who we are, sir,' Tom said. 'You have the advantage of us.'

'Jaswant Patwardhan, at your service. I wish I had known you intended to visit our boat. I could have offered you better hospitality. And more convenient ingress.'

His voice and manner were entirely serious, but there was a glint in his dark eyes. Tom was floundering in surprise and embarrassment, so I took a hand.

'We were looking for a boy,' I said.

He looked at me, assessing.

'Any boy in particular, Miss Lane?'

'His name is Anil. He worked for Mr Griffiths.'

Tom was annoyed with me for stepping in, but it had given him time to recover and take up the conversation as we'd planned.

'Mr Patwardhan, I assure you that we do not intend to pry into your activities, but Mr Griffiths was a good friend of mine and I owe him a duty to find out what I can about how he died.'

'Will that give him life again?'

The glint was still there, but Mr Patwardhan's question seemed serious rather than mocking.

'In our country, taking your own life is considered dishonourable,' Tom said. 'Isn't it right to try to protect a friend's honour?'

A nod of the turbaned head conceded the point.

'You came to his funeral,' Tom said. 'Was that out of respect for him?'

'Respect was due to him.'

'Was he a friend of yours?'

'I met him only recently. But he was a friend of a very good friend of mine.'

'Was one of the times you met him the Saturday before he was found dead?' I asked.

I could see Tom was annoyed with me for butting in, but at this rate Mr Patwardhan and Tom would go on exchanging careful courtesies until the pigeons roosted. Mr Patwardhan turned to me, not seeming at all put out by the question.

'Yes, that is so.'

'Why did you go to see him?'

The silence that followed my question wasn't discourteous. Mr Patwardhan was considering. In the course of it I noticed a tall groom on a bay cob giving a riding lesson to a boy on a pony. He had the pony on a leading rein. Amos had said nothing about keeping close by when we met the Indian gentleman, but I wasn't surprised to see him. Mr Patwardhan made up his mind.

'If you would condescend to take a short journey with me, I shall be better able to answer your questions.'

He raised a hand. Although he wasn't even looking in its direction, a plain carriage that had been waiting further up the ride came towards us. I recognized it as the livery stable vehicle from Richmond. When it stopped beside us, Mr Patwardhan politely opened the door and got in behind us. As soon as we'd sat down, and without further directions being given, the carriage turned round the reservoir, trotted northwards up the ride, then headed west along the upper boundary of the park. Looking out from the window, I saw Amos and the pony cutting across the grass to keep up with us, his pupil getting a probably premature lesson in trotting. After a few minutes we stopped by a grove of trees. Mr Patwardhan had his hand out to help me to the ground. Usually it would have been an unnecessary courtesy, but this time it was just as well because I nearly fell backwards into the coach in surprise at what was there. A ray of sunshine had come out between clouds like a light in a pantomime and was illuminating a scene from the east that had somehow been picked up and transported to Hyde Park.

The trees, in pale young leaf, were what English trees always were. A small flock of sheep grazed on the far side of the grove. Barouches and phaetons with people out for a Sunday morning airing went gliding past only yards away. But here, on the edge of the trees, was a pavilion like something from a fairy tale or, at the very least, a shelter for fine ladies at the most aristocratic sort of picnic. The fabric was royal blue, embroidered with silver stars. The flaps of the pavilion were turned back, revealing a lining of paler silk. A small pennant in silver, black and blue flapped from the top of the pavilion in the breeze. Further off, on the far side of the grove, a plain *fourgon* carriage was resting on its shafts, proving at least that this splendour had arrived by mortal means. Mr Patwardhan walked up to the pavilion and stood aside, indicating that Tom and I should go first. The entrance was high enough to walk in without stooping. Inside, the light was dim, sun filtered through layers of silk. The air was full of a strange, spicy smell. At first I could see nothing. It must have been the same for Tom, standing beside me. I was aware that there was at least one person inside the pavilion, and that he or she must be getting a good view of us while we were at a disadvantage. Then a throaty chuckle, unmistakeably female: 'Welcome. Won't you sit down, please.'

The first thing I saw were the eyes, gleaming like a tiger's out of the dark. The voice, with a strong Indian accent, had come from waist height. Gradually I made out a figure sitting on a pile of cushions, leaning against a kind of carved bedhead, comfortable as a cat. The folds of her sari spread round her like water. Green and red jewels glowed on her fingers in the dim light. Nearer us, on a carpet, were carved stools with cushions, designed to be folded up and carried as camp chairs, but richly carved and gilded. I sat and so did Tom. Mr Patwardhan stood between us and the tent flap. As my eyes adjusted to the dim light I saw that the woman's face was sharp, skin stretched tight over prominent cheekbones, creased round the mouth and eyes, but the eyes themselves were as large and bright as a girl's. They moved unblinkingly from Tom to me. There was a challenge in them.

'You're Mr Griffiths's princess,' I said.

It had come to me that second and there was no time to think whether it was wise to say it or not. It was partly the setting and the way she was sitting, but more than that. Since reading Mr Griffiths's story, the woman at the centre of it had stayed in my mind. Beautiful, of course, but daring and ruthless as well. She'd have had to be, to plot on such a grand scale. There'd been cruelty there too in the way she used people. I'd seen all of those things when this woman looked at me, but then she hadn't been trying to hide them. Behind me, Mr Patwardhan shifted his weight, surprised. Tom was looking at me as if I'd gone mad.

'I was many people's princess,' she said.

I tried to keep looking at her as steadily as she was looking at me.

'Why have you come here?' I said.

'He will explain.' She gestured towards Mr Patwardhan and added, 'He's what you might call my prime minister.'

It was ridiculous, of course. She had no country to rule. Even in Mr Griffiths's account, her estate was no more than a castle, servants and animals, and it would almost certainly have dwindled rather than grown. And yet it didn't seem ridiculous. Even here in a foreign country she was creating her own setting. Meeting in some ordinary room might have diminished her, so she kept court in a tent in the park. Mr Patwardhan spoke from behind us.

'The Rani knew that your parliament were discussing things that concerned her. She decided she should be present in London.'

'Did Mr Griffiths ask you to come here?' Tom spoke direct to the woman – or rather the Rani – but the answer came from Mr Patwardhan.

'The Rani makes her own decisions.'

With her eyes turned to Tom, mine were free to take in more of the surroundings. A curtain from floor to ceiling divided off another part of the tent. Servants' quarters, presumably. In the shadowed angle between tent wall and curtain, another woman was sitting on a cushion, legs folded, sari over her head, eyes modestly downcast and hands together. The Rani's maid, probably.

'Is my sister right? You're the Rani Rukhamini Joshi?' Tom said.

Apart from anything else, that would make her heir to quite a large sum of money under Mr Griffiths's will. Or perhaps not so large by her standards.

'That's so,' Mr Patwardhan's voice confirmed from behind us.

I was growing tired of this game. Perhaps the Rani sensed that, because she glanced at me.

'Why wouldn't you talk to me when I came out to Richmond?' I said.

'Because we didn't know who you were.' From Mr Patwardhan again.

I kept my eyes on the Rani.

'I think you knew very well,' I said to her. 'You knew a lot of things. You knew Mr Griffiths was dead and you knew about the funeral. I saw you in the coach there. You must have had somebody keeping watch on Tom.'

'And you on us.' The Rani said it without resentment, as if it were only to be expected. 'What did you expect to find in my ship?'

'The body of Mr Griffiths's servant, Anil,' I said.

The tent was quiet, apart from the harness jingle and wheel swish on the carriage drive a few hundred yards away. Goodness knows what people out for a Sunday drive made of the sudden appearance of an eastern pavilion. Some fête, probably. The Rani considered and made her decision.

'We shall have some tea.'

I'd have expected the maid to get up and attend to it, but it was her prime minister who disappeared behind the curtain. While he was gone she didn't attempt to make conversation and sat looking down at her rings, with no sign of tension or even acknowledgement that Tom and I were still present. Nobody moved until the curtain was drawn aside and Mr Patwardhan came back, followed by a boy carrying a tray. The boy was dressed in trousers, tunic and turban. Carefully, he set out cups and a brass pot on the table. Over his head, the Rani's eyes met mine.

'I'm glad to see Anil again,' I said.

Tom spoilt the calm effect I was aiming for by giving a gasp of surprise, but then he hadn't been paying much attention to the boy. For some reason, his eyes were on the maid who hadn't moved. Anil served us tea, giving no indication that anything out of the way was happening.

'I think we should trade,' I said to the Rani. 'What we know for what you know.'

Vulgar, I knew, but guessed that straight talking was the only hope of getting anything from her. The slightest down and up movement of her chin gave agreement.

'You first,' she said.

No point in arguing.

'Mr Griffiths had always felt guilty about what happened to you,' I said. 'He was angry about opium too. He was making a last attempt at putting things right, as far as he could, by publishing his story. The merchant Alexander McPherson – you knew him – didn't want that. Among other things, Mr Griffiths was as good as accusing him of stealing your jewels.'

In point of fact, her brother's jewels or her state's jewels, but nobody seemed to be worrying about that any more. I waited for some reaction from her, but it didn't come.

'Somebody killed Mr Griffiths,' I said. 'Whoever it was made it look as if he'd killed himself. Your prime minister visited him on a Saturday evening. On the Monday morning he was found dead. His servant disappeared then reappeared with you in Richmond. At the very least, you know more about how and why Mr Griffiths died than we do.'

The Rani's eyes closed. The skin of her eyelids was thin and papery. Until then I hadn't even seen her blink and thought it was a first sign of distress, even guilt. But when she spoke, the chuckle was back in her voice.

'Are you saying I had him killed?'

'Did you?'

'Why should I?'

'If you were planning to smuggle opium and he found out about it, he'd feel angry, betrayed even. He'd try to stop it.'

Another surprised movement from Mr Patwardhan, but the Rani was smiling.

'And I'm smuggling opium, am I?'

'We found a chest of it yesterday night, on board the *Calypso*.'

'Did you take it away?'

That urgently from Mr Patwardhan. Even the Rani seemed anxious for an answer.

'No.'

'Or tell some officials?'

Tom cut in before I could answer. 'We told nobody and left it exactly as it was.'

He might even have gone on to apologize if I hadn't spoken first.

'We don't want to pry into your affairs except as far as they concern Mr Griffiths's death. That's all we have to trade. Now it's your turn.'

This time she spoke to us directly, not through her prime minister. Her tone was measured and unemotional, as if she'd worked out all she was going to say in advance.

'Mr Griffiths discovered that I had come to London. He was distressed to hear that we were living in most unsatisfactory accommodation and offered us the use of his small serai.'

So that was why Mr Griffiths had moved out of his comfortable cottage. It might also explain the money order waiting to be sent on his desk, if the Rani had been temporarily or permanently embarrassed for money.

'When we met, Mr Griffiths told me of his determination to see that I was compensated for my loss and the pamphlet he intended to publish. I approved it, but there were some points that were not altogether as things happened. I considered this for some time, then sent Mr Patwardhan to tell him. It was too late. The pamphlet had gone to the printer. But Mr Griffiths was interested in what I had to say. He said he would think about it and asked Mr Patwardhan to return in two days.'

I'd have liked to ask what was the new information she'd sent to Mr Griffiths, but she wasn't the kind of person you interrupted.

'Mr Patwardhan went to his lodgings the following evening.

He found another person present. The man was Alexander McPherson.'

This time I couldn't help interrupting.

'In Mr Griffiths's lodgings? When was this?'

'As you said, the Saturday.'

'And McPherson was actually there with Mr Griffiths? What was he doing?'

While she was speaking, Mr Patwardhan had come to stand beside her. Now she nodded to him to take up the story.

'Drinking sherry,' Mr Patwardhan said.

'Just standing there, drinking his sherry?'

'Not standing. Sitting opposite Mr Griffiths. They were both drinking sherry.'

I was imagining confrontation, even violence. The picture faded, leaving total puzzlement.

'As if they were friends?'

Mr Patwardhan considered. 'I shouldn't say friends. Rather two opponents who had agreed a necessary truce. Which indeed was the case. Mr Griffiths introduced us, then he said something that I remember word for word. "I still abhor what this man is doing in the way of trade, but I think he will keep his word, particularly since he has very little choice." Mr McPherson was not pleased, not pleased at all. He said choice or not, he was a gentleman and always kept his word. I drank a cup of tea, then Mr Griffiths said I should please go away and come back the following day, the Sunday. He said they – meaning himself and Mr McPherson – were going to do something which the Rani should not know about until it had taken place. He asked me to come in the evening after dark, on foot, so as not to be noticed.'

A silence. I was trying to adjust to this picture of Mr Griffiths as a plotter. I think Tom was too, because when he spoke his voice was like somebody coming back from a long way away.

'And you went back the following evening and found Mr Griffiths dead?'

'No. I went back and found Mr Griffiths very much alive and pleased with himself. His last words as he saw us off in the carriage were to tell the Rani that he'd do himself the honour to call on her in the next day or two.'

'Who's "us"?' I said. 'And what carriage? He'd told you to send your carriage away.'

'There's an alleyway beside his lodgings, and a back gate. He had another carriage waiting there. The boy Anil came with us. The Rani found it impossible to get proper servants here, so Mr Griffiths said he would lend Anil.'

'"Us"?'

'Myself and Mr McPherson.'

I almost howled with confusion.

'You mean you and Mr McPherson drove off together? Where to?'

It was the Rani who answered. She seemed amused.

'To Richmond, of course. Mr McPherson spent the night with us.'

She'd skittled us, and she was enjoying it. There were a dozen questions I wanted to ask, but few of them made sense in the light of what she'd just said. I asked her to repeat it, to make sure I'd heard aright, and she did, with a look on her face that wasn't quite a smile but showed that if she were a cat, she'd be purring. Or in her case, a tiger more like.

'But why?' I said.

'Because it was far too late for him to go back to town.'

Which was a fair enough answer, but not how I'd meant the question, and she knew it.

'So is Alexander McPherson a friend of yours?'

'I had not seen him for twenty years. I doubt if I shall see him again.'

'Did he kill Mr Griffiths?'

'No. There was no need. As Mr Patwardhan told you, they'd agreed a truce.'

'Do you know who did kill Mr Griffiths?'

'No.'

'You said there were some points in Mr Griffiths's account that were not how things happened. Did they concern Alexander McPherson?'

'One of them, yes.'

The glint in her eye showed that somehow I'd hit a question that mattered and she was deciding whether to say more.

'So where was he wrong about McPherson?'

'Mr McPherson hadn't taken my jewels. He never had the jewels apart from that one hawk I gave him. When I heard that Mr Griffiths was accusing him, I told him he was wrong.'

'What did he say to that?'

'That he would apologize to Mr McPherson, in public if necessary. That's why they made their truce. Now, I hope you will both kindly excuse me. I am an old woman, and all this is very tiring.'

She took no trouble to sound convincing. Tom was bending to pick up his hat from the carpet when I tried a last question, more or less at random.

'Did you really come all the way to London because of this committee?'

If that were the case, she'd surely overestimated the importance of any parliamentary committee.

She nodded. 'That. Also to show my only daughter the country her father came from.'

As if that were an agreed signal between them, the girl I'd taken for a maid lifted her head and let the fold of her sari fall back from her face. I couldn't help gasping. It wasn't just her beauty – though she was one of the most beautiful girls I'd ever seen, with skin the colour of creamy coffee and eyes like the sky on the kind of summer night you want to last forever. The real shock was the way that her beauty completed the picture of Mr Griffiths's princess. Some of it had been there in the Rani's pride and force of character. The daughter's face showed what an irresistible force the mother must have been when younger. Poor Griff. Something was happening to my brother. Tom had grasped his hat and been on the point of standing up when the girl's eyes met his. He dropped his hat, sat back down on the stool then jumped up again as if it were suddenly red hot, all without taking his eyes off her.

'I'm honoured . . . delighted to meet . . . Miss, or I should say, Kumari . . .'

'My daughter's name is Chandrika,' the Rani said.

Chandrika smiled. Tom bowed. Mr Patwardhan had recovered Tom's hat and was trying to hand it to him. The boy Anil was holding back the tent flap. Somehow we said our goodbyes and walked with Mr Patwardhan to where his carriage was waiting. Anil walked behind us. On the way, I hung back and imitated Tom's clumsiness by dropping my reticule. Anil was there at once to pick it up. As he handed it back, I whispered to him.

'If you're in fear or danger, say so now and we'll get you away.'

It wasn't an empty promise. Amos, with the boy on the leading rein, was practising circles within calling distance.

'I'm in no danger, memsahib. The Rani says I can stay with her and go back to India with her.'

No fear or guile in his voice. I waved to Amos as a sign that no help was needed. Mr Patwardhan was willing to drive us anywhere we wanted, but I asked him to set us down by the reservoir where we'd met.

'It makes no sense,' I said to Tom. 'Why should she be in league with Alexander McPherson?'

Tom didn't answer. He was watching as the carriage drove away, towards the tent in the grove of trees, now out of sight. At last he gave a long sigh and said something, though nothing to the purpose.

'That poor girl. Did you understand, Libby? She must be Griffiths's daughter.'

NINETEEN

'Libby, just try and entertain the idea that they might be telling the truth.'

The middle of Sunday afternoon, with Mrs Martley out visiting, so Tom, the cat and I had the parlour to ourselves. We were well into our second pot of tea and a discussion that couldn't, so far, be called an argument because we were both too confused to take sides. Tom's plea followed a theory, proposed by me, that the Rani and McPherson were involved together in a plan to smuggle quantities of opium into Britain.

'I've tried to,' I said. 'I simply can't envisage Mr Griffiths and McPherson sitting down and plotting together.'

'I've thought about it, and I can see it might have happened. Griffiths was open and honourable to the core. If he was convinced he'd done the man an injustice, he'd say so. I could imagine him walking back into Westminster Hall and telling the world he'd been wrong and McPherson hadn't stolen the jewels.'

'Only, by their account he did nothing so straightforward. He tells Mr Patwardhan to go away and come back secretly because something's going to happen that the Rani shouldn't know about. Then there's that carriage he has waiting in a back alley. Does that all sound open and honourable?'

'If Griffiths did that, then I'm sure there was nothing dishonourable about it,' Tom said, the stubbornness coming back into his voice.

'*If* he did. That's the whole point. You can't say it must have been honourable because he's honourable, when it might not have happened at all.' I could hear the annoyance coming back into mine.

For once, Tom was the peacemaker.

'All right, it's a circular argument. But let's test their story as far as we can. Griffiths finds out they're in London, in straitened circumstances. He immediately offers them his cottage. Is there anything incredible in that?'

'If they have several hundred pounds worth of opium with them, they shouldn't have been in straitened circumstances.'

'It would take time and contacts to convert that to money in a city they don't know.'

'Very well, I withdraw that objection. But there is another one. Are we quite sure that the Rani is Griffiths's princess?'

'You were, as soon as you set eyes on her.'

'I might have been wrong.'

'You weren't. You could see that just by looking at her . . .' By the pitch of his voice, he'd intended to put another word after 'her' but he left it hanging. 'In any case, would Griffiths have given his cottage and his servant to just anybody?'

'So the Rani is his princess and he tells her that he's doing everything in his power to right the injustice done to her. He's too realistic to think he can get the princedom back and besides it wasn't hers in the first place. So that means the jewels?'

'Yes. So he's naturally taken aback when the Rani tells him McPherson didn't take them. It does make sense so far.'

'I wonder how she can be so certain,' I said. 'That implies she knows who took them. As far as Griffiths was concerned, there were two suspects, The Merchant and The Soldier.'

Tom gave me a sideways look.

'All right, Libby. I know what you're going to say next. That dratted library. I simply haven't had time.'

'It would be useful to be able to rule The Soldier out, if we knew who he was and that he'd died.'

'I'll start tackling those old army lists tomorrow.'

'So, how far have we got? Mr Griffiths knows now that he's been barking up the wrong tree and makes a truce with McPherson. Then he actually sends McPherson off, in conditions of some secrecy, to spend the night in the Rani's household at Richmond. How does that make sense?'

'Part of righting the injustice perhaps, so that she could tell him in person that she knew he hadn't stolen her jewels.'

I thought about it. 'Possible, but why do it at the dead of night? Couldn't it have waited till morning?'

'That's a problem,' Tom admitted. 'But there must have been some reason.'

'We're back with the *if* again. Of course, even if McPherson really did spend the Sunday night at Richmond he could still have sent an underling to kill Mr Griffiths.'

'Except there'd have been no point. Mr Griffiths was no threat to him any more.'

'Yes. And we don't suppose he was so mortified at being wrong about McPherson that he killed himself after all?'

'No.'

'I agree. No.'

On that note of agreement, we agreed to shelve the discussion for the day. My brain felt squeezed out and Tom needed to get back to Mr Tillington, who'd had a bronchitic attack that morning. I walked with him part of the way along the mews.

'Of course, there'd be one way of disposing of some of the *ifs*,' I said.

'Talking to McPherson you mean? I was thinking that too.'

'I can't see why not. After all, if he really came to a truce with Mr Griffiths, that should apply to you as Mr Griffiths's friend.'

'I don't suppose he cares about me either way.'

'Is it worth trying? You could probably get in touch with him through the East India Office.'

'Yes. I'll think it over. I might try.'

'Let me know if you do.'

I resolved that if the meeting took place I'd somehow contrive to be there, but didn't say that to Tom. In the last few steps before we parted, he surprised me with something different altogether.

'Libby, you have a memory for poetry. What was that bit of Byron about walking and the night?'

I quoted: '"She walks in beauty, like the night
Of cloudless climes and starry skies;
And all that's best of dark and bright
Meet in her aspect and her eyes."'

'Yes, that's the one.'

He didn't turn back to wave to me from the corner. Probably too busy trying to memorize it.

Overnight, a whole new aspect occurred to me. If we allowed the hypothesis that the Rani's story were true, there had to be another way of accounting for the destruction of Mr Griffiths's pamphlet. McPherson would have nothing to fear from it, even if knowledgeable readers guessed the identity of The Merchant. Even with Mr Griffiths gone, he could appeal to the Rani herself to prove his innocence of jewel robbery. Which meant that whoever had stolen a carriage-load of pamphlets from the printer, searched Tom's lodgings and attacked Mr Tillington to try to prevent the story being aired was another person altogether. In that case, the one thing I knew about him was that he'd used Eckington-Smith as his cat's paw. I even toyed with the idea that Eckington-Smith himself might be The Soldier, but that didn't survive the light of day. There was nothing military about him and I knew enough about his career from earlier investigations to be sure that he'd never served in India. The man was in financial trouble, willing to work for anybody who would pay him. Following him might be the way to discovering who had wanted so very much to have the pamphlet suppressed. But I knew there was another reason, which might be distorting my judgement: following Eckington-Smith might lead me to Tabby. Or *vice versa*. If Tabby had been following him, then she'd know more than I did about whom he'd been meeting and when. So I set about finding her.

I worked at it over the next three days and discovered many things. That the financial heart of the country that is the City of London may cover no more than a square mile, but is so crammed with small streets and alleyways that you can walk round it for hours on end and not tread on the same stretch of wood, stone or cobble paving twice over. That the smell of coffee from the doors of the dozens of coffee houses is almost unbearably enticing when you know you can't walk into one without affronted male eyes turning towards you. That businessmen, in their uniform dark suits, tall black hats and general air of being responsible for keeping the world revolving, look so much like each other from a distance that sighting one in particular is like trying to pick out one rook in a rookery. That it's even worse when it rains, because they vanish under identical black umbrellas and become turtles. That if you happen to have come out without your own umbrella there comes a point where you don't care about getting wet any more, because you're soaked through to the corset and petticoats. That doormen at the Bank of England and various other banks and exchange houses are mostly retired soldiers and observant, particularly of women on their own, and not inclined for casual conversations. (No question, of course, of going near the one at Capel Court. The doorman there would have recognized me in an instant.) Above all, I discovered how greatly I was lacking in the virtue of patience. Of course I'd watched and waited before, but never so long and with so little prospect of anything happening. It made me realize that Tabby was much my superior in that respect. Time had never seemed to fret her in the way it does most of us.

I never found her. I looked carefully at every group of urchins or draggle-skirted girl and gave away a small fortune in pennies. I even recognized some of the lads who'd witnessed Tabby's attack on the doorman's hat. They hadn't seen her for days, they said. I wondered if my failure to find her or Eckington-Smith meant that he'd moved elsewhere and she'd followed him. It didn't seem likely. The little I knew about men of business suggested that they needed to keep with their kind. If I hadn't spotted him so far, that was because I'd underestimated the difficulty. Sometimes, particularly on the rainy day, I would have a sudden feeling that Tabby was somewhere close at hand, tracking me, but then I'd turn and find nothing but more umbrellas.

Unlike Tabby, I went back to Abel Yard in the evenings. Quite early in the evening, because the streets of the City became almost deserted by five o'clock. Always I hoped to find my brother there. On the first evening there was no sign of him. On the second he sent a boy with a note saying he'd intended to call, but Mr Tillington had suffered another bad turn and shouldn't be left. Frustratingly, not a word about researches in the library of East India House. After dark on the third evening he arrived at last, tired and hungry. I let

Mrs Martley fuss over him with tea, cold pie and a glass of wine, then took him through the low doorway to my study.

'Have you made any progress?' I said.

'I'm not sure if you'd call it progress. There were so many small battles going on around that time, it took me a long time to find the one that Griffiths was writing about.'

'But you have?'

'Yes, an engagement almost exactly as he describes it, with few casualties. And it does correspond with the civilian records of when he was serving in the territory.'

'And the captains?'

'Four of them. Octavus St Clair, Peter Morris, Horace Smith and Angus McWhitty.'

'And was any of them invalided home soon afterwards?'

He looked pained. 'Give me a chance, Libby. Medical discharge certificates are another set of records altogether.'

'I wonder about McWhitty. Could it be a case of Scots keeping together? You might try him first.'

'When I get time. They do expect me to do some occasional work, you know. Then there's poor Tillington to look after.' A small hesitation. 'And I did go out to Richmond this afternoon.'

He didn't meet my eyes, pretending a sudden interest in an engraving of the Parthenon on the wall.

'To see the Rani?'

'It seemed only polite to call, after their hospitality.'

A cup of tea in a tent hardly seemed to merit a coach ride to Richmond and back, but I didn't say so.

'Did she tell you any more about the jewels?'

'For goodness' sake, it was a social call. I didn't go to cross-examine her.'

'Was Mr Patwardhan there?'

'Yes, and before you ask, I didn't pelt him with questions either.'

'And the daughter?'

'If you expect me to question her about this miserable business you must be—'

'I only asked if she were there.'

'Yes.' Another hesitation, then a stream of words. 'She's

amazing, Libby. She's spent most of her life in a castle – more of a fort, really – in the middle of nowhere but she has more poise and intelligence than any woman in society. She knows as much Shakespeare as you do, probably more, sketches and plays the sitar, speaks four languages . . .'

And had eyes that a man could wander in forever, particularly a man who'd never been in love before. I didn't say that, of course, only remarked that she sounded very accomplished and registered that my brother, as a source of sensible information on the Rani's household, was a lost cause.

I tried to bring him back to business by asking if he'd found time to ask for a meeting with McPherson.

'I wrote yesterday and had a note back this morning. No go there, I'm afraid.'

His mind was still with the cloudless climes and starry skies.

'What exactly did you write and what exactly did he reply?' I said.

He wrenched it back reluctantly. 'Pretty much as we agreed. I said I understood that Griffiths had retracted some injurious implications, and if my small services could help in repairing any damage done, I'd appreciate a chance to talk to him.'

'Good. And his reply?'

He took a piece of folded paper from his pocket and passed it to me.

> Mr McPherson thanks Mr Lane for his communication, but sees no need for a meeting. If Mr Lane wishes to do him a service, it will be by not gossiping about this business and strongly discouraging anyone else from doing so.

'Curt,' I said.

'You can't blame him. He must be sick of the whole affair.'

'You'd think he'd be glad to have his name cleared.'

But something was beginning to stir in my mind that I couldn't understand myself yet, let alone discuss with Tom. I expected him to be anxious to get back to Mr Tillington's sickbed, and indeed he was on edge, but there was something else on his mind.

'The parliamentary committee's almost finished taking evidence.'

'I suppose it will be months before it produces a report,' I said.

'Yes, but according to the men that know, they've pretty well reached a decision.'

'On whether Griffiths had McPherson's assistant killed? Surely that's out of the question now. They'd have never made their truce otherwise.'

'I don't think they even know about the truce. They'll let the whole business lie as something on which they can't reach an agreement. I meant they've already decided on what matters most to McPherson and his friends – the compensation.'

'Are they getting it?'

'Not until after the war with China, then it will be exacted from Peking as part of the peace settlement.'

So Disraeli had been well informed as usual.

'I suppose the Calcutta men aren't pleased about that.'

'Furious. From their point of view the war is only a means to an end. They want their compensation now. Without it, some of them will be ruined.'

'McPherson included?'

'Possibly, but the really worried ones are the smaller men who put more than they could afford into the Eastern trading companies. It looked like easy money, but now the shares are going down and down.'

Tom looked more gloomy about it than you'd expect for somebody with no capital.

'You realize what that means, Libby?'

'That our family fortunes are wrecked? Woe and alas.'

'I mean if the game's lost, the merchants will be going back to see what they can do in Calcutta and there's no reason for Company men to stay either. We could all be sailing in two or three weeks.'

It really was woe and alas now. I'd known a parting must come, but had managed to push the thought away as something weeks or even months in the future. I'd hoped to be back on unclouded good terms with Tom before it happened. A smaller sorrow was that, with Tom and the rest of them gone, we might never know the truth about Griffiths's death.

'I'm sorry,' Tom said, as if guessing my thoughts.

'Not your fault. Shall you come back tomorrow?'

'If I can, yes.'

I didn't go back to the City next day. I'd failed entirely in Tabby's craft, either in finding her or Eckington-Smith, so had to fall back on my own. I made myself neat for visiting and walked across the park to Kensington.

'You must come and visit me, any time you like,' Mrs Eckington-Smith had said to me when I'd finished my work for her.

She didn't mean it: we'd both known that. It was when she was on the point of moving out of the house she'd lived in with her husband in St John's Wood. She wanted to leave that and the memory of her marriage to him behind for ever. I was part of that. She was grateful to me for helping to free her, but I'd seen her at the darkest time of her life and she could never look at me without thinking of it. I was aware of that when I stood on the doorstep of her cottage – not far from where Mrs Glass lived – and gave my card to her maid. Still, she came to meet me bravely.

'Miss Lane, such a pleasure. I've been hoping you'd find time to call.'

Her parlour was comfortable but not ostentatious, lilacs in a vase on the table and a child's wooden horse and cart on the carpet. I think she and her small daughter had been playing with it when I arrived. When our coffee was served, the child and the horse and cart were sent to play with the maid in another room. We sipped our coffee and made conversation – about her son, away at school, the new piano she'd ordered. She was interesting herself in charity work and beginning to make new friends.

'I've introduced myself to them by my maiden name,' she said. 'Not that it makes much difference.'

The wounds were raw, but healing. Still, she winced when I mentioned that I'd heard her husband had left the house in St John's Wood.

'He had to, I suppose. He has debts.'

'Do you happen to know where he moved?'

She shook her head.

'Somewhere cheaper, I suppose. I did hear he'd been travelling round the country a lot. Trying to get fools to lend him money.'

'Does he have investments in the East India Company?'

'He certainly did at one time. He was trying to build up enough shares to be a director. He said there were fortunes to be made from India.'

'But he never went there, did he?'

'No. He's scared of any sea voyage longer than to the Isle of Wight.'

She changed the subject, wanting my valuable opinion of whether to plant geraniums or penstemons in her window box. After half an hour I left. She came to the doorstep with me and urged me to call again soon, managing to sound as if she meant it. Since that attempt had failed, I needed some other means of finding Eckington-Smith's present address. I went home, folded a sheet of paper, wrote on it the address from which I knew he'd moved and marked it 'Urgent'. Then I put on a plain grey dress and bonnet and walked to Westminster. It took some time to find the entrance used by MPs so I arrived there looking suitably confused, like a timid conscientious servant. I inquired of the official in tailcoat and breeches standing at the door if somebody could kindly give me the address of Mr Eckington-Smith MP.

'You could leave it here if you want to, missy.'

'Is he here today, sir?' I hoped not.

'No. Haven't seen him for a while.'

The messengers had prodigious memories for the comings and goings of MPs.

'It's urgent.' I showed him the address. 'He used to live here, only they say he doesn't any more. I don't know what to do, sir.'

He liked being called 'sir' and maybe even the timid smile I gave him from under my bonnet rim. Perhaps he was bored, or even kindly by nature. At any rate, he decided to help. He told me to wait, beckoned up a younger messenger and asked him to cut along to the post room and inquire for Mr Eckington-Smith's present address. I waited. A few members came and went. Luckily Mr Disraeli was not among them. After a quarter of an hour or more, the younger man came back with a slip of paper. My messenger read it out painstakingly.

'You know where that is, missy?' Then, mistaking my look of surprise for ignorance. 'It's in the City, not far from where the Bank of England is. You can get an omnibus from over there.'

I knew it well. Mr Eckington-Smith's current address was two streets away from where Mr Griffiths had died. Probably not a coincidence.

I took the omnibus to the Bank and walked along Cornhill and Leadenhall Street, past the offices of the East India Company. A small detour took me to Mr Griffiths's late lodgings. There was an alleyway beside it and a place at the back where a carriage might have waited. At least the Rani's story did not fall down on that point. The address given to me was only a few minutes' walk away. Eckington-Smith lived at number five: a plain terraced house of sooty brick and faded cream paintwork, respectable but not impressive. The basement area was deserted with nothing in it but a water tub and an old broom, no sign of servants. I walked round the corner to the back of the row of houses. A narrow alleyway ran along the row, just wide enough for handcarts delivering goods or clearing cesspits. From the smell, some attention was needed. A wall with a line of narrow wooden gates closed off the backyards of the houses. I counted along, opened the gate and walked into the backyard of number five.

They'd had a bonfire, fairly recently, but not since the downpour of two days ago. The ashes were heavy and sodden, pieces of unburnt paper glued to the trodden earth. I took off my glove and prised up a couple of them and read . . . *profits for the City of London. It has been a process of gree* . . . and . . . *even the opium-dulled consc* . . .

Judging from the ash pile, it had been a large bonfire, but then it would have needed to be to consume a carriage-full of Mr Griffiths's pamphlets. I checked that nobody was watching me from the back windows and looked round the yard. Nothing much to see except brick walls on either side and a lean-to against the right-hand wall, probably for coals or logs. The door wasn't locked. I lifted the latch, opened it and knew I was on the trail at last. I was looking at a nest of sacks. It could have been a refuge for almost anything: a large dog or an exceptionally badly housed kitchen maid. I knew, as surely as if she'd engraved her name over it on a brass plate, that the nest was Tabby's. It was exactly the way she'd made her sleeping place in the shed near the cows in Abel Yard, before I had the cabin built for her. She had a way of rolling two sacks into a bolster. You could even see the imprint of her head in the middle of it. I picked up a long brown hair and flicked a flea off my wrist. Oh Tabby. There was nothing else of hers, but then I didn't expect anything. She'd returned to her old life, where you kept your possessions on your person.

I went back to Abel Yard, guessing that Tabby wouldn't be back in her lair till after dark. By eight o'clock I was back in the alley. I went into the yard of number five to make sure she wasn't back. The shed was unoccupied. Inside the house, a dim light showed from a window on the first floor. I let the latch down softly and took up position in the alley, wrapped in my cloak, leaning against a wall. At this time of night, there was no reason for anybody else to be there, so I had it to myself apart from the occasional scavenging dog or mousing cat. Now and then hoofs and carriage wheels sounded faintly from the street. Darkness came down. A variety of clocks from banks and counting houses doled out nine strokes, then ten. Two fighting dogs rolled across my feet. A few houses down, a knife scraped across several plates then a bin lid clanged. Pig bin, I supposed. I walked up and down the alley several times to keep from getting stiff and cold. Eleven o'clock. Another walk up and down. The faint light was still showing in number five. It must have been near midnight when it happened. A dark figure turned off the street and into the alley. It was moving cautiously, but as if it knew where it was going. I drew back against the wall, not wanting to scare her off before I had a chance to say anything. From where I was standing, I'd be about ten yards away from her when she got to the back gate. The advancing figure was no more than a black shape against the dark. It was at the gate before I realized that it wasn't Tabby.

Not very tall, but too tall for her. A man, breathing wheezily as if unaccustomed to walking. I could smell the fumes of strong tobacco from his greatcoat and cheap brandy as he fumbled at the latch, cursing under his breath. A rough voice, not Eckington-Smith's rotund tones. So our man had a visitor who came by the back gate. He managed the latch, pushed the gate open and walked into the yard, leaving it open. He was carrying a bag that looked heavy in his left hand. I moved so that I could see into the yard. He went to the back door, knocked on it with his fist, but not loudly. The light on the first floor waned then the window went dark. Somebody had picked up a candle in its holder and was carrying it down to the door. I was wondering whether to risk moving into the yard to overhear anything that was said when somebody pushed me roughly aside and rushed past. Tabby, running. I don't think she even knew who I was. I was simply an obstacle. Inside the gate, she hesitated for a moment. The visitor was still at the door. It opened, and there was Eckington-Smith standing inside it in a dark flannel dressing gown, his face with its broad forehead and narrow chin as pale as a peeled pear in the light of the candle he was holding. He started saying something to the man at the door. It sounded like a complaint of some kind but he didn't finish it because Tabby bounded forward and something flashed in the candlelight.

She pushed the visitor aside, making for Eckington-Smith. The visitor stumbled. His arm swung out with the heavy bag he was carrying. Whether it was intentional or an accident, it hit Tabby, knocking her off balance. It gave me the two seconds I needed to catch up with her. I grabbed her by the shoulder. Cold air hit me as her knife ripped through my cloak. We were stumbling on something. Sovereigns, spilled from the visitor's bag, hundreds of them glinting in the candlelight. The light was wavering because Eckington-Smith was swinging the candle around, shouting, 'Police, police.'

'Come away,' I said to her. 'For heaven's sake, come away.'

It shook her, hearing my voice. Up to that point, she'd been straining away from me, still trying to get to Eckington-Smith. The visitor was on hands and knees, scrabbling sovereigns. Taking advantage of her moment of confusion, I dragged her back towards the gate. Eckington-Smith was still yelling.

Distantly, the clack-clack of a police rattle sounded, like a startled pheasant.

'Run. Just run,' I said.

Running from the police was a natural instinct for Tabby. We ran back along the alley, in the opposite direction from the way we'd entered. I only hoped it wasn't a dead end. For a bad moment it looked as if we were making straight for a blank brick wall but an opening to the side gave just enough space to squeeze through. Tabby found it first and turned a pale face to me to make sure I was behind her.

'Yes, go on.'

We came out to a street, quite a wide one. Police rattles were clacking from two directions now, but still some distance away. Tabby dived up another alleyway. I followed. She knew the territory better than I did. It came out in Leadenhall Street. A few lamps burning outside buildings made it look alarmingly light after the alleyways. We were the only people in it.

'Walk,' I said to Tabby, and turned us westwards.

She'd have gone on running but I had a stitch in the side. In any case, respectability was now our best hope. As we walked, I slipped off my mistreated cloak and made Tabby wrap it round herself and put the hood up.

'Don't need it,' she said.

But that wasn't the point. If the police encountered us now, I'd do my best to pass for a lady out late with her maid. What we were doing on the streets of the City late at night should be no business of the constables. Luckily, we didn't meet one. At Cornhill a cab came grinding towards us, probably on its way home. Two half-crowns in hand persuaded the driver to change direction and take us as far as Charing Cross. We walked back to Abel Yard from there, without attracting much attention. At Abel Yard I took her upstairs to the parlour, sat her down on a chair (trying hard not to think about fleas) and stirred up the fire to make tea. When I found some bread and cold meat for her she ate wolfishly, her slowly acquired table manners quite gone. I waited, drinking my tea, until she was finished. Then: 'You'd better explain,' I said.

TWENTY

'You should've let me kill them.'

'You'd have hanged.'

'Wouldn't matter.'

Tabby hunched in the chair, hair flopping, eyes burning.

'I thought you were going to get him stopped, that time you found out about him,' she said. 'I waited for you to do something, but you didn't, so it was up to me.'

Her anger against me was so fierce I could feel the heat of it, like standing too close to the fire. No use pretending I didn't know what she was talking about.

'I didn't know you knew, Tabby. I suppose I was trying to protect you. That's why I took you off following him, as soon as I found out what he was.'

'You thought you took me off.'

Six words like so many punches. I didn't know my work. I didn't know Tabby.

'So all the time, that house in Clerkenwell . . .?'

'Yes.'

'He had to close it, you know. I made sure influential people knew about it, so it closed.'

'And opened again three doors down, a week later.'

She said it like a fact of life, sure as rain falling.

'I didn't know.'

'Lot of things you don't know.'

No answer to that, so I didn't try. She sat staring at the fire for a long time before she spoke again.

'I'd worked it out, how to get both of them. Thursday nights, he always brings the takings round to the back door.'

'The man with the bag of money?'

A nod.

'Is he the manager of the house?'

Another nod.

'You wouldn't have got away.'

'Yes I would, if it hadn't bin for you interfering.'

'For heaven's sake, was I supposed to stand there and let you knife them?'

'Nothing to do with you.'

More silence. She was forcing me back, making me defend myself. I tried to keep my voice level.

'You think I didn't do enough,' I said. 'You're right. If that wicked place has opened again, I didn't do enough. But we did manage to do a lot of harm to him. If he'd managed to trick us into thinking his wife had gone mad and was trying to kill him, he'd have got all her money. Without it, he's overstretched financially and nearly running out of credit.'

Silence. I might as well have been speaking Greek.

'And he'd have managed to take her children away from her.'

'*Her* children,' Tabby snapped out. 'What about the others?'

No use pretending I didn't understand her. She was right. I'd been too pleased with myself for what I'd managed to do for the man's unfortunate wife, too ready to believe that the brothel in Clerkenwell had closed for good.

'How did you know?' I said.

'How do you think I knew?'

The eyes fixed on mine weren't burning any more. They'd gone dull as pebbles.

'You?'

'I got away, three years ago it was. There were girls there younger than me, a lot younger.'

Tabby was never sure about her own age, but I guessed that three years ago she'd have been not much older than twelve.

'How long were you there?'

'Weeks, months, what does it matter? I told you, I got away.'

'So when we started investigating Eckington-Smith, you recognized him?'

She shook her head. 'Nah. He made sure he never showed his face there. It was when you set me on following him and I saw him with the man what managed the house. I'd have known that one out of all the demons in hell.'

I remembered. She'd come back one night and told me how she'd seen Eckington-Smith secretly meeting a man in a cab and getting out with a bag that clinked. She'd given me an address in Clerkenwell where the other man lived. At the time, I'd praised her for her clever tracking. When Amos told me what he'd discovered about the brothel in Clerkenwell I'd taken Tabby off the case, or thought I had.

'Why didn't you tell me?' I said.

'I'd put you on to what I knew. What business was it of yours how I knew it?'

'Tabby, I'm sorry. I can't tell you how sorry.'

I went over to her and put a hand on her shoulder. It was like touching granite. I went back to my chair and tried to put on a businesslike tone, though I felt anything but businesslike.

'Very well, you think I've failed you and I have. But that's in the past now. The question is what we're going to do about Eckington-Smith.' The silence seemed marginally less hostile, so I went on. 'As it happens, he's come up in quite a different case. A friend of mine's been murdered and Eckington-Smith is running errands for a man who wanted him killed. If we can find out who that man is and prove that Eckington-Smith's an accessory to murder . . .'

'Accessory?'

'Somebody who knew about it and helped. If we could prove that, he'd probably go to prison for a long time.'

'My way would have settled him quicker.'

'Well, that's no use now. For better or worse, what happened tonight will have put him on his guard, so why not try my way?'

'What is there to try?'

'In all honesty, I don't know. But we're getting near to something, I'm sure of that. Stay here, or at least let me know where you are, and I promise I'll let you be part of anything that happens to him.'

She considered it, then gave a reluctant nod of the head.

'All right, but I'm not waiting forever.'

As a sign of truce, I used the last few coals in the hob to rouse up the fire and brew more tea. After a while, I risked asking her whether she'd been living in the backyard den all the time she'd been away. She shook her head.

'I've bin to Birmingham.'

In spite of everything, there was just a touch of pride in her voice. To the best of my knowledge, she'd only ever been out of London in my company, then no more than a few hours' coach drive.

'Why in the world did you go to Birmingham?'

'Following 'im.'

It took a while to piece together. She'd followed Eckington-Smith to a coaching inn, then paid to take an outside place on the same coach. He'd taken a room at an inn in Birmingham and visited several offices the next morning, a Saturday. As far as she could tell, he hadn't completed his business because he was in a bad mood when he booked two more nights at the inn, stayed there on the Sunday and visited more offices early on the Monday before taking the coach back to London. By then Tabby had used up her small store of money – it couldn't have been more than a few shillings in the first place – and gone back to her old trick of clinging to the back of the coach, losing him somewhere along the way when a post-boy spotted her. She'd taken some time to pick up the trail again back in London.

It fitted with what Mrs Eckington-Smith had said about his travelling and trying to raise loans, and all the time there was Tabby, clinging to him like a barnacle to a rackety ship.

'Why?' I said.

'Didn't want to lose 'im when I'd found 'im.'

She'd had the knife with her all the time, but decided not to use it because she'd have less chance of escaping afterwards in a place she didn't know. That suggested she wasn't as careless as she'd pretended about whether she hanged or not. Perhaps that was encouraging in its way. Then, back in London, she'd formed the idea of accounting for him and his brothel manager at the same time and spent many days watching and waiting. While I was drawing all this out of her, a depressing idea was in my mind. I fetched a calendar and tried to pin down the days when Eckington-Smith had been out of London. Dates and even days were foreign to Tabby's way of living, and it took some time. We managed to work out that it had been about a week before I'd caught sight of her outside Capel Court. By the time we'd established that, Tabby was more than half asleep. Reaction from the events of the night and probably the first food she'd eaten for days were catching up with her at last. It was hard work for both of us, pinning down for certain those days when she and Eckington-Smith had been in Birmingham, and brought no satisfaction. At the end of it, she was so drowsy that she even let me go with her to her old cabin and see her settled on her pallet that was at least more comfortable than sacking.

I went back to the embers of the fire and some uncomfortable thoughts. Tabby's account of Eckington-Smith's travels fitted well with what I knew. If his trip had been unsuccessful in raising loans, he'd have returned to London desperate enough to do anything for money, easily bribed to arrange for Mr Griffiths's pamphlets to disappear. I might have gone further and concluded that he'd been paid to commit the murder itself. I'd have liked that, only there was one great obstacle. Unmistakeably, and on the evidence of a girl who wanted him dead, Eckington-Smith had the strongest of alibis. On the night Mr Griffiths died, Eckington-Smith had been spending the night at a coaching inn at Birmingham, around twelve hours' travelling time away, with Tabby watching the entrance from a doorway across the street. If Tabby knew that, she'd be gone again, with no trust at all that I'd bring Eckington-Smith to account. She hadn't dropped the knife. From the careful way she'd moved when she stood up, even half-asleep, I was sure she was still carrying it. Of course, I should have taken it off her, but she'd only have refused and run away. And, as she'd told me, Tabby wouldn't wait forever.

TWENTY-ONE

The Indian Orphans' Society is holding a GRAND BAZAAR and Sale of Work at St Mary's Church Hall, Kensington, this SATURDAY. Doors open promptly at 2p.m. The Ladies of the Committee hope all their FRIENDS will attend and generously support this GOOD CAUSE.

The invitation had been delivered while I was out, with Mrs Glass's name on it. I vaguely remembered that she'd mentioned some such event. Normally, I shouldn't have given it a second thought, but by Saturday I was so desperate for ideas that I decided to attend. My brother had not called on Thursday evening, when I was out, or on Friday when I'd waited in. Tabby was still resident in Abel Yard, but lingering around and looking at me in a way that suggested she wouldn't be there much longer if I didn't think of something. I'd neglected Mrs Glass, I knew. If somebody had tried to poison her to stop her talking to me, it followed that she knew something. Getting to it was another matter.

'So glad you could come, my dear. Now, you must see Miss Bradley's lace. Simply fairylike. Taught by a French governess. Miss Bradley, a customer for you.'

Mrs Glass delivered me into the hands of Miss Bradley and rushed away to greet another arrival. I bought the least expensive thing on the stall, a tiny lace mat to accommodate a scent bottle, and worked my way back to Mrs Glass to inquire after her health.

'Yes, thank you, I'm entirely recovered. Just a passing upset. I do hope you said nothing to Mrs Talbot about the punch. I saw her two days ago when I was delivering our invitation and she didn't mention it.'

'No, I didn't tell her. Is she well?'

'Very well. She has guests, otherwise she'd be here. She's still a little disappointed about that dinner, but I told her gentlemen will have these little political differences and I'm sure nobody takes them too seriously. Of course, it was embarrassing at the time, but . . .'

Then, just as I hoped we might be heading in a useful direction, she spotted somebody else.

'Excuse me, dear, that's Mrs Eckington. Just moved here. I'm hoping she'll join our committee. Now, you must look at dear Philly's beautiful painted goblets. Philly dear, a customer.'

I pretended to admire the dreadful things the girl Philly had inflicted on some innocent drinking vessels while keeping watch on Mrs Glass. I'd no intention of imposing my company on the former Mrs Eckington-Smith for the second time in three days and was glad to see her out in society. Sad, though, that her attempt to revert to her maiden name did not seem to be having much success. When they finished talking I made my way back over to Mrs Glass, with the least objectionable goblet added to my haul.

'I gather some of them are very annoyed about a pamphlet,' I said. 'Mr McPherson included.'

Mrs Glass was keeping a shrewd eye on the stalls and had to drag her mind back to what we'd been talking about, until my mention of Mr McPherson's name produced a reaction. Unfortunately, it wasn't the one I'd wanted. She beamed.

'I'm afraid some people are very unfair to that gentleman. He may seem a rough diamond, but after all he has spent most of his life in the Far East, associating with all sorts of characters. And he has been most generous to our orphans.'

'Generous?'

'Yes. I took the liberty of approaching him after that dinner party and he subscribed more than anybody else to our new school. Much more. Just look.'

She pulled a folded list of subscribers from her reticule and showed it to me. As she said, Alexander McPherson's name headed the list with a donation of one hundred pounds. Nobody else was giving half as much.

I didn't recover in time to ask her another question, as a committee member arrived with a despatch that they were running out of change on the tea counter. Mrs Glass left in a rush, throwing a question to me over her shoulder.

'Shall you be going to the reception at East India House this evening? I expect your brother's been invited.'

It took me an embroidered linen handkerchief and a sachet of spices to find out more about the reception and then Mrs Glass disappeared behind the scenes, probably to count the takings. I left, thinking I'd learned very little. In fact, Mrs Glass had handed me a vital part of the puzzle, though I didn't find that out until much later.

If you need to attend some function to which you haven't been invited, it's an advantage to be female. The footman standing at the top of the steps between the classical columns of East India House might have asked for an invitation card from a gentleman he did not recognize. In my case, he bowed and opened the door. Admittedly, I'd taken some care in dressing for the occasion: my best midnight-blue silk with pointed waist and bishop sleeves, matching pumps with bows, simple pendant of lapis lazuli. I'd have liked to wear my lucky dragonfly in my hair, because I certainly needed luck, but it would have made me too conspicuous. I slipped into the main reception room along with a large and noisy group, gratefully accepted a glass of champagne. I'd deliberately arrived late, so the room was crowded, the level of noise high. A string and wind band on a dais was playing airs from Donizetti, almost drowned out by the buzz of conversation. No dancing on this occasion, which was probably just as well given that most of the guests were well into their middle years. A preponderance of gentlemen, many with red faces that might have come from years of service in India or long sittings over the directors' port. The women were mostly wives, bearing with stoicism the double burden of heavy jewellery and having to listen to husbands' familiar jokes.

The first essential was to make sure that my brother was not amongst those present. I was gambling on the hopes that he'd be too junior to be invited or, if invited, too disgusted with the Company to attend. A quick circuit of the periphery of the room confirmed my hopes. After that I lingered on the edge of various groups, watching and listening. I gathered that the evening was, unofficially, a celebration of the Company's having come through the latest ordeal by parliamentary committee more or less unscathed. Its directors were confident again, looking forward to pickings from the forthcoming war with China. The guest I was interested in arrived even later than I had. Suddenly, there he was in the centre of the crowd, surrounded as usual by a male chorus of hangers-on. Eckington-Smith was not one of them. I wasn't the only one to notice McPherson's arrival. Conversation dipped then rose again, heads half-turned then snapped back. It wouldn't be easy to get McPherson alone.

The band played a march. One of the directors made an optimistic speech. We all filed into the supper room. It was buffet style, which from my point of view carried less risk of discovery than a formal meal, but was still dangerous. A lady sits down on one of the gilt chairs by the wall and waits for her gentleman to bring food. A lady sitting on her own risks having three or four spare gentlemen converging on her with unwanted gallantry and even less wanted things in aspic. I remained standing, half hidden behind a fern in a pot. McPherson and his coterie weren't interested in eating either. They'd managed to exchange their champagne glasses for tumblers of whisky and soda and were talking together in the far corner of the room. Fern by fern, I moved towards them. One of the hangers-on crooked a finger for a waiter. He was evidently ordering more whisky, because the waiter disappeared through a door and came back with a loaded tray. I stopped him on his return journey with a trayful of empty tumblers.

'When you've taken those back, would you be kind enough to tell the gentleman in the middle there that somebody wishes to talk to him urgently about a lady at Richmond.'

He looked surprised, but did as I asked. I watched as he delivered the message, saw McPherson's head turn in my direction then walked through the service door.

It opened on to a stone-flagged passageway, dimly lit, probably leading to the kitchens. Within seconds, the door from the supper room clattered and McPherson was beside me.

'You again. What do you want this time?'

His tone had no pretence of manners. Evidently, he remembered snubbing me at Beattie's dinner.

'A talk,' I said. 'It shouldn't take long.'

'So what does she want this time?'

'The Rani? Nothing, as far as I know. She didn't send me. I just needed to attract your attention.'

'What is this? What are we supposed to be talking about?'

I looked at him, making him wait.

'Jewels,' I said.

I missed his reaction, because the door from the supper room swung open and another waiter hurried out, obviously surprised to see us there.

'We can't talk here,' McPherson said.

'Where, then?'

He turned without answering and led the way along the kitchen corridor, then right through another door that led back to an anteroom in the grand part of the building. Either he knew the place very well or he had a good sense of direction because a door off the anteroom took us into the library. It was a cavern of a room, two floors high with a gallery round it, deserted but softly lit by two oil lamps. The marble fireplace had no fire in it, but from habit McPherson strode across to the rug and turned to face me, as if master in his own home.

'So.'

'Your secret is safe with me,' I said. It was a line I'd always wanted to try, but never had the opportunity till now. 'On conditions,' I added.

'And what is this secret supposed to be?'

The posture hadn't changed, but just a shade of doubt was on his face.

'That you're not a jewel thief,' I said.

I think the words 'jewel thief' penetrated his mind first because he'd been expecting them. What he hadn't expected was the 'not'. When that sank in the change in his expression went from doubt to shock.

'You never had the princess's jewels,' I said. 'Only that hawk, and she gave it to you freely. It's worked hard for you, that hawk. I wonder where your credit would have been without it.'

He wasn't a stupid man and knew when it was no use blustering. He did tell me I was talking nonsense, but only as an automatic response while he was thinking. I didn't want to give him time to think.

'Why don't we sit down and I'll tell you what I think happened,' I said, settling myself into one of the leather armchairs on either side of the fireplace.

He remained standing.

'And why don't I have you thrown out?'

'Do, by all means. It will make an excellent column in the newspapers: A certain well-known trading gentleman throws a lady into the street for defending his honour.'

'*You*, defending my honour!'

'But then, the last thing you want is your honour defended, isn't it? You had to choose between honour and credit. Or should I say, creditworthiness. You made sure that everybody knew how angry you were about that paragraph pretty well accusing you of jewel theft. That was as good a way as any of spreading the story all round town. Like back in Bombay, hiding your hawk on poor Mr Griffiths's desk.'

'*Poor* Mr Griffiths!' Now he was genuinely furious. 'Why will you and everybody else persist in regarding that man as some sort of saint? There are things I could tell you that might make you think differently about your beloved Mr Griffiths.'

'Yes, I'm sure you could. So why don't you?'

That took him by surprise. I looked up at him and nodded at the vacant armchair opposite. He sat down as if he couldn't believe he was doing it. We both waited.

'You were going to tell me about Mr Griffiths,' I said. He said nothing. I let the silence draw out before speaking again. 'Very well then. Shall we start where he started, in his pamphlet?'

'I haven't read the confounded thing.'

His irritation sounded genuine.

'It starts with three young men sailing to India', I said. 'He calls himself The Griff and the other two The Merchant and The Soldier. It's pretty clear that you're The Merchant.'

A shrug, as if he didn't care one way or another.

'Much later, the three meet again by chance in a small state in the Maratha that the Company's pretty well taken over. At least, it was chance as far as he was concerned. He hints that The Merchant may have been there by arrangement with The Soldier. The prince has a beautiful and ambitious sister. There's a small war, then an unsuccessful uprising against the prince. Does that sound familiar?'

He was still managing to look bored.

'I've spent most of my life in the East and travelled all of India from Ceylon to the Punjab. The circumstances you describe are things I've witnessed a dozen times or more.'

'The prince had an amazing collection of jewels,' I said. 'They vanished. It's no surprise to you that Griffiths thought you were in possession of them. He came very close to accusing you in public.'

'The man was practically insane on the subject. Some people told me I should have sued him for slander, but it was of no account to me.'

'Except that you deliberately provoked him by wearing that diamond hawk in public. Just as you did in Bombay, by trying to make it look as if he'd stolen it and even killed your assistant for the jewels. Very clumsy, that was – and I don't think you're a clumsy man.'

That surprised him. He recovered almost at once, but not before I'd caught that reassessing glance at me.

'So let's move on to the night before Mr Griffiths died,' I said. 'You visited him.'

'If you're going to accuse me of murdering the man, please come to the point so that I can rejoin my friends.'

'A few days ago, I might have done exactly that. But I didn't know then what Mr Griffiths told you. More to the point, I didn't know what you said to him.'

His eyebrows joined in a black bar over angry eyes.

'It was a conversation between the two of us. Nobody knows what we talked about.'

'Are you sure?'

And no, he wasn't sure. I could sense his mind moving fast, wondering if they could have been overheard. By the boy Anil, perhaps. I pressed on while he was still wondering.

'Mr Griffiths had asked you to meet him so that he could apologize. He'd learned from a source he trusted that you did not have the prince's jewels and never had them. He was an honourable man . . .'

'Honourable!'

'In that respect at least. He offered to make public amends in any way you wanted. At the very least, he was determined to tell all your friends and business acquaintances that you were innocent and write to the newspapers.'

A snort from McPherson, but no other attempt to interrupt.

'A very formal letter it would have been, I suppose,' I said. '"Mr Griffiths would like it to be known that he entirely withdraws any imputation he has made, directly or indirectly, against the honour and integrity of Mr Alexander McPherson." Still, more than enough to do the damage.'

'Damage? Miss Lane, do you realize what nonsense you're talking? Even if I accept your account of what Griffiths said to me – and I don't – how could a public acknowledgement that I'm not a thief possibly do me damage?'

'Because it was a choice of being thought either a thief or a bankrupt,' I said.

His fists were clenching and unclenching on his knees. Big fighter's fists. If he could have solved his problems by punching the life out of me, I don't think he'd have hesitated. But a man doesn't make fortunes without being able to think several moves ahead. He'd assume I'd have told somebody all this before confronting him. I only wished I'd thought of it. Faintly, the music of another march drifted into the library. Supper was over.

'You needed that opium compensation money urgently,' I said. 'You can't pay your debts. If you have to wait a year or more for it, you can only survive if people think you still have assets – like a fortune in jewels. If the world believes that, you may just be able to hold out. You've been keeping up appearances very well – donations to orphans and so forth. The last thing you wanted was Griffiths declaring to the world that you didn't have the jewels.'

'So I killed him to stop him, did I?'

'No. I should have thought that once, but I know you left him alive and spent the next night at Richmond with the Rani.'

'She's not a rani.'

'Princess, then. Your old friend, the princess.' He didn't deny that at least. More than friend, I suspected. 'Mr Patwardhan took you to her. He's the witness that you couldn't have killed Mr Griffiths. But somebody killed him. That's my only interest. If you help me by telling what you know, then I'll give you the promise you wanted from him. I won't tell the world that you're poor and honest.'

I could do that. In their different ways, both Tom Huckerby and Mr Disraeli would love the story. McPherson must have guessed that I wasn't bluffing. Fists unclenched, hands flat on his thighs, he started talking. Once he'd decided, he told his story unemotionally, as if reporting to shareholders.

'I'll start from when my assistant Burton was killed. Griffiths wasn't responsible. In case you're wondering, I wasn't either. It was just what it seemed to be, an attack by robbers. I'd ridden out alone to meet him and talk to him before he arrived in Bombay. I knew we had to talk up my assets – such as they were – and the old story about the missing jewels had come into my mind. I was sorry Burton was dead, but as I was riding back it came to me how I might use it. I put my hawk on Griffiths's desk, assuming that he'd find it and immediately make a song and dance by accusing me of trying to blame him for Burton's murder. It worked better than I'd expected because your brother found it first, Griffiths went straight off to the governor and the whole of Bombay was talking about the jewels, just as I'd hoped. By the time we all arrived in London, the idea that Burton had been attacked because of the jewels and that most of them were in my possession was as firmly fixed as I could have wanted. Griffiths couldn't have managed the thing better if I'd been paying him for it.'

'Then the princess arrived in London,' I said.

'Then the princess arrived in London. I don't know why, but one thing I do know is that woman has been scheming about one thing or another ever since she opened her eyes in the cradle. She's as devious and ruthless as Cleopatra and Lady MacBeth combined and she ate men as casually as sugar almonds. Griffiths was besotted with her.'

And not only Griffiths, I thought. Talking about her, McPherson had lost the reporting to shareholders tone. It took him a few deep breaths to get it back again before he went on.

'She was the one who told Griffiths I didn't have the jewels. Pure mischief-making, I suppose. That would be like her. So that's the story. You wanted it. Whether it helps you to find out who killed Griffiths or not, I don't care. But I've kept my side of the agreement and I expect you to keep yours.'

His hard dark eyes looked into mine.

'Not completely,' I said.

'Not keeping your agreement completely?'

The fists had clenched again.

'I meant you haven't kept yours. In two respects. One is that you haven't told me why you went out to Richmond that night to see the princess.'

'Her man, Patwardhan, suggested it. She wanted to apologize to me for any part she had in the misunderstanding.'

'And you cared enough to see her late at night? Wouldn't it have waited till morning?'

'I don't care for waiting. Your second objection?'

'You haven't told me about The Soldier.'

The fists unclenched, but it was an effort.

'What am I supposed to tell you? I don't even know who he was.'

'According to Griffiths, you were all there together. The princess was using all three of you, or trying to, in the plot against her brother.'

'Did Griffiths write that?'

'Not in so many words, but it's obvious. According to Griffiths, you'd sailed out to India together.'

'You'll excuse me if I don't put as much trust in what Griffiths wrote as you appear to do.'

'The Soldier was a captain. There were only four of them with the company. You must have known him.'

'Yes, and hundreds of other captains at dozens of different places. How am I supposed to know which one would figure as a hero in Griffiths's romancings?'

'Not a hero exactly. I think he's here, in London. If you didn't set Eckington-Smith to steal his pamphlets . . .'

'So that was the Eckington-Smith business. No, I didn't set him or anybody else to steal them. Why should I? If you think about it, you'll see that it was in my interest to let that jewel story circulate as much as possible. I'd have paid him to publish the damned things.'

That sounded convincing.

'Then, as far as I can see, the only person with an interest in suppressing them is the man he called The Soldier.'

'Possibly. But since I can't help you in that respect, I can only wish you good hunting.' He spoke with sarcastic courtesy. He'd sensed that we'd come near the end of things I knew for certain, which meant I was running out of trading currency. 'So if you'll kindly permit me to leave you, Miss Lane . . .'

He paused at the door.

'We have an agreement?'

'Yes.'

I didn't add that the agreement was conditional still, because I was certain he hadn't told me all he knew.

I lingered in the library for a while, not wanting to face the raised eyebrows of McPherson's hangers-on, who'd probably put the worst interpretation on our seclusion together. A pile of East India Company annual reports stood on one of the tables, for anybody who wanted to take one. I opened a copy and turned to the list of stockholders. The list was starred with asterisks according to the amount of stock each person held. McPherson was at a comparatively modest two stars, which meant over three thousand pounds but less than six thousand. I turned to Eckington-Smith, not expecting anything, and was amazed to find four stars against his name, the maximum possible, denoting an investment of over ten thousand. Four stars carried voting rights that would make Eckington-Smith a considerable power in the Company. It did not go at all with a down-at-heel man who received brothel takings at his back door and scurried to Birmingham and back looking for loans. Something was seriously wrong. I puzzled over it in the cab on the way home, found no answers and decided to talk it over with Tom on Sunday, but he didn't come. On Monday morning, I woke up with an idea in my head. I rushed downstairs to meet Amos, determined on an early morning errand to the other side of the park. And fell over a brick.

TWENTY-TWO

Not a serious fall, though I caught my toe in the hem of my riding skirt. I put my hands out to protect myself so my gloves took most of the damage from the cobbles. As usually happens when you trip, shock transferred itself to anger against the thing that had caused it. An ordinary household brick, raw and new, left carelessly just where I could be guaranteed to fall over it at the bottom of my staircase. Only it wasn't an ordinary brick because something white was wrapped round it, and it hadn't been left carelessly because the white thing was a small package for me. It was simply addressed *Miss Lane* and tied with a piece of coarse string. Amos had come running in case I needed picking up, reins of both horses in hand. He watched as I untied the package and read the note inside, and he must have moved to catch me when I looked like falling again because I found myself leaning against his shoulder, struggling to speak.

'Tom. Oh Amos. Tom.'

I gave the note to him and watched his face change as he read.

'Oh the buggers . . . I'm sorry . . . oh the . . .' Then, recovering a little, 'What's that came with it?'

I opened my hand to show him the thing that had been in the package: a gentleman's silver watch, small and plain. Even before I opened the cover I knew the inscription inside: *To my son Thomas Fraternity, at the start of his journey. J. Lane.* The watch my father had given him before he sailed away to India. Tom would never have parted with it willingly.

I took the note back from Amos and read it again:

> We have your brother. He will be exchanged for ascertainable information about the location of the jewels. A message may be left at Robinson's print shop. If you

do not wish harm to come to him, the message must be received by midday tomorrow.

The writing was clerk's copperplate – a thousand ledgers all over the city could show similar samples – the paper plain white.

'Robinson's,' I said. 'Somebody knows I know the place. That takes us back to Eckington-Smith and The Soldier.'

My mind was starting to move again, but slowly.

'So what are we going to do?' Amos said.

My first reaction was to go with him to Eckington-Smith's house in the City and tear it apart, but they'd expect that so wouldn't be holding him there. If they were holding him anywhere.

'They may be lying,' I said. 'The first thing to do is to see he isn't at work or at Mr Tillington's house.'

I didn't believe it, because of the watch, but it might just have been stolen from him. We agreed that Amos should take the horses back to the stables while I took a cab to Holborn, then meet me in two hours at Abel Yard. Before I left, I went to the cabin and roused Tabby.

'Get dressed and come with me. Don't bring the knife.'

She knew from my voice it was serious and didn't ask questions. In ten minutes we were in a cab together, making for Fleet Street.

'I'm going to drop you at Tom Huckerby's,' I told her. 'He'll show you a printer's shop near Ludgate Hill called Robinson's. I want you to watch and remember everybody coming in and out of that shop until I tell you otherwise.'

I took the cab to Mr Tillington's house. I had to wait a long time on the doorstep before he came downstairs and answered the door himself, in his dressing gown and leaning on a stick, an invalid smell of camphorated oil hanging around him.

'No, my dear. Your brother's not here. I assumed he was staying with you.'

'How long has he been away?'

'I haven't seen him since he left for the office on Friday morning. I was becoming worried. It's unlike him not to send a message. Is something wrong? Won't you come in?'

'No.' I gave him one of my cards. 'If he comes back, or if you hear anything at all about him, please get word to me here as soon as you can.'

I left him standing at the open door, looking mazed, and took the cab on to East India House. I told the desk clerk in the entrance hall that I needed to speak urgently to my brother. They kept me waiting for a long time before a man who looked like the head clerk came down and told me, with annoyance, that Mr Lane had failed to arrive at work that morning or Saturday morning.

'Was he here on Friday?'

A frown, as if that were confidential information, then a reluctant nod.

'Did he stay all day and leave as usual?'

'To the best of my knowledge, yes.'

'Would anybody else know more?'

'If there had been any irregularity in Mr Lane's attendance on Friday, I'm sure it would have been brought to my attention. If you see your brother, I'd be grateful if you'd remind him that absence from duty is entirely unacceptable unless caused by illness or close family bereavement.'

He marched back upstairs, as if every minute away from his ledgers had to be marked down as time wasted.

Amos didn't have to ask if I'd had any success.

'So where now?'

'Richmond.'

'Ascertainable information about the location of the jewels' was what the note demanded. At least not the jewels themselves. But I didn't care about them. I'd give elephant loads of anybody's jewels to have Tom back and glaring at me. The person who must know something about the jewels was the princess. If she was so sure that McPherson had not stolen them, that should mean she knew who had. Surely she could tell me enough to buy Tom's release. I rode pillion behind Amos on his cob, to get to the stables and collect Rancie. We got some odd looks as we went across the park, but I was beyond caring about that. I carried Tom's watch in the pocket of my riding skirt, a reminder of how the hours were draining away. It was ten past twelve when we came to the livery stables, half past by the time we were riding away on Rancie and a fresh cob for Amos. At the pace we rode, even Rancie was tiring when we got to Richmond Green. Amos stayed within calling distance of the cottage, holding the horses, while I went up the path and knocked on the front door. Anil opened it so promptly that somebody must have been watching from inside. The scene in the main room was much as it had been in the tent in the park, except that the Rani was sitting upright in an armchair instead of on piles of cushions. Mr Patwardhan was standing beside her, her daughter Chandrika on a stool in the corner. Chandrika raised her head when I came in, looked over my shoulder and lowered it again when she saw I'd come alone.

The Rani invited me to sit, offered tea.

'No time for that,' I said. 'My brother's been kidnapped. Whoever's holding him wants to know where your jewels are.'

A gasp from Chandrika. She was staring at me, wide-eyed. Then she caught a glance from her mother and looked down. Her hands were twisted together so tightly it must have hurt.

'My jewels were taken a long time ago.' The Rani's voice was calm as her eyes looked unblinkingly at me.

'But you know who took them. You must do. You told Mr Griffiths it wasn't McPherson.'

'That does not imply that I know who did.'

'Perhaps not, but I think you do know. Who is The Soldier?'

'Soldier. What soldier?' She looked at Mr Patwardhan, as if I were speaking riddles and he might interpret.

'When you were plotting against your brother,' I said. 'You were using three of them, Mr Griffiths, McPherson and a captain in the army.'

I was beyond being tactful.

'Plotting?' She made another appeal to Mr Patwardhan. 'Was I plotting?'

She was playing with me. I was furious.

'All I'm asking you for is a name. Or even a guess at where those jewels might be now. Anything. I've got until midday tomorrow to tell them something.'

'I wish I could help you.'

The way she said it was like a door closing. I tried

everything I could think of in the way of appeals, persuasion, but it was like hammering my fists against teak.

'I hope one day you know what it's like when you love somebody and he's in danger,' I said.

But it was an admission of my defeat. Anil showed me out. At the door he said, under his breath, 'I hope you find your brother.'

I paused on the step, hoping even at that point that he might have something to tell me, but he only bowed and closed the door.

The ride back to London seemed endless. The horses were tired and the quiet ticking of Tom's watch against my hip seemed to vibrate through my body. Amos didn't have much to say after I reported my failure to him. As we came near the park in the dusk, he asked me what we were going to do next. I tried to drag my mind back from panic.

'When you've taken the horses back, would you mind going to Robinson's print shop near Ludgate Hill and bringing back Tabby.'

It was twenty past seven by then, with no more comings or goings to be expected at the print shop. There was just the faintest chance that she might have seen something useful. Amos expected to take me back to Abel Yard, but I went with him to the livery stables. It was a short step from there to Kensington. For once, I didn't even stay to see Rancie untacked and fed. I told Amos I'd see him later and went to pay another call on the lady who had been Mrs Eckington-Smith. She was on the point of taking her little girl upstairs to bed and looked alarmed when she saw me at this unconventional hour for callers. No point in burdening her with the worry for Tom. I simply asked her my questions there in the hall, with the child in her nightdress sitting on the stairs.

'You told me you were going back to your maiden name but Mrs Glass called you Mrs Eckington. Was that a mistake?'

'No. Eckington is my maiden name. My husband simply added his own name to mine when we were married. They were such snobs, his family, they hated being just Smith.'

'So your husband's name was Smith?'

'Yes, does it matter? Has he done something worse?'

'Does he have a brother?'

She was looking alarmed at my urgency. Even the child sensed it and was chewing her fingernails.

'Yes, an elder brother.'

'A soldier?'

'A long time ago. Long before I knew him.'

'In India?'

'I think so. Soldiers go everywhere, don't they? I was never very interested in him.'

'Where does the brother live?'

'He has a house somewhere in Buckinghamshire, out in the Chilterns. I only visited once, a horrible gloomy place. I remember that he and my husband talked the whole visit about money. They're obsessed with it.'

'You don't remember where exactly?'

'No. It was a long time ago.'

She'd have remembered if she could. She wanted to help me but was scared and bewildered. I apologized for intruding and left. It was dark by the time I came out, but I walked straight home across the park, not caring. Four captains on the list, one named Smith. For what it was worth, I now knew the identity of The Soldier. Captain Smith. Brother to Eckington-Smith. Holder of more than ten thousand pounds worth of shares in the East India Company, using his brother as nominee. A covetous, secretive man who knew about the jewels. If I found him, I might find Tom, but had no idea where to look. Locating a man named Smith somewhere in the Chilterns would take days, and we had sixteen hours left.

At nine o'clock, Amos came back to Abel Yard, bringing Tabby with him.

She ate, drank and, from her remarkable memory, ran through everybody who'd visited Robinson's print shop that day, but no description matched anybody in the case. Besides, it had moved on now.

'Eckington-Smith has a brother,' I said. 'I don't know where he is, but he's got Tom.'

'That house,' Tabby said, munching bread.

'Would they keep him there? If Eckington-Smith recognized us, he'll know it's not safe.'

But it was a big if. It had been dark in the yard. He might have supposed it was no more than a simple attempt at robbery. Our talk became a council of war, with Mrs Martley observing. It was a measure of her partiality for Tom, and her anxiety about him, that she tolerated without complaint the unwashed presence of Tabby in the parlour. Tabby insisted that her place was back there in her woodshed den behind Eckington-Smith's house, watching. It was hard to deny, although she looked beyond tiredness, her face white and pinched.

'I'll take her,' Amos volunteered. 'Then come back here and decide what to do next.'

He'd brought a cob with him, tied up below in Mr Grindley's carriage workshop with a pile of hay borrowed from the cows at the end of the yard.

'No knife,' I said to Tabby. 'And don't go inside that house whatever happens. We'll come for you first thing in the morning.'

I went down to see them off, Tabby riding pillion. Upstairs, Mrs Martley had fallen asleep in her chair. I persuaded her to go up to bed, made up the fire and sat with my heart beating in rhythm with the ticking watch that was still in my pocket. If there was even the faintest chance that Tom was being kept prisoner in Eckington-Smith's house, we'd force our way in early, before people were awake. It was possible. Amos could always whistle up half a dozen strong-armed grooms. Two things worried me. The first was that if Tom were inside the house, the first reaction of his captors might be to kill him to stop him giving evidence against them. The second, less logical but stronger, was my belief that Tom wasn't there. I'd missed something. I still couldn't see what it was, but if I could only think of it, he might be safe. I was no nearer it when Amos came back, just before midnight. I'd left the door unlatched for him.

'She's there watching,' he said. 'Not a light on in the place. You'd say it was empty.'

'I'm afraid it might be,' I said.

I brewed tea. We discussed what we should do. Amos was all for a raid on the house at first light. No need for anybody else, he said. Just say the word and he'd be through the door like a badger through a hedge. With no other plan, I had to agree. At about two in the morning, Amos went down to see the cob was all right and smoke a pipe in the yard.

I must have been dozing in the chair, because I woke with a start to hear his voice on the staircase. He wasn't alone. He was gently encouraging somebody up the stairs, the way he might have spoken to a weary horse. I jumped up and opened the door, thinking the miracle had happened and Tom was back. As they came in, Amos was practically carrying the person with him. Swathes of dark silk trailed round his corduroy shoulder. Two dark eyes stared into mine.

'Chandrika!' I said, disappointment and amazement hitting me together. The gold embroidered hem of her sari was torn, her feet bare and bleeding.

'Tom,' she said, looking at me as if the one word explained everything. For a while, it seemed to be all she could say. I fetched a glass of water and knelt down at her feet, waiting.

'My mother. I'm so sorry. I wanted to say then, when you were there, but I knew how angry she'd be.'

Her eyes were on me, as if I should understand without being told.

'To say what?' I said.

'She has the jewels. I know where they are. We can take them, then they'll let Tom go.'

'Your mother's had the jewels all along?'

'Not all along, no. Only for a little while. Mr Griffiths made Mr McPherson steal them back for her.'

'Steal from where?'

'East India House. The man you call The Soldier was keeping them in the vaults there. But that doesn't matter. I can take you to where they are now and you can take them to the men who have Tom.'

'So where are they?' I said, still not quite believing.

'We have a boat on the river. There's a big wooden chest in it.'

'The boat with the sea horse?' I said. She nodded. 'But there's only one chest there and it's full of opium balls.'

'The jewels are there.'

Amos was standing beside her chair. He caught my eye.

'Back to the boat, then?'

'Yes,' I said.

'I'll go down and see to something. Give me half an hour or so.'

While he was away, I persuaded Chandrika to drink some tea, well sugared, and got from her the story of how she'd managed to get the eight miles from Richmond to Mayfair alone and in the dark. She told it simply and without dramatics, though the risks she'd taken astounded me. Soon after Amos and I had left, she'd walked out of the back door of the cottage while her mother and Mr Patwardhan were in conference and asked the first person she met the way to London. After the first mile or two, her sandal strap had broken and she'd gone barefoot. By good luck, she came to some inn along the way just as a London coach was about to leave and persuaded the coachman to let her ride on the outside.

'I had no money, so I gave him a bracelet,' she said.

Judging by the ornate silver bangles on her arms, he'd been well paid. In her light sari, Chandrika must have been cold and shivering when she got down in Piccadilly, but had enough presence of mind to ask the coachman to call her a cab. Another bracelet had gone for the fare. I supposed it was a tribute to the comparative honesty of the coach driver and cabbie that she had any left.

'How did you know where to find me?' I said.

'Tom told me.'

It sounded as if she'd hung on every word he said.

'Won't your mother be angry when she finds out?'

'I shan't be able to go back to her, ever.'

Again, no drama in her voice, but complete certainty. I felt pity at the way she'd burned her bridges, but was anxious to know if she were telling the truth. It was a relief when Amos called up to us from the yard. He'd borrowed a fine Stanhope gig that had come into Mr Grindley's workshop for repairs and harnessed the cob to it. It was a crush for the three of us, Amos driving in the middle, with myself and Chandrika on either side. I'd found a good thick cloak for her and a pair of slippers for her narrow feet. We'd have looked a strange trio, if there'd been anybody alert enough to notice us on the London streets at three o'clock in the morning.

By half past four, we were rowing out again to the *Calypso*. After searching along the wharfs, Amos had borrowed a rowing boat in the same cavalier way that he'd borrowed the gig. Luckily, the rope ladder was down, as we'd left it. It looked as if nobody had been to the boat since our visit. I went up first, fearing for Chandrika in slippers and sari, but she left the slippers in the boat, hitched up her sari and climbed like a cat. Amos followed with the lamp and we went down into the hold. The opium chest was still there. Amos opened the lid and I showed Chandrika the neat rows of petal-wrapped opium balls in their separate compartments. She picked up one of the balls and rapped it sharply against the planks, the noise echoing round the empty hold. The opium ball cracked open like an egg, showing a dark core inside, a wooden sphere about the size of an apricot. When Chandrika took the sphere into her hands and twisted, it came into two halves. She held one of them closer to the lamplight so that we could see. Nestled in raw cotton, a great ruby flashed fire like the heart of a volcano. She went on, until the planks where she was kneeling were scattered with fragments of opium crust and wooden hemispheres, with more rubies, diamonds and an amazing emerald shining out. Then she looked up into our wondering faces.

'Enough for Tom?'

Right up to then, I'd been half alert for a trap, but the simplicity of her expression and the tone of her voice convinced me. It was a ransom for a prince and to her my brother was worth it.

'Enough,' I said.

'Then let's take them to whoever wants them so much,' she said.

Gently I picked up the great square-cut emerald. As it moved out and in of the lamplight it transformed itself from the dull glow of a green bottle to the blaze of beech trees in midsummer sunlight. And yet it was the bottle, not the emerald, that came into my mind. A dull green bottle, so as not to show any change in appearance from the arsenic. An elderly woman who almost fainted when a man she had not seen for some time walked into a drawing room. I might have made some sound, because both Chandrika and Amos were staring at me.

'What's wrong?' Amos said.

'Nothing wrong, except that I'm a fool. Come on, let's go and get Tom.'

Chandrika started knotting the jewels into a fold of her sari as if they were of no more account than pebbles.

'No,' I said. 'Put them back in the chest, for the while at least. We may need them, but I don't think so. Your mother might keep them, Chandrika.'

She'd been prepared to sacrifice everything for my brother. If it turned out to be necessary, I'd still accept the sacrifice as freely as it was offered. But there was another way, less brutal to her, and I knew Tom would have wanted me to try it.

'So where are we going?' Amos said.

'To Tom's lodgings.'

He stared at me.

'So you think he's come back?'

'I think he never went away. Come on.'

TWENTY-THREE

Grey daylight was just beginning to show the outlines of banks and merchants' offices as we drove up from the river to the heart of the City. We were the only vehicle on the roads, with the cob's hooves echoing along chasms of buildings. We stopped by the alley at the back of Eckington-Smith's house. I got down, walked along the alley and called softly to Tabby. She was with me as soon as I'd spoken.

'He's not there. Nobody's in there.'

'No. Something else to do.'

I told her as we walked back to the gig. There was no room for her inside so she hung on to the back as we went along Cheapside, past Newgate and into Holborn.

'Quieter for all of us to walk from here,' Amos said.

'Quiet's not what we want,' I said. 'Right up to the door, close as we can get.'

The front of the house was dark and blank like all the others in the street. Amos handed the reins to Chandrika. She looked from him to me, puzzled.

'Just keep hold of them like that. He won't go anywhere,' Amos assured her.

It was his way of making sure she stayed in the gig, away from trouble. He'd guessed that was what I wanted. He stationed himself on the pavement, by the cob's head. To anybody looking out of the house, he'd look like any ordinary groom. I whispered to Tabby to keep out of sight on the far side of the horse and not move till Amos did. On the first floor of the house, a spark flared, then candlelight. A curtain shifted and dropped back. I went up the step, hammered on the door knocker and shouted up to the window with the candle.

'It's me. Tom's sister.'

The window sash lifted. A face in a nightcap looked out, confused and blinking.

I called up: 'Is he back? Have you heard from him?'

Mr Tillington shook his head and replied in a quavering voice, 'You haven't found him, then? My poor girl. Wait, I'll come down.'

We waited. I glanced across at Amos. To look at him, you'd have said he was relaxed to the point of being half asleep.

The door opened. I stumbled against it, trying to look as if I were fainting, but in reality to make sure it didn't close.

'My poor—'

I suppose he was going to call me poor girl again, in that weak quavering voice, but he never got that far because Amos hurtled like a comet across the pavement, up the step and crashed with all his considerable force into my brother's kind, sick friend, Mr Tillington. Alias Captain Smith. Alias The Soldier.

Mr Tillington went down like a sack. Tabby, who'd been close behind Amos, trod on him as she followed me upstairs. I called Tom's name as I went. The house sounded echoing and empty, the stairs dark. The first door I opened from the landing let us into what was evidently Tillington's room, window up, bed disordered.

'Found him?'

Amos's voice, then his heavy footsteps upstairs. He came into the room with us.

'What about him?' I said, nodding downstairs to where Tillington had been felled.

'He won't be troubling us.'

'Dead?'

My heart lurched.

'No, but good as for a while. You two stay here while I make sure there's nobody next floor up.'

His footsteps went on up. I pulled back the curtains, found a lamp on the bedside table and lit it. The room looked and smelled like any sickroom, a smell of camphor and beef tea, a row of medicine bottles on the mantelpiece. He'd acted his role of invalid very thoroughly. I remembered Mrs Glass's voice: *Amateur dramatics can be very dangerous to the feelings in sultry climates.* His acting skills must have swept her off her feet many years before, since she'd been so badly affected when she caught sight of him at the dinner party. If he and Tom hadn't happened to walk in at the same time as McPherson, I'd have tumbled to it sooner. The former Captain Smith had kept up his acting skills well enough to deceive Tom completely. It must have been a bad moment for both him and McPherson when they'd met at the Talbots' dinner party. McPherson could have destroyed 'Tillington' in a moment. But then, McPherson was a man with several things to hide and could only guess what game his old associate was playing. In both cases, they'd followed their devious instincts and played bluff and counter-bluff.

I opened the door on the other side of the landing. Another bedroom, window well-curtained. The smell was strange, sickly. A figure wrapped in a blanket lay unmoving on the bed. Light from the lamp in my hand lurched from the bed across the walls and back, as if the room had turned into a ship's cabin in a gale.

'Tom.'

Tabby was behind me. Amos came thundering back downstairs and pushed her aside. By then, I'd pulled back the blanket and was kneeling beside him.

'Oh Tom.'

His eyes opened and looked straight into mine. Strange eyes, full of night. Then his forehead creased as if the lamplight hurt him and his eyes closed again. Amos was kneeling beside me.

'Doped,' he said.

'Is he dying?'

'No. Long as we can wake him up and keep him that way.'

'Coffee,' I said, remembering.

'Yes, there'll be a kitchen. Can she make coffee?'

He glanced towards Tabby.

'No,' I said. 'I'll have to do it.'

'Wait while I go downstairs and tidy up a bit, then I'll give you the word.'

We waited. Shuffling sounds came down from the hall, then Captain Smith's voice raised in useless protest. Even so, it sounded stronger than the quavering tones of Mr Tillington had been. A door slammed. A key turned in the lock.

'All safe,' Amos called up.

The kitchen was in the basement, in a state of bachelor disorder. If there'd been domestics in the house, they'd been turned away some time ago. Luckily there were a spirit lamp, coffee beans in a tin, a grinder. I set Tabby to grinding the beans. It seemed an age before the kettle boiled.

'So who is he?' Tabby said, gesturing upstairs with her chin.

There was no sound from the room where Captain Smith was imprisoned. Men tied up and gagged by Amos were guaranteed to stay quiet. All the same, we both jumped round when the door to the kitchen suddenly opened. Chandrika was standing there, Tabby was gaping at her as if she were the genie from the lamp.

'Have you found him?'

'Yes. You were supposed to stay with the horse.'

From the gesture she made, she wouldn't have minded if the cob had taken wings and flown away.

'Where is he?'

'Upstairs, not well. Open that cupboard and see if you can find a clean cup.'

When I went upstairs with the tray, they both followed me. Amos had managed to get Tom sitting up in a chair, but his eyes were still closed, head flopping. I poured water into the coffee to cool it and held it to his lips. He drank a drop, shook his head as if he resented the efforts to wake him. Chandrika was kneeling on the floor, looking up at him.

'Tom,' I said. 'Tom, please.'

His eyes opened and fastened on Chandrika's.

'You? Here?'

His eyes stayed open. He drank. For a moment, an ignoble feeling of annoyance hit me. Who'd found him, after all? For that matter, who'd brewed the coffee? But the knowledge that he was going to live swept it aside.

'Yes, we're here,' I said.

Chandrika and I stayed there, feeding Tom sips of coffee, until he was capable of standing and walking. He wanted to ask questions, showing particular concern for his poor friend, Mr Tillington. He thought somebody must have broken into the house and attacked them both, drugging him and doing goodness knows what harm to the old man.

'Don't worry,' I said. 'He's alive and being well looked after.'

In fact, Amos had looked in to check on him before driving the gig away so that he could bring back a more robust vehicle. In a whispered conversation on the landing, Amos told me that he'd removed the gag long enough to give our prisoner a drink of water, then left him securely tied with the door locked. I'd no idea what to do with the man. If we'd taken him to the local police station with our story, they'd probably have released him and arrested us.

'Leave it till later,' Amos had said. 'It'll sort itself.'

By the time Amos drove back in a two-horse closed carriage, Tom was far enough recovered to be demanding some answers.

'The fact is, he's not Mr Tillington,' I said. 'He's The Soldier, Captain Smith that was. And he's certainly not your friend. He was the one who drugged you.'

I'm not sure he'd have believed me, but Chandrika told him I was right and he wasn't to waste his strength in talking. If she had faith in me, and he in her, that would have to do for a while. At least it worked well enough to get us all downstairs. As we passed the locked door on the ground floor, I glanced a question at Amos.

'It's all right,' he said. 'I'll come back for the goods once I've dropped you off.'

We were almost rolling, until I remembered something.

'Where's Tabby?'

She'd been with us when we were looking after Tom, then at some point she'd disappeared. I'd been too occupied to worry. Amos came back into the house with me.

We searched the basement kitchen and the two upstairs floors. No sign of her. I was beginning to think she'd disappeared again when I noticed a ladder leading up to the loft. The opening above it looked too narrow for Amos's shoulders, so I went up. Faint daylight was coming through a skylight in the roof. As my head came up into the opening I saw Tabby. She was sitting on the floor in a thin shaft of light, unmoving, hands linked round her drawn up knees. She was staring at something sprawled on the grey blankets of a narrow divan bed. A hand was hanging drown from the bed, the sleeve that flopped over its wrist set hard as plaster with dried blood. The iron smell of blood hung over everything. When I pulled myself through the opening and stepped towards the bed, congealed blood pulled like tar at my shoe soles. The body was on its back, eyes closed, face as white as the underside of a flounder. Mr Cyril Eckington-Smith MP.

'Like that when I found him,' Tabby said.

I pulled the arm up by the sleeve. The arm was stiffening, the wrist slashed almost to the bone. When I made myself touch the neck above the stiff collar it was cold. She was right. He'd been killed hours before Tabby or the rest of us arrived at the house. She looked up at me and must have seen that I believed her, but it didn't bring her any satisfaction. Grief and reproach were on her face.

'It should've been me that killed him,' she said.

TWENTY-FOUR

'And then you killed your brother,' the Rani said to The Soldier.

She made it sound like the least of his crimes. In her eyes, perhaps it was. Two days after our forcible entry into Smith's house, we were assembled in the main room of the Rani's cottage in Richmond. That was Amos's doing. Faced with the problem of what to do with a bound and gagged Captain Smith, he'd simply kept on driving and delivered him to Richmond, along with an ex-pugilist acquaintance of Amos's with orders to see he didn't stray. From Amos's report, the Rani and her prime minister had reacted as if such things were a matter of course. Now Amos and his friend were keeping watch outside, just in case Smith should try to make a run for it. It didn't look likely. Anybody looking into the room would have thought this was nothing but a slightly unorthodox social gathering, with everybody on best behaviour. The Rani was at the centre of it, Mr Patwardhan standing beside her, daughter Chandrika sitting demurely on her pile of cushions in the corner, the very picture of a dutiful daughter, except that her eyes kept straying to Tom. Tom's attention was divided between her and the man he'd known as Mr Tillington. When Tom understood, he'd been furious at Smith's trickery, more so with himself for bring tricked. That was unfair to himself, I'd told him. That cool and ruthless old man had known exactly how to take advantage of Tom's isolation to keep watch on what followed Griffiths's death.

Even now, he was sitting back in his chair looking at the Rani as if she were putting some doubtful business proposition to him.

'My poor brother killed himself,' he said. 'He had suffered recent personal and financial troubles.'

'He had more than ten thousand in East India shares,' I said. 'As your nominee, of course. He'd become greedy and wanted to keep them for himself. He knew or guessed you'd killed Mr Griffiths, so thought you couldn't argue.'

Smith ignored me completely. He'd been doing that ever since we came into the room. He was sticking to the line that he was an innocent man, attacked and taken prisoner and would have the law on all of us.

'It's possible that you didn't intend to kill Mr Griffiths,' I said. 'What you wanted was to know where he'd put the jewels he and McPherson had stolen from you . . .'

'They didn't steal them. They were restoring them,' the Rani said.

'Captain Smith saw it as stealing. Those jewels had been in his possession since he came back from India all those years ago . . .'

'Stolen from me,' the Rani said.

'. . . he'd kept them safely hidden, disguised as a chest of opium, in the vaults of the East India Company. Possibly, he'd even paid in the chest of opium as security for a loan. McPherson somehow found out about that, but it suited him to keep quiet. Maybe he and The Soldier knew too much about each other.'

At first, Smith had simply tried to deny that he was The Soldier, until one look from the Rani settled that issue.

'Then McPherson and Mr Griffiths both came back to London and the whole picture changed,' I said. 'Mr Griffiths knew he was a sick man and he was determined to get the princess back her jewels, if it were literally the last thing he did. He learned from the Rani that McPherson didn't have them and Smith did. But McPherson's financial survival depended on his creditors believing they were in his possession. So Mr Griffiths summoned McPherson and put to him a simple proposition – steal the jewels from Smith and give them back to the Rani, and I'll let the world believe you have them. McPherson had very little choice. He knew his way round East India House and probably how to bribe some of the staff there. After all, nobody there knew there was a fortune in jewels in the chest. As far as they were concerned, it was just another consignment of opium. As instructed, he took the chest from the vault and delivered it to the Rani.

That was why he made that late night journey out here on the Sunday.'

The Rani nodded. 'He kept faith. In that respect, at least.'

For once, Chandrika glanced at me instead of at my brother. The jewels were an anxious subject for her. She and her mother had managed to make peace after Chandrika's sudden absence, but it wouldn't last if the Rani ever found out that her daughter had been willing to sacrifice the whole chest of jewels for Tom's life.

'Smith found out or guessed what had happened,' I said. 'He went to Mr Griffiths and demanded to know what he'd done with the jewels. He lost his temper, probably started shaking him. Mr Griffiths fell and hit his head. He was probably dead already when Smith put him in the bath and slit his wrists.

Smith spoke directly to the Rani.

'I hope you don't believe this.'

She stared at him for several heartbeats. It was as if the rest of us had ceased to exist and something that had happened between the two of them a long time ago was as raw as it had ever been.

'I'd believe anything of you,' she said. Her words were like a judge's sentence, and for the first time Smith dropped his head and wouldn't meet her eyes. She let a few more heartbeats pass before adding: 'In any case, we have a witness.'

She picked up a small silver bell and rang it. This was her idea entirely, the danger point. A door opened. Anil came into the room, neat in white tunic and trousers, put his palms together and bowed to the Rani.

'Look at this man,' she said, pointing to Smith. 'Do you recognize him?'

'Yes, Rani.'

'Is he the man who visited Griffiths sahib?'

'Yes, Rani.'

'What did you see him do?'

'I saw him put Griffiths sahib into the bath. I saw it from the landing, through a crack in the door.'

'Was Griffiths sahib alive or dead?'

'He looked dead, Rani.'

'What happened then?'

'I don't know, Rani. I ran away. I was scared he'd kill me if he knew I'd seen.'

The Rani turned back to Smith.

'I'm sure you'd like to kill this boy too. I promise you, that if any harm comes to him I shall with my own hands cut out your heart and feed it to a dog.'

Unwise to try a line like that unless you mean it. The Rani meant it, and Smith knew it. He admitted defeat in the words that came most naturally to his miser's soul.

'How much do you want?'

The answer turned out to be ten thousand pounds worth of East India Company shares to the Calcutta orphans, gifted in the name of the Rani. Mrs Glass, knowing nothing, was ecstatic. I didn't like it. My wish would have been to see Smith answering for Mr Griffiths's death in the dock, but then we could hardly ask Anil to perjure himself in court. He'd done well as it was, showing almost as promising a talent for amateur dramatics as The Soldier himself. I hope the Rani rewarded him well. But at least there was something I could do. I sent a polite note requesting a meeting with McPherson. This time he left his usual territory in the City and came all the way across town to my office in Abel Yard. If this were some sign of humility, the rest of his bearing was as arrogant as ever.

'So what do you want from me now, Miss Lane?'

'To reassure you. It's over.'

And I gave him a severely edited version of what had happened.

'And who else knows about this?'

'Nobody, except those who were there. As I said before, your secret is safe with me – conditionally.'

'Still conditionally?'

'Yes, if you do what we're asking. You know how to ruin a man?'

'Ruin a man?'

'Yes. I'm sure a business gentleman like you will have done it several times over.'

He took that as a compliment. A brief smile came to his bruiser's face.

'So what's your condition?'

'Just that. Ruin Smith.'

A month later, Mr Disraeli cantered up to me as I was riding in the park.

'I dare say you've heard from your brother about the latest doings among our East Indians.'

'What?'

'Eckington-Smith's brother has been hammered. He's had to flee across the Channel to escape his creditors. A boarding house in Boulogne, so I'm told.'

The way he said Boulogne made it sound like a cooler suburb of hell, which was probably how Smith would see it.

'And that rogue McPherson seems to be flourishing again, in spite of not getting his compensation. Useful things, jewels.'

'Very useful,' I said, wondering as usual how much Mr Disraeli guessed. Quite a lot, judging by his next question.

'Odd business about the brother, don't you think? I'd have said Eckington-Smith was too shameless to kill himself.'

'Yes.'

'But then, no man's death is entirely regrettable if it produces an interesting by-election.'

'In his case, not regrettable at all.'

'I agree. As ever, a pleasure to meet you, Miss Lane. Please give my best wishes to your brother.'

As he raised his hat and turned away, I said: 'And is there still going to be a war against China?'

'Indeed. Quite settled.'

And off he cantered.

Two days later, I went down to Gravesend to see Tom off to India. His departure had been delayed for two weeks because he was to sail with the Rani and her party to see them safely back home. He'd spent a fair part of those two weeks showing Chandrika around London, with myself in the unusual role of chaperone. He was head over heels in love, for the first time in his life. Goodness knows how it would end, but when I remembered Chandrika on the night of the rescue I knew he hadn't fixed his love unwisely. The idea that she was Griffiths's daughter seemed to him to give his old friend's approval to their love. I didn't hint to him, and never would, that on my reading of Griffiths's story, she might equally well owe her getting to The Merchant or The Soldier. Some questions are better left unanswered. The day before they left, the Rani had given me a bracelet set with small diamonds and rubies. When I'd told her that Smith was financially ruined, she'd smiled.

'I'm glad to hear it. He betrayed me twice over.'

From her face, I knew it was no use expecting more.

At Gravesend, our party took a launch out to the boat that was to carry them to India. Tom saw everybody safely settled below then came up on deck with me. The launch was waiting to take back to shore those of us who were not sailing. We stood side by side, looking at the bustle on the quayside. It was hard to find words.

'I've given Tom Huckerby Mr Griffiths's manuscript,' I said. 'He's going to shorten it into a pamphlet against the opium trade.'

'I'm glad to hear it. Liberty . . .'

I waited. He was still looking towards the quay.

'I'm sorry for some of the things I've said. You've made a life. It might not be the life I'd have wished for you, but I think our parents would have been proud.'

I couldn't talk. Tears were running down my cheeks. He hugged me suddenly, very tightly.

'You'll think of coming out to see us, Libby? Not to stay I mean, if you don't want to.'

'I'll think about it, yes.'

The launch blew its steam whistle. He watched as I joined the other passengers on board. As we drew away, Chandrika came and stood beside him at the rail. His white handkerchief and mine fluttered back to each other until they were no more than dots in the bright dazzle from the water.